MEATHEADS

Steve Brown

Cover design by: Art Painter
Library of Congress Control Number: 2018675309
Printed in the United States of America

For Carmen, Luke and Jasmin.

In memory of
My friends and fellow soldiers who are no longer with us. You
are not forgotten.

With special thanks to
Colin Towell and John Hudson for your
encouragement and support.

CONTENTS

CHAPTER ONE

First Impressions

It was like a scene from the exercise yard of a 1970's American prison movie thought Reece. Men gathered in small groups or by themselves, were spread about the dusty compound. Some sat relaxing in the shade of their faded olive-green tents, which had been bleached by the scorching desert sun and battered by sandstorms, rendering them closer to beige than their original colour. A few played cards, sometimes disagreeing with each other's versions of the rules, which had been learned in different parts of the UK, or sometimes abroad, until an agreed set was established that satisfied everyone at the table. This would then become another set of rules, that future visitors would have to learn while at that location. Others quietly read books about the German paratroopers of World War 2 and the Soviet-Afghan war. A paperback copy of Harry Potter and The Half Blood Prince lay abandoned on a well-worn camp bed, the page saved for later reading by being splayed open and weighed down with a half empty bottle of water. Books that had been read by their original owner and passed on, slowly grew worse for wear with torn covers and pages scarred from being turned down at the corners for future reference. One man he noticed, sitting alone on a brown wooden ammunition crate was carefully sharpening a large fixed blade knife on an oilstone that was nailed to a similar box in front of him, grinding it slowly up and down the blackened metal with an expression of deep concentration etched on his face. Others were doing physical training, hitting punch bags with a ferocity that would break a man's ribs, skipping ropes and doing seemingly endless amounts of press ups on the sandy floor. A bare-knuckle fight between a prime Clint Eastwood and Charles Bronson would not have looked out of place here.

As he approached, although noticed by all, he was barely acknowledged by the paratroopers who carried on with their business, a quick glance was enough for them to assess him as a non-threat. These guys looked tough he thought, almost all had shaved heads and appeared to be in peak physical condition, their bodies lean but muscular and tanned from the combination of living on rations whilst working hard in the intense climate. Some had grown beards, but most were clean shaven. Several bore a tattoo of The Parachute Regiment cap-badge on their right shoulder as proof of their pedigree. There was an air of arrogance about them and it was obvious why the Royal Engineer who had given him directions to the Brigade Reconnaissance Force compound had branded them "Meatheads." These soldiers were intimidating. Reece stood still and searched for eye contact or a friendly face as there was no obvious option of who to approach. The man hitting the punchbag had his back to Reece but stopped and turned around as if suddenly aware of his presence. Sweating heavily, he approached him, removing his black leather boxing gloves as he walked. "Who are you looking for mate?" he asked abruptly.

CHAPTER TWO

The Journalist

Reece Carnell was not the stereotypical journalist. Where many of his peers found success through ruthlessness and apathy, Reece had used integrity and empathy as the building blocks for his reporting. Remaining objective was something that he found quite natural as he had always done his best to see both sides of a story. As a young boy his parents had divorced, both blaming each other for the failings in their marriage and when his father left, he stayed with his mother. Throughout his childhood and into adulthood Reece never fully understood the circumstances of their divorce as his mother accused the father of having an affair, and his father blamed it on her alcoholism. Both stories were equally convincing and told with equal sincerity by his parents, but they were also very contradictory and vehemently disputed by both. This early experience had taught him that there were always at least two versions of every story. Suffering from asthma from an early age Reece had been deterred from playing sports, instead focussing on technology and academics, which he excelled at. However, despite his awareness of his disease he still smoked cigarettes and ate a very poor diet of mostly sugary snacks and takeaway food which accounted for his somewhat boyish, underdeveloped physique. At 24 years of age, his body looked like that of a 14-year-old boy, but he was surprisingly strong for his frame. His face however, told a different story, with a wrinkled forehead and crows-feet with dark circles around his eyes from the long days and nights of research and many hours he'd spent sat staring at screens, frowning with concentration. His hair was receding, much to his embarrassment, and he tried in vain to disguise it by brushing it forward.

In his last year at school Reece had completed two weeks of "work experience" with his local newspaper "The Gazette". He had chosen to do that, not because he had an interest in journalism, but because he thought it would be the easiest. The other options made available to him were a general building company, a local hospice and a second-hand shop which was managed by an old lady, locally known as "The Old Witch." The other jobs were filled by friends of his, all of which regretted their choice and decided to choose alternative employment after leaving school. The boy who took the placement with the building company was treated like a child slave, digging out foundations, shovelling sand and cement and carrying heavy loads of bricks up ladders for his so-called mentors for over a week before being withdrawn by his parents after coming home with blisters and open sores on his hands. He had single handedly dug a soak-away on a building site that was six feet deep and four feet wide. Another boy, a close friend of Reece's who had chosen to work at the hospice lasted only one day before quitting. Unfortunately for him, within hours of him starting a patient had died in their bed while he was talking to them, looking him directly in the eyes as they took their last breath. The haunting image of the gaunt old man staring at him with dark sunken eyes would stay with him forever. A girl went to work with the old witch in the charity shop and fared much better, enjoying her time and even receiving a small cash payment as a thanks for her efforts. However, three weeks afterwards she was killed after falling into a river and drowning during a storm, fuelling the illegitimate stories of the old witch and the curse she wielded. Reece's work experience turned out to be the perfect fit for him and he enjoyed it more than he could have imagined. Although he was given the menial tasks he expected, such as making the teas and coffees and emptying the bins, he was also challenged daily and given responsibility like he had never experienced before, rising to the occasion every time. In fact, he impressed the editor so much that he offered him an apprenticeship.

On returning to school Reece worked with a new-found energy, focussing on the subjects that he knew would serve him in journalism. English, computer studies, geography, politics and geography all became interest to him, and he also read a newspaper every day, deliberately alternating between the tabloids and broadsheets to experience a broader perspective. He also invested in an expensive high quality SLR camera which his grandmother helped him buy and spent much of his spare time taking, editing and developing his photographs. Photography came naturally to Reece and he could often see drama or beauty in the most innocuous settings, capturing breath taking landscapes and portraits in everyday situations. He even managed to earn a small income by working at a few weddings and parties. The week after he left school, he began full time employment at the newspaper, quickly earning himself a regular column reporting on local events and gaining a good reputation for his work ethic. During his time at The Gazette he also managed to establish himself as a photographer and would regularly be tasked to take pictures by the other reporters on the team to accompany their stories. Before not too long his photographic work had caught the attention of other publishers and he was able to undertake some freelance work for several magazines and publications before receiving a call one day from the Daily Telegraph in London with an offer of some work. Initially the job was as the photographer for a well-known reporter covering a story on people smuggling and extortion rackets in London, but when the job was almost cancelled because the reporter couldn't make it, he pleaded with the editor to give him a chance, and he did. The report that Reece produced far exceeded the expectations of everyone at the newspaper, not only receiving excellent reviews, but also resulted in a huge Metropolitan Police investigation which resulted in several high-profile arrests and convictions. The upside was a job offer at one of the UK's most prestigious broadsheet newspapers that had been running for over 150 years. The downside, however, was that his part in the prosecutions was public knowledge and not appreciated by the criminal gangs that had been adversely affected. His report and accompanying photos were used extensively as evidence by Scotland Yard.

At 20 years old, he left home and moved to London to pursue his career with the Daily Telegraph, initially renting a room in a house owned by a very nice Hindu family in Shepherds Bush. His room was in the basement of a four-storey town house and had its own external door at the bottom of a small spiral staircase accessed from the street above. The room had its own small en-suite shower room and a microwave oven that he had bought so he was totally independent from the family above who were always very helpful and considerate if he needed anything. At least once a week, usually on a Friday evening the lady of the house would bring him a hot dinner, immaculately presented on a large plate, covered in tin foil. She would always say that she had cooked too much food and would throw it away if he didn't eat it. He knew she was lying to protect his pride, but he wasn't embarrassed, in fact he looked forward to it, there was usually enough for him to keep for lunch the next day too. Furnishings in the room consisted of an old, metal framed single bed which sagged pathetically in the middle where the springs had capitulated, a small bedside table that was strangely secured to the wall by a metal chain, a dented steel waste paper bin and a free-standing clothes rack where he hung his shirt and trousers for work on the only functioning coat hanger of the 8 he'd inherited, the others all bent, snapped and contorted. The remainder of his clothes lay draped over the rail in a disorganised pile that threatened to topple the flimsy aluminium and plastic contraption at any moment. On the first night in his new quarters, while giving it a quick clean and organising his stuff, Reece had also found a small pile of magazines tucked under the bed. The top one was called "Train Enthusiast" and the cover picture was of a pristine green and red steam train travelling through a high sided valley, an impressive trail of white steam trailing in its wake. Reece quickly tossed it towards the bin in the corner, misjudging the force required and knocking the bin over noisily. "Boring!" He said out loud. The magazines underneath were quite the contrast, "Submit & Serve" showed a picture of a person kneeling in a leather one-piece suit with the caption "How to make a Gimp suit," the second, "Fetish Lovers" showed two female dwarves dressed up as police officers and covered in custard and at the bottom of the pile was a sex toy catalogue with many items inside circled in black ink for future reference. These three publications also ended up in the bin, but not as hastily as the first, his curiosity got the better of him. He wondered who had occupied the room prior to him and based on the evidence decided it was either a fat, perverted train spotter or an angry dwarf that wore extremely heavy clothing. Either way, he would be buying a new mattress.

Living in the hustle and bustle of London was an eye-opening experience for Reece and he quickly realised that he would need to either adapt to the dog eat dog environment of the city or fall prey to it. Navigating the streets and public transport of the buses and underground railways was an unsociable affair, nobody talked, nobody made eye contact and they certainly didn't display any kind of politeness or consideration for each other. Initially he tried to maintain the high standards of etiquette and manners that had been drilled into him from childhood but simple gestures of good will such as holding a door open or giving way to someone in a busy thoroughfare would not only go unacknowledged by the recipient, but would also be immediately pounced on by anybody else within striking distance. In London, to yield was a sign of weakness and any weakness was exploited. An open door was like a bright light to a moth to the throngs of people within every building, causing them to divert from their current trajectory to take the path of least resistance, and there never seemed to be an opportunity to let go once you'd opened it, without feeling as though it was slamming in to someone's face. Soon he succumbed, only touching doors when he had to and never checking behind before letting go, hoping that an old lady or child wasn't following behind. Anyone who gave way was clearly not from London, either a tourist or visitor of some sort and they would end up stuck, pinned against a window or wall by the incoming tide of people from the other direction, much to the anger of those behind them, who would become immediately agitated and start protesting aloud. The only way to regain right of way was to hope for another unfortunate "outsider" on the other side to make the same mistake and exploit it mercilessly before they were pressured into changing their minds by those behind them.

After a year in the city, Reece had adapted his behaviour and personality enough to survive comfortably in the fast-paced ultra-urban environment. Moving through the streets he fixed his gaze straight ahead at shoulder height, walking with purpose like a horse wearing blinkers he was not distracted by anything outside his immediate frontage. Headphones inserted, music drowned out the noise, with only the sounds of police sirens and car horns interrupting his playlist. He had moved from the room in Shepherds Bush and was now renting a one-bedroom flat on the 6th floor of an apartment block in Camden Town. The cost was much higher but he had grown out of his old room and become increasingly concerned for his safety after being confronted outside the house by an aggrieved criminal that had been affected by the extortion racket story. The new place was much more secure, six stories up from the street, electronic security access, CCTV cameras and a residential security guard who he shamelessly befriended quickly for his own peace of mind.

Although he enjoyed his work, Reece realised he had become somewhat stagnant and predictable in his routine, catching the same bus every day, working his regular shift, buying lunch in the same place and socialising on the same nights in the same pubs every week. The pay was good, and he had made some great friends but looking around the office one day he realised that he was being consumed by the machine, he was a carbon copy of everyone else.

Overseas reporting opportunities were regularly awarded at the newspaper, but there was a hierarchy to who got them. The most desirable, well paid and exclusive were given to the senior reporters who had been there for years and were well established with reliable information sources and connections to the establishment. These were the top of the tree, the people that would also be seen on the T.V news, giving an expert opinion. The jobs that they rejected were handed down to their closest allies and friends who were trying to get themselves to the top. The jobs rejected by them, the leftovers that were not expected to receive any worthwhile recognition would eventually be advertised to the remainder via email. The only way to secure the best jobs was to bide your time and work your way up the ladder or create your own opportunity and convince the editor to let you go. Reece was far too impatient to wait and spent all his free time searching for the next scoop. Using the internet, magazines and newspapers he was constantly updating himself on local, national and international events looking for incidents on the peripheries of the headlines that were under reported.

In 2002 the British army deployed a battle group to Afghanistan to support a U.S invasion to overthrow the Taliban. The excitement at the Daily Telegraph and every other media outlet was

huge and Reece had a ringside seat to watch how the journalists jostled for position and competed for information, resources
and column space. As the new guy he had no chance of deploying to the Middle East, not even as a photographer, so instead he
watched and learned. With such a big event happening abroad it
presented opportunities for the junior reporters to step up and
take on domestic news, an opportunity he grasped with both
hands. In March 2003, the U.S led coalition had invaded Iraq
and quickly dismantled its military with overwhelming superior force. Although elevated in status from his first year of hard
work Reece was still not ranked high enough for this event and
again watched from the side lines as reporters were deployed to
follow the army into another war zone.

During the summer of 2004 Reece was tipped off by a friend at
a rival newspaper about a covert police and MI5 operation into
home grown Islamist terrorists in England. After a few days of
digging around, he learned that Operation Catapult was a huge
operation involving over a thousand personnel from the police
and secret services to route out a UK based terror cell affiliated
to an organisation called Al Qaeda. The chief suspect in the case
was a well-known extremist called Abu Hussein, an Iranian born
cleric who was the Imam of a Mosque in London. It was thought
his group were planning a terror attack in the city at Christmas.
Reece managed to arrange a meeting with Abu under the guise
of writing an article about the effect of Middle Eastern conflict
on British Muslims and hoped he could elicit information from
him on his ideology.

After work one evening he stopped at his local pub for a drink
and sat at a table outside to enjoy a cigarette with his pint of bitter. He took out his cigarettes from his pocket and opened them
one handed, raising the packet to his lips and withdrawing a cigarette with his mouth. Placing the pack onto the table he then
took a lighter from the same pocket and lit it, drawing in hard
to light it. As it started to smoke, he replaced the lighter into his

pocket then took a long puff, closing his eyes and savouring the moment. As he exhaled the grey smoke, he opened his eyes to find another man, that he did not recognise, had joined him at the table, sitting uncomfortably close and looking him straight in the eye.

"Can I help you?" Reece said sharply.

The man picked up Reece's cigarette packet from the table, flipped open the lid and took out a cigarette. Returning the pack, he placed it between his lips then spoke, the cigarette flapping up and down as he did so.

"Sure, you can help me. Can I get a light?" He said dryly. Reece immediately noticed he had a Scottish accent.

Unnerved Reece withdrew his lighter once more and offered it to the stranger, who sat still, eyes flicking from the end of the cigarette to Reece and back again. Reece struck the lighter and held the flame up to the end of the Marlborough Light and the man puffed on it until the tip glowed bright orange.

"Thanks." He said, eyes still fixed on Reece.

"Oh, my pleasure." He replied sarcastically. "Can I get you anything else? I've got a pint of bitter here, or maybe you'd prefer a lager?"

"We can help each other." The man said cryptically.

"Sorry mate, but I'm straight." Reece stated, looking around the pub to assess the clientele. If it was a gay bar, he had no idea. Several mixed couples sat together assured him it wasn't.

"Operation Catapult." The man said quietly. "You need to back off."

"Or what?" Reece replied.

"It's a very dangerous game." Said the Scotsman. "Lives are on the line here. For the safety of you, your family and a lot of operators and civilians, you need to back off!"

"Are you MI5?" Quizzed Reece. "Are you threatening me?" He was intimidated but tried to portray otherwise.

"Yes." Said the man. His eyes had not even blinked as they stared intensely into Reece's. "That story needs to come out, but not until I say so. This is a lot bigger than you can comprehend my friend. Bad timing here will result in a lot of casualties, and you don't want to be one of them and neither do your parents. This is the only warning I'm going to give you, but if you stand down, I will provide you with information that will blow your fucking socks off, exclusive to you."

"How long?" Reece asked.

"Three months, and I guarantee you'll be front page." Said the agent, taking a last puff of the cigarette and stubbing it out in the ashtray in the centre of the table. "You have my word."

"Okay, deal." Said Reece reluctantly, extending his hand to shake on it. "How do I contact you?"

The mystery man stood up, gripped his hand firmly and shook it briefly. "You don't." He said. "I'll call you."

"What's your name?" Reece asked as he turned to leave.

The mans eyes looked down at the table momentarily, then back up to Reece. "John Smith." He replied before walking away.

"Okay John. Well I'll wait for your call then. Goodbye." Reece called out as the man left. He sat back down and picked up his pint glass, downing the remainder of his drink in one go. Placing the glass back on the table he noticed the branding on the side of it "John Smith's Bitter"

"Fucking Psycho!" He muttered.

As instructed Reece stepped away from his investigation work into Al Qaeda, focusing his efforts on whatever taskings he was given and working diligently. Every time he checked his emails, he hoped there would be a message from MI5 or a coded message with details of a covert rendezvous at a secret bunker or safe-house. Ten weeks after the meeting at the pub Reece was at his gym getting changed after a long swim in the pool. He pulled his coat out of the locker he was using then closed the small metal door.

"Jesus Christ!" He exclaimed, jumping backwards a couple of paces in shock. "Why do that? Why sneak up on people like that?"

Behind the door stood "John Smith" who had not intended to sneak up either time, just happened to have terrible timing. He understood how it probably looked and rolled with it, correctly assuming it might add to the mystique that came with MI5 work.

In his hand was a large brown envelope which he offered to Reece.

"For you." He said. "Be careful how you use it. Good luck."

Reece took it and placed it inside his bag. "Thanks John." He said. They exited the changing room together and went their separate ways.

Reece hurriedly headed straight to his apartment and on entering, locked the door and shut the curtains before delving into his bag to open the package.

John Smith was right, the story was bigger than he could have imagined, even with the large amount of redaction on the documents and pictures the story was huge and the promise of exclusivity had been kept too. None of the information he was reading was public knowledge, but with Reece's excellent awareness of current affairs he was able to connect a few incidents and personalities to piece recent events together with this investigation. Over a two-year period, there had been undercover agents, foreign intervention, fraud, corruption, and terrorism involved, not only in the UK but in America, Afghanistan, Pakistan and Iraq too. The result was over one hundred arrests, millions of pounds worth of recovered assets, the dismantling of a bomb making cell in London and the successful interception of a massive improvised explosive device destined for the city that would have had disastrous consequences if not halted. The report that Reece produced was so shocking that the Telegraph serialised it over an entire week at the beginning of 2005.

When the dust settled from the story Reece realised he had made it to the next rung of the ladder within the newspaper when one of the most senior reporters at the paper, the political editor approached him with an opportunity. It was spring 2005 and the fighting in Afghanistan was escalating once again with different ethnic and political and militia groups vying for power in the vacuum caused by the rapid withdrawal of the Taliban and subsequent failure of the ANA and coalition to affect command and control. His friend had turned down the job, explaining that he wanted to investigate a story in Turkey that was a higher priority. Apparently, there were hundreds of foreign fighters joining the jihad from Europe, using the Turkish border to enter the region. The real reason was a justified fear of being kidnapped. Several reporters had been taken hostage in both Afghanistan and Iraq in recent months and used by Islamist extremist groups to spread fear and propaganda. Some had been held to ransom at millions of dollars, some had been forced to make videoed confessions to being a spy or to slander their own governments for their illegal occupation of Muslim lands. Governments from countries such as the UK and US did not negotiate with terrorists, so hostages from those places did nor fair well. So far only one hostage, an aid worker from Italy, working in Kabul had been released. Although they would neither confirm nor deny, it was widely known that the Italian government had paid 1.5 million dollars for her release. Of the five hostages taken in a nine-month period, 1 Italian aid worker, 1 Indian construction worker, 1 British aid worker and 1 American journalists and a U.S Marine, two had been beheaded, one had been released and two were still missing, fate unknown. The two beheadings had been broadcast live on the internet and had a huge psychological impact on everyone involved in the conflict, especially those who had watched it who would never forget the horrific brutality. Soldiers were angered and sickened, civilians were shocked and frightened. Everyone understood that if they were ever captured, they might receive the same gruesome end. As far as psychological warfare went, the beheadings were a master stroke by the terrorists.

The job on offer was in Kandahar Province, Southern Afghanistan, close to the Pakistani border. A militia group, thought to be involved in kidnapping and bomb making and closely affiliated to the Taliban were operating out of a base in an undisclosed location in the mountains and had agreed via connections in Pakistan, Turkey and Georgia to the interview. The incentives for them were not only the money they were unofficially receiving, but also the opportunity to raise their profile and push their agenda of anti-western politics and Islamic fundamentalism.

When offered the job, Reece considered it overnight. He knew it was dangerous and he saw through the façade his colleague was portraying, but to be successful in his chosen profession, risks had to be taken. After consulting with his friends at the paper and researching the reliability of the multiple information sources and connections he decided it was worth it.

Getting to the secret location was a complicated affair and the following week he took a flight from London to Pakistan, initially landing in Jinnah International Airport in the capital city Karachi, then transferring to a domestic flight to Quetta Airport. From here he was collected by a Pakistani journalist named Mok who was a regular BBC foreign news contributor and drove him to the Afghan border town of Chaman, about 100km north. The drive was long but pleasant enough, following the N25, a well maintained arterial road through a mixture of open desert, cultivated land and winding mountain passes, they stopped several times along the way to purchase food and drinks from roadside stalls and for Reece to smoke a cigarette. Due to the high altitude Reece was struggling to hear very well and kept trying to clear his ears by holding his nose and blowing hard, but despite this they got on very well and talked throughout the journey. Mok was incredibly knowledgeable about the political situation in the region and briefed Reece on the dynamics of the many different factions and parties in the area.

It was late when they arrived at the hotel and Mok ensured a smooth check-in before they made their way to their separate rooms which were next door to each other. Breakfast started at 0530hrs and they agreed to meet in the lobby then, before entering the rooms.

"Remember what I said in the car. There are eyes everywhere." Mok said, as he walked through his door.

"Will do." Replied Reece. "See you in the morning." Mok had been telling Reece about the Pakistani Secret Service and how corrupt they were. He was certain that Reece would have been followed from the moment he landed in Karachi and that their hotel rooms would have some kind of surveillance on them too. Reece entered his room cautiously, not sure what he would do if he found something suspicious inside like a microphone under the bed or video camera hidden in the air vent. Worse still there could be a man sat in the shadows waiting for him, like in the movies. He walked in slowly his emotions a mixture of excitement and nervousness and turned on the light expectantly. No one was there, just a very inviting bed, half covered in pillows which he threw onto the floor as he got into it after a quick shower. Despite his apprehension he slept well and woke to the sound of a ringing telephone at 0500hrs. Having not noticed a phone in his room he sat up and turned on the bedside lamp. He could hear it but could not see it and stood up to walk around the small space to find it. Following the sound, he opened the top drawer of the cabinet and sure enough there it was, next to a copy of the Quran. He picked it up and held it to his ear.

"Hello?" He grunted.

"Good morning Mr Carnell, this is your morning call, thank you, goodbye." Said the chirpy voice at the other end before promptly hanging up.

Reece sat on the bed and took out a cigarette. He'd noticed the lack of no-smoking signs in the hotel and the presence of an ash tray assured him it was ok to smoke. He glanced up to the ceiling to check for a smoke detector and then lit it when there wasn't one.

Mok was waiting for him in the lobby and they made their way to the restaurant for something to eat. Both ordered coffee and Reece copied Mok's food order as he had no idea what anything on the menu was and enjoyed a delicious traditional Pakistani breakfast called Nashta, which consisted of scrambled eggs, fresh baked bread, mincemeat and a selection of fruit. As they finished their coffee Mok and Reece were both given a packed lunch in a white paper bag which they took and left, stopping at reception to check out. Receiving the bill Reece was surprised at the amount and queried it with Mok, asking him to interpret the receipt. Mok pointed to the list as he spoke.

"Rooms, breakfast, lunch, movie, phone call, tip." He explained.

"What movie?" Reece asked. "I never even had a T.V in my room."

The porter spoke. "Sir, all rooms have T.V."

"Inside the wardrobe!" Mok explained. "Did you not find the T.V? It's in the wardrobe."

Reece shook his head. "Obviously. Silly me, of course it is." He said sarcastically, turning to the porter. "And the telephone is in the drawer, right?"

"Yes, of course sir." He replied happily. "Very good."

Reece asked no more questions and paid the bill on the company credit card.

It was a short journey to the Afghan border and Mok made sure their crossing went smoothly, entering Afghanistan and continuing the drive northwards for another 45 minutes before arriving at the pre-arranged drop off point in plenty of time. It was arranged to meet at 0900hrs but Mok received a phone call to tell them there was delay so they waited patiently. By 1100hrs Reece could no longer resist temptation and ate his packed lunch, finishing just as a white and red Toyota Hilux approached them from the north and parked in front of them on the roadside. three men got out of the vehicle and approached, exchanging pleasantries with Mok in Arabic and then introducing themselves to Reece as Mok translated.

One of the Taliban searched Reece's equipment and clothing removing a few items he was unsure of before gesturing for him to get in the vehicle.

"See you in five days." Said Mok. "You'll be fine. Have fun."

Reece had been given a set of goggles that were covered in tape as a makeshift blindfold. Before putting them on he looked at Mok nervously. "Don't be late!" He said. "Five days!"

As promised, Mok was there to collect him five days later and Reece was relieved to see his smiling face as the blindfold was removed. The Taliban escorted them most of the way back to the border, pulling over about a mile short and waving them on. Mok continued past at speed as he and Reece waved from their open windows, passing back into Pakistan and stopping again at the same hotel, where they rested, ate and discussed the last few days. The following morning, they drove back to Quetta Airport and Reece began the first leg of the flight home arriving back in London the next day.

CHAPTER THREE

No Bluff Too Tough

It was now August 2006 and Reece was about to begin an attachment to a Logistical Support Regiment as an embedded reporter for The Daily Telegraph newspaper. He was due to work with a supply squadron, and report on the steady flow of troops and equipment into and out of Kandahar Airfield, the main ingress and egress point for coalition forces in Afghanistan on Operation HERRICK. The soldiers were already four months into a six-month deployment and fighting had been the most intense the British Army had seen since the Korean War. He had never heard of the Brigade Reconnaissance Force before, until he overheard two soldiers from Britain's elite 3rd Battalion the Parachute Regiment, 3 Para, talking in the dinner queue outside the canteen. The topic of conversation was a firefight that had taken place the previous day in a town called Kurzak, involving a British patrol and a large group of Taliban fighters. One of the paras, a Scottish Lance Corporal was excitedly recounting the story as it had been told to him by his Platoon Commander that morning. The Scotsman's' strong Glaswegian accent made it difficult for the reporter to eavesdrop but he managed to decipher enough of the tale and accompanying hand gestures to gather that a small group of paras were based in an outpost West of Kandahar in the lawless Helmand Province, and were carrying out offensive operations against the Taliban. He was fascinated that he had never heard of these soldiers, who the Scot referred to as the "BRF" and that detail of this apparent battle had not been released to the press in the daily updates. The soldier spoke of heavy machine guns, anti-tank missiles and apparent heavy casualties on the Taliban side from an air strike. Reece had heard enough and decided to give dinner a miss, instead heading for the 16 Air Assault Brigade HQ building in search of the Media Operations Officer. He left just in time to miss the young paratrooper tell his favourite story of how he once bedded a mother and daughter he'd met in a nightclub in Aldershot.

On arrival at the HQ Reece presented his Press I.D card to the disinterested Cpl at the reception desk who seemed too busy playing with his mobile phone to take any notice of the picture it showed. The Royal Signals NCO looked no more than fifteen years old with a bright red spotty face and round black rimmed glasses that made him look more like a high school prefect than a soldier, thought Reece. For all he cared it could have been Osama Bin Laden himself, but he waved him through, gesturing toward a well-thumbed folder, mumbling "sign the book" as he fixed his gaze back onto his phone. Reece did as the Corporal asked and signed in the big green lever arch folder that was the media ops visitors' book and as he did so noticed that there were no other reporters visiting at that time. This was good news he thought, he did not want anyone else poaching his idea.

The Media Ops Officer was a tall gangly Captain from the Household Cavalry Regiment, a unit that prides itself on being the senior regiment in the British army and holds international fame for its grand, ceremonial horse parades in London. His name was Tarquin Smythe-Brockett, typically posh for an officer in the Guards Division and he was undoubtedly the most pompous and arrogant person Reece had ever met. The young working class reporter had taken an immediate dislike to him when they were first introduced a few weeks before in Colchester, but knew it was in his interest to humour him and pretend to like him in order to get the stories he wanted. As Tarquin approached, Reece managed to feign a smile and extended his hand in a false act of friendship. His father had always told him that you could judge a man by his handshake and Tarquin's was like a wet fish, just as he remembered, reenforcing his preconceptions of the man. "Hello old chap, what can I do you for?" Tarquin bellowed predictably. This was just one of his mannerisms that annoyed Reece to distraction and was promptly followed by another as the Captain ran his right hand through his greasy black hair, pausing to rest it on top of his head, with his left hand on his hip. "Have to make it quick old boy, the ruggers on in the Mess, England v's France!" Reece remembered it was the quarter finals of the Six Nations Rugby Championships and got straight to the point. "I've just got off the phone to my editor" he lied "and he says there's a story in Kurzak with the BRF that he wants me to cover. I need to be embedded with them up there where the action is." He knew he was sticking his neck out but felt confident that the officer wouldn't check his story, and he was right. Tarquin was at the end of his six-month tour of duty in Kandahar and his only concern was arranging his flight home in 10 days' time. Reece also knew that The Daily Telegraph was one of the few newspapers respected by the Ministry of Defence for its accurate and positive reporting on the army during its operations in Iraq and Afghanistan, at a time when the war on terror was losing public support in Britain and more and more politicians were calling for a withdrawal. Tarquin moved his right hand to his chin, gripping it tightly as he considered the request. "What do you know about the BRF?" he replied quietly, clearly surprised that Reece knew of their existence in Kurzak. "I know that they've been in a firefight with the Taliban up there" he replied confidently. "And I also know that if this story gets published by some of my rivals before all the facts are known, it could be another PR disaster for the MoD back home." He was thinking on his feet now and knew that the army wanted nothing less than for some of the British newspapers to start scare-mongering so early in the campaign.

The PR disaster he was referring to was an incident that had taken place in Iraq two months before, when soldiers from the 2nd Battalion The Parachute Regiment had killed a group of terrorists who had carried out a drive by attack on their patrol. The terrorists, who were dressed in traditional women's clothing in order to avoid suspicion, had pulled alongside the patrol as they walked through a market and opened fire with AK47 rifles. Miraculously none of the paras were hit by the hail of bullets, but their reaction had been swift and devastating. They returned fire instinctively and between six men fired over 200 rounds into the car as it tried to speed away. All four occupants of the Toyota Corolla were riddled with bullets to a point where their clothes were saturated in blood and the interior of the car was painted with blood and fragments of brain and bone. The paras had reacted the only way they knew how and met violence with violence, but during the violent exchange of gunfire an innocent bystander had been killed and another seriously wounded. This event had turned the people of the town against the British and some of the media exploited it to the full publishing headlines such as "Trigger Happy Paras Gun Down Shoppers in Iraq". Some reports didn't even mention the fact that the known Al Qaeda rebels had fired on the Para patrol first and the whole situation took the MoD and government a lot of time and money to rectify.

The officer looked at his watch, the game was starting in fifteen minutes "o.k. you can go, but anything you report has to be cleared by me personally before it's sent or I will make sure you never work with the army again, do you understand?"

"Absolutely, you have my word," Reece replied happily, his mind games had worked.

"There's a helicopter leaving for Kurzak tomorrow at 0300hrs Zulu, be on it and travel light." Tarquin was shouting again as if giving an order. "I will sort out the details and warn off the

BRF that you are coming. You will need to link up with Major Johnny Hill, he's the BRF boss and a bloody good chap. Any questions, no, good." At that Tarquin turned sharply and set off at a brisk walk for the Officers Mess. Reece did have a question, but it would have to wait; "What time was 0300hrs Zulu?" Although he had worked with the military many times over the years, he had never quite got used to the way they worked in different time zones. Zulu was the most common; this was GMT and used to avoid confusion with any aircraft that might have to fly from countries where the time zone was different. It was 3 ½ hours behind local time in Kandahar, so that meant his flight was leaving at 0630 in the morning. He worked it out again in his head to make sure then went outside to call his boss back in London to tell him of his coup.

0600hrs. It was like a fire alarm going off right next to his ear, but Reece tried to ignore it and get an extra couple of minutes lie in. He knew that if he turned it off he would most likely fall back to sleep and miss his flight so he endured the old-fashioned ringing alarm clock as long as he could before sitting up begrudgingly to turn it off, his bare feet resting on top of the battered flip flops that he kept on his cold bedside floor. He was not a morning person and started the day with his usual, well established routine. Reaching under his pillow, he retrieved his cigarettes, turning the packet upside down before shaking out a lighter and cigarette into his hand. Eyes still closed, he put the cigarette into his mouth, momentarily withdrawing it to lick his dry, sticky lips, when the filtered tip stuck to them. Holding his lighter in his right hand he primed it by gently rolling the steel roller forward with his thumb three times before quickly striking it backwards and lighting his Marlborough Light, a routine he'd been doing since he started smoking at 14 years of age. He sat on the edge of his bed in silence thinking about the day ahead, slowly awakening, aided by the nicotine hit. Cigarettes were cheap in Kandahar and as a result, he was smoking at least a pack of twenty every day, compared to his usual six or seven back in England. He took a last extra-long puff and stubbed it out on the rough concrete floor, adding to the pile of butts and black ash already there from previous mornings. Now he was ready to get up and get dressed. His clothes lay in a crumpled heap on the floor, where he'd discarded them the previous night so he was dressed quickly, finishing off by donning a Norwegian army woollen jumper that he'd bought from an Army surplus store in London during his student years. Faded to a pale green with frayed hems and a few small holes, the heat retaining properties of the weathered jumper were almost completely placebo. Reece brushed his teeth, using his electric toothbrush like a manual one as there was nowhere to recharge it and the battery had run flat. Every morning he promised himself he'd buy a new one, but always forgot. He placed his wash-kit into his holdall and zipped it up before slinging it over his shoulder and leaving for the helicopter landing pad, which was only a short walk away from his accommodation. As he had no idea how long he would be in Kurzak Reece packed the blue helmet and body armour he'd been issued by the army and enough clothes and supplies to last a couple of weeks but his bag was still only half full. The way he saw it, as long as he could brush his teeth and change his socks every day then he had everything he needed. The most important things he carried in his jacket pocket, his waterproof notebook, pencil, spare pencil, Marlborough Lights and lighter. His large Nikon camera hung from his neck on a sling, always at the ready for an opportune snapshot.

At the heli pad the R.A.F Chinook helicopter was being refuelled, and mechanics were busy carrying out routine checks on the engine before it could be started. A group of ten men had gathered in a circle at the back of the aircraft, also destined for Kurzak. One of the men, an R.A.F sergeant beckoned Reece over with a wave and after checking his I.D began a comprehensive brief on where he was to sit, what he would wear and rather worryingly what actions he should take in the event of the Chinook being shot down or crashing while on board. The brief brought home the reality that he was about to leave the relative safety of Kandahar Airfield and enter a hostile and violent place, where Taliban fighters ruled the towns with an iron fist and the people lived in a society more akin to the 13th century than the 21st. Immediately after the brief, he hastily donned his helmet and body armour and spent the next few minutes nervously adjusting straps and clips to make sure they would not come off. By the time the passengers were called forward Reece's fidgeting had attracted the attention of the waiting soldiers and they quietly mocked his obvious nervousness for their own amusement.

The Loadmaster beckoned the passengers on board and directed them individually to where he wanted them to sit, using hand gestures rather than shout over the noisy engines. He wore a set of green coveralls with black boots and what seemed an oversized helmet with a microphone touching his lips. The waistcoat that he wore looked cumbersome, the pockets and pouches straining at the zip due to ill-fitting contents. On the top of his thighs were white plastic pages, covered in illegible scrawl that he'd written while talking to the pilot over the intercom and on his right ankle a small pocket housed an aircrew emergency knife. Along the middle of the floor were metal boxes, the passenger's baggage and other stores bound for Kurzak, including mail from the UK, all secured to the floor by well used, faded yellow ratchet straps. The Loadmaster busily carried out his checks, regularly speaking into his microphone to communicate with the cockpit before he too sat down at the rear of the helicopter.

The aircraft's engines became louder and the whole vehicle shook as it generated the power required to lift its 13 ton mass off the ground, taking off exactly on time, tilting forward steeply as it quickly accelerated toward the airfield boundary The pilot was flying as fast and low as he could to minimise the chance of being shot at by rebels in the towns and villages and as a result, Reece's stomach felt like it was in his mouth on several occasions. The shooting down of a coalition aircraft was a known ambition of the Taliban and the Squadron Leader did not intend to become the first. The situation was surreal as he twisted in his seat to gaze through the porthole behind him. Beyond the deafening noise of the engines the scenery was magnificent, below the desert was unspoiled and as flat as a billiard table, the landscape unchanged for thousands of years. In the distance rugged mountains rose proudly from the floor, dominating the early morning horizon, casting great shadows for miles across the barren plains below. Some still had snow on the peaks as a reminder of the harsh winter gone by, the white caps contrasting with the reds, greys and blacks of ancient rock formations. The sky was clear blue with not a cloud in sight, the sun shining brightly as it slowly rose in the east between two distant mountains. From up high, in the sanctity of the helicopter it all seemed so beautiful, so peaceful and inviting, but that was far from the case, as he would soon discover. After 30 minutes, the loadmaster, who had been sitting behind a Machine Gun on the tailgate throughout the flight, stood up and turned around toward his passengers. Clapping his hands together to attract their attention, he held up two fingers, slowly rotating his body from left to right as he made eye contact with all on board, to warn them that they would be landing in two minutes, Reece looked across to the others to check if he should be doing something but no-one moved so he relaxed. Two minutes later everyone was contorting their bodies so that they could observe the ground, looking through the round porthole windows behind them as the pilot made his final approach to the Landing Site. The Loadmaster lay on the tailgate, his head peeking outside the airframe in order to give final instructions to the pilot as he descended the last few feet. The landing was soft and the loadmaster quickly lowered the ramp at the back until it touched the ground, followed by a thumbs up signal, at which point all the soldiers stood up, grabbed their kit and sprinted out the back of the aircraft leaving the inexperienced reporter behind. Reece panicked, thinking that he would be left aboard and taken back to Kandahar and quickly tried to stand up, forgetting in his haste to undo his seatbelt and then struggling to locate the quick release buckle that would free him. The loadmaster casually moved over to the embarrassed, sweating civilian, placed a hand on his shoulder and held up the palm of his other hand to tell him to stop. He reached down and undone the simple clasp with a flick of the wrist, trying to suppress his laughter as he did so and set him free. Reece got to his feet, slung his bag over his shoulder and ran down the ramp onto the stony surface, stopping after about fifty feet, hoping to see someone who would tell him where to go next, but there was no-one. The helicopter took off creating a dust cloud that covered him from head to toe and sandblasted the back of his neck and he realized why the other passengers had run a lot further away than he did. After standing alone helplessly for a couple of minutes, it became clear that there was no welcoming committee to meet him and as he had no idea where to go, he made his way to the first person he saw.

The camp perimeter was constructed of metal cages that stood six feet high and four feet thick, which were lined with canvas sheets then filled with earth. On top of this grey wall, a coil of razor wire lay along its length, with another overhanging beneath it on the outer wall to prevent anyone climbing over. The wire glinted in the sunlight, an entanglement of razor-sharp teeth that would slice and shred the clothes and skin of anyone foolish enough to try to breach it. The construction of Camp Price was still in progress and a group of soldiers from the Royal Engineers was busy shovelling earth into the cages close to where Reece stood. The men stripped to the waist with desert camouflage shorts and boots worked busily to fill the cages with earth brought across to them by a dumpster and all were covered in a thick layer of grey dust. The soldiers were shovelling at a steady rhythmic pace. Bent forward at the waist, they all adopted the exact same method as they worked, mirroring each other's movements like clones, switching from right to left-handed spontaneously. The shovels were swung slowly rearwards, then accelerated forward into the earth, pause, push shovel forward assisted by their back knee, pause, slight push down on the handle, pause, lift, swing to the rear whilst pivoting, swing forwards ejecting earth. Repeat. Reece tapped one of them on the shoulder to get his attention and asked directions to the BRF.

"Excuse me mate, I'm from the Daily Telegraph, could you tell me where I can find the BRF please?" He asked politely.

The man, a stockily built Lance Corporal was breathing heavily, and took the opportunity to drop his shovel on the ground, resting his hands on his knees before catching his breath. As he stood up, he made a loud throaty groan, his lower back aching as he straightened it for the first time in about half an hour. The lost reporter waited patiently as the fatigued engineer reached across to retrieve a half empty bottle of water from a group of five seemingly identical bottles. His dirty hands unscrewed the lid, before he put the bottle to his mouth and gulped thirstily, small particles of dust were visible at the bottom of the bottle where the movement had unsettled them in the water. Satisfied, he lowered the bottle with a relieved sigh, before pointing toward a Union Jack flag, which flew high above another walled compound, fluttering slightly in the gentle breeze. "Aahhhh. Don't you just love a nice drink of warm water?" He exclaimed sarcastically. "BRF you say? .... Them meatheads live over there... See that compound? ... That's where they are mate. Through that blue gate." He said, still pointing.

"Thanks mate, much appreciated, have a good day." Reece replied, turning 90 degrees to his left and setting off towards the gate. It looked more like green than blue to him, but he didn't want to get into a debate about it.

The engineer returned to work, shovelling the earth and yelled out to Reece as he walked back across the helipad, stones crunching beneath his feet.

"You might want to keep that body armour and helmet on if you're going into that place!" He warned. "Bunch of lunatics!"

Reece extended his arm out to the side with his thumb up to acknowledge the advice as he walked away, chuckling quietly to himself, the soldier was so covered in dust he resembled a clay model, Reece could not even tell whether he was black or white, or young or old, and the thick West Midlands accent had only made him seem even more bizarre. Unsure what to make of the final comments he kept his protective clothing on and made his way to find the BRF.

The dilapidated green gate hung open at 45 degrees on one contorted hinge, the weight of it slowly bending the iron fixing downwards. Evidence of two other hinges was visible on the wall, but they had capitulated long ago and been scavenged as scrap metal by the locals. Reece walked through the entrance and into the small compound. Within the walls was a dishevelled, single storey, concrete building, riddled with bullet holes, broken gutters and rotten wooden window frames. The glass from the windows had long been smashed with some remnants of broken glass still laying on the ground beneath them. In its place now were sandbags, which were great for protection, but not so good for letting in daylight or enjoying the scenery. The flat roof was fortified all the way around its perimeter with more sandbags, stacked neatly about two feet high and 3 sandbags deep, as if prepared for some heroic last stand. The roof housed a mast that stood 5 metres high, on top of it sat what looked like an old car CB aerial from the 1980's which swayed from side to side in a large arc with every passing gust of wind. Several black antennas and satellite dishes also littered the roof all pointing in the same direction expectantly. Reece had anticipated more, the compound seemed quite dormant. In his mind, he'd imagined a hive of activity, something more like a gladiator school or ninja academy. Underwhelmed he walked to the wooden door and knocked three times, doing his best to ensure it was loud enough, but not obtrusive. The door rattled in its fragile frame,

although it looked heavy, it was poorly made from cheap ply-
wood, and moved open a few inches just from the force of the
knock. After waiting a polite amount of time, he tried again, this
time holding the door closed with his left hand while knocking
slightly louder with the right, using the point of his knuckles
this time for a sharper sound. After a few seconds the door
slowly opened inwards as a bearded man pulled on it and presented himself in the doorway. Dressed in different camouflage
to the others he`d seen, the huge soldier crouched slightly to fit
under the door frame, his broad shoulders barely squeezing into
the space. Reece introduced himself. "Hello, I'm Reece Carnell
from the Daily Telegraph. Here to cover your guys story for the
people back home." With a stern expression on his face the man
looked Reece straight in the eye, his bright blue eyes clearly visible through the mass of hair that surrounded them, his gaze
momentarily dropped to Reece's feet, before returning eye to
eye, like some kind of cyborg with laser scanner eyes. Reece returned his gaze, smiling flatly with a closed mouth and his eyebrows raised, waiting for a response. The man broke into a
broad, surprisingly friendly smile as he spoke.

"No shit! Well come on in buddy, welcome to our palace." The
man mountain extended his hand and pulled Reece towards him
through the door as he shook it firmly. Turning his head towards
the inside of the room he boomed. "Yo! Guys there's a British
dude from the Daily Telegraph here to do a story on us. How bad-
ass is that?"

The British Army had many foreign and commonwealth soldiers, but Reece had never before come across an American serving in the ranks, but this man was definitely American, by his
accent Reece guessed New York or at least east coast. The door
closed behind him as he stepped inside, pulled shut by a piece of
green bungee cord tied to the frame.

As his eyes adjusted to the relative darkness of the indoors Reece
immediately noticed a large amount of paraphernalia displayed
on the walls and ceiling. On the back wall, behind a large round

table hung a huge American flag. Next to that, hanging slightly off centre and tilted to the right, was a framed picture of George W Bush, the President of the United States. More soldiers approached, dressed in the same digital camouflage material as the first. As one reached out to shake Reece's hand, he noticed another American flag, this time attached to the man's shoulder sleeve on a Velcro patch. One thing was certain, these were not the BRF!

"We gonna be famous boys!" Cheered one of the soldiers.

"We're fuckin rock stars now bitches!" Shouted another excitedly.

One man appeared in the corner dramatically, stepping one foot up onto a chair. Standing with his shirt unzipped, mirrored sunglasses on, and a cigarette hanging from his mouth, in a strong Spanish accent he declared "If you're looking for a poster boy, look no further amigo!" He tilted his head forward to look over the top of his sunglasses at Reece, then walked away dramatically disappearing through the small cloud of smoke he had exhaled.

The atmosphere was buzzing with excitement, everyone in the building was energised by the thought of getting some public recognition for their hard work. Some sought fame, others the chance to share their story. Either way there was no going back now for Reece, he couldn't face the idea of telling them he`d got the wrong place.

After a lot of introductions and vigorous handshakes, Reece finally sat down with a few of the soldiers that had been selected by the behemoth he'd originally met. He was the Gunnery Sergeant who everyone addressed as "Gunny."

Reece was being offered food and drink from all directions, declining most but eventually accepting an ice cold can of Coke and a packet of Cheetos crisps.

He rested his notebook on his thigh and took a mouthful of Coke before placing the can on the ground by his feet. The condensation from the can made his hand wet and he wiped it on his trouser leg then reached into his breast pocket for his pen, removing the lid with his teeth before starting his unprepared questions.

"Right, gentlemen, let's get started, thanks for having me, it's a pleasure to meet you all. First things first, how exactly do you spell the name of the unit?" He asked. He still had no idea who these soldiers were.

"How do we spell it?" Queried Gunny.

"Yes. Just to make sure I get it right." Confirmed Reece.

"How do we spell it?" Repeated Gunny, looking puzzled.

"Ahem, yes, just to make sure I spell it the US way, not the English way."

"O...D. ..A." Replied Gunny. "I don't see how there's any other way to spell it. O.D.A."

"Excellent. Exactly as I thought." Said Reece convincingly, writing down the three letters at the top of his page then underlining it twice with an over exaggerated swipe of his pen and exclamation mark.

Reece spent the next hour talking to the ODA and learned that Operational Detachment Alpha was the primary fighting force of the US Special Forces, Green Berets. They were very forthcoming with their stories, discussing some real feats of bravery and tales of the chaos of battle. Their most recent mission was to recue a captured U.S Marine called Sergeant O'Malley that had been assumed dead after a helicopter crash near Kandahar. The coalition became aware of his survival when the Taliban posted a video of him on the internet. Wounds to his face and head were clearly visible, possibly from the crash, possibly from being beaten and he was made to read out a statement demanding the immediate U.S withdrawal from Afghanistan. The spectacle of a broken, battered American soldier on television has caused a massive reaction from the U.S military who made it their highest priority to recover him. Personally overseen by the senior officer of the coalition, General McGraw, himself a Marine, everything was thrown at it, satellites were diverted to focus on possible holding locations and eavesdrop on communications, electronic warfare aircraft were deployed to intercept radio transmissions, CIA agents followed up on intelligence leads and special forces units mounted search and rescue missions. The ODA had launched twice based on intelligence received through covert sources. The first being a total waste of time into a deserted warehouse complex, the second being their most recent. The second mission was thought to be the closest anyone had come to finding O'Malley and the ODA were convinced that they only missed him by a couple of hours.

Inserting by helicopter and supported by U.S Apache and Super Cobra attack helicopters the ODA had flown low-level into the target area and fast-roped onto the roof of a modern compound in a suburb south of Kandahar. The insertion had been met with fierce resistance from Taliban fighters inside and the ODA suffered several injuries before securing the target, killing ten enemy and taking two others prisoner along with several mobile phones and laptop computers seized at the scene. DNA tests on blood stains taken from the building also confirmed that O'Malley had been there. When the fighting started three vehicles were seen fleeing the scene, two motorcycles and a van. The two motorcycles were destroyed as they sped down a dirt track away from the town, but the van was only monitored as it could have contained O'Malley. Frustratingly the van drove into a densely populated area on the city outskirts and video footage from the attack helicopters in pursuit clearly showed a person being bundled out of the vehicle and into an apartment complex. Analysis of the footage was inconclusive, but it was thought highly likely that the person seen was indeed O'Malley and despite a massive follow up operation to secure and search the area, he was not found. Gunny pointed to a black and white flag hanging on the wall, at the top were the acronyms POW

* MIA which stood for prisoners of war and missing in action and at the bottom were the words YOU ARE NOT FORGOTTEN. Below the flag were several photographs of U.S servicemen and women that were either unaccounted for or known prisoners in Afghanistan. Reece moved closer to study their faces. "Is it ok if I take a photograph of this?" He asked politely.

"Absolutely, go right ahead." Gunny replied, placing a hand on his shoulder and pointing to one of the pictures of a U.S Marine in his ceremonial uniform of white peaked cap, dark blue jacket and gold buttons. His left breast adorned with several rows of medals. "That's him. That's Sergeant O'Malley right there." He said. "We won't give up until all these guys are back home, safe with their families." Reece took a photo of all the soldiers separately and one more of them all together beneath the flag.

Although unintended, this material had turned out to be a real golden nugget, a great story in its own right, but it was totally unauthorised and Reece knew he would have to retrospectively seek permission to publish any of it, with a high risk of being refused. After the interview he was given a quick tour of the compound and took some more photos of the men, promising to forward them copies once he had access to his email account. Most of their equipment was stored in an adjacent compound, but he wasn't allowed to see it for security reasons, as some of it was classified SECRET. Before leaving he exchanged telephone numbers and email addresses with Gunny, then collected his kit and said his farewells.

"I'm also doing another story on a British unit called the BRF. Do you know where I can find them?" He asked Gunny.

A voice quickly replied from one of the side rooms "Make sure you ask them how to spell that too!"

Laughter erupted.

Reece nodded his head, accepting the jibe. He deserved that.

Gunny answered. "Go back out through the gate, turn right and you'll see a blue gate 50 yards away. Those crazy mother fuckers are in there".

"Crazy?" Reece Queried.

"Don't worry, they're great guys. Just a bit crazy that's all." Gunny reassured.

"Those gringos are fucking loco!" A familiar voice interjected. Reece looked up to see the poster boy standing in exactly the same place as before in exactly the same pose. "Good luck amigo."

"Erm, thanks." Reece replied.

Stepping outside, there was a definite increase in temperature as the day began to warm up, the Sun's rays beaming over the walls, heating the concrete and metal structures of the compound. Reece walked back through the green gate and turned right as instructed. Sure enough, there it was, 50 yards away, a blue gate.

Behind him a voice shouted. He turned around to see a man stood on a wall shouting and gesticulating in his direction. He tried to hear what was being said but the noise of the generators and machinery was overpowering him. He turned around to check for anyone behind him but nobody else was around. Concluding that it must be him the person was shouting at, he made his way towards him, holding his hand to his ear and turning it towards him as he walked. "I can't hear you." He shouted back. "Hang on, I`ll come to you." He yelled pointing to himself and then towards the other man to emphasise his words. He walked up to the wall beneath where the man stood, the stones crunching underfoot all the while, adding to the din and scuppering any chance of him hearing anything. "What are you saying?" He asked.

The man bent down into a squat to get closer. It was the same guy that gave him directions earlier. "I said blue gate mate, not green" He stated clearly, pointing back across the heli pad. "The green gate is the American ODA compound. You want the BRF, that's' the blue gate mate."

It had already been a long morning. Reece feigned a smile and reluctantly gave a thumbs up to the Engineer. "Thank you. I'll try the blue gate this time. Have a good day." Turning around he retraced his steps back across the helicopter pad, past the green gate and entered the BRF compound through the blue gate. Tucked away in a corner of the camp with its own perimeter wall and only one entry / exit point the place was rarely visited by outsiders and easy to monitor people coming and going.

CHAPTER FOUR

Welcome To The BRF

The BRF compound was an old Afghan jail facility that had been allocated to house the men and their equipment. The main building was made of concrete and steel and contained twenty-four solitary confinement cells over two floors which some of the soldiers had commandeered as sleeping quarters, preferring them to the tents outside. The other cells were used as stores, one full of rifle, pistol and machine gun ammunition, one packed to the ceiling with anti-tank rockets and grenades. Others kept the rations, water, and maps etc. In the corner, with an improvised curtain made from an old blanket across the doorway, one of the cells housed a small table, piled high with an impressive selection of pornographic magazines. The jails' original purpose was to house Afghan army offenders, when it was part of a small garrison that had since been consumed by the British base. Typical inhabitants would serve short sentences of up to 28 days for crimes such as petty theft or being AWOL. However, the blood-spattered walls and floors along with numerous shackle points and chains served as a constant reminder of the jails more recent history after the camp had been occupied by the Taliban. They had used it as a torture and execution facility where the Sharia Courts sent men found guilty of crimes such as treason, blasphemy and homosexuality. Many women had also been flogged and executed for adultery or improper behaviour.

Naturally suspicious, the BRF platoon sergeant stopped his workout on the improvised punch bag made from mail sacks and rope and filled with sand, to approach the nervous looking reporter as he stood sheepishly in the middle of the compound.

"Who are you looking for mate?" He quizzed sternly, sweat pouring from his body and breathing heavily as he took off his boxing gloves and began unwrapping the red bandages that were wrapped around his hands.

"Hello, my name is Reece Carnell from The Daily Telegraph, I'm here to do a story on the BRF, can you tell me where I could find Major Johnny Hill?" Reece offered his hand to Frank as he introduced himself, but Frank didn't take it. Instead he raised his eyes to the sky and through gritted teeth snarled "Oh fucking really, says who?"

This wasn't quite the reaction Reece had hoped for and it was apparent his arrival was unexpected.

"The Media Operations Officer, Captain Smythe-Brockett arranged for me to be embedded with your unit, to cover the great work you guys have been doing out here, Major Hill cleared it yesterday." Reece tried in vain to hide his nervousness as he spoke to Frank, but the sergeant's obvious disapproval only made him worse.

"No shit!?" He said turning around. "Has anyone seen the boss?" Frank shouted his question towards the other men in the compound, his fists tightly clenched by his side.

"He's gone up the tower Frank," came the reply from the soldier sharpening his knife, who spoke without taking his eyes off the razor-sharp blade.

"Right, you!" Frank said sharply, pointing at Reece. "Follow me, we'll get this shit sorted out right now!" With that Frank brushed past Reece parrying him to the side with the outside of his forearm, heading back through the blue gate with long, fast strides, his arms swinging from side to side. Reece followed obediently, almost running to keep up with Frank as he marched off angrily toward the tower which stood over 100ft high in the centre of the camp.

The tower was a steel construction of two levels. The top level was manned by two soldiers 24 hours a day and was fortified with sandbags and draped in camouflage netting. Inside this bunker was a machine gun, a sniper rifle, two anti-tank rockets, a thermal imager and night viewing devices. From here the sentries could see for miles in all directions and only three days before a sniper had killed a suicide bomber as he drove toward the front gate on a motorbike wearing a vest full of explosives. The bullet hit with such force it took his head clean off his shoulders stopping the attack over 400m from the camp perimeter. Since then the Taliban decided not to attempt another suicide attack on the base. The crazed motorcyclist was the 34th victim of the 3 Para Sniper Platoon, though their eventual total kills would be well over a hundred by the end of the tour. Halfway up the tower was another platform which was sometimes used by the officers for briefings. From this elevated vantage point commanders could point out key locations and reference points on the ground when giving orders for patrols in the local area.

This was also the place where the BRF platoon commander Major Johnny Hill went to clean his weapons, away from interruption and the incessant banter of his men. His superiority complex had always prevented him from asking advice from anyone of subordinate rank and as a result he didn't know how to correctly strip and clean his weapons. Up the tower he could muddle through without being caught out and avoid being compromised by his men. Reaching the foot of the ladder, Frank stopped and grasped it with both hands before calling out. "Boss, are you up there?"

Johnny heard Frank's voice and sensed the anger in it. Quickly he began to reassemble the machine gun. "Yes, roger that, I'm nearly finished, wait there and I'll come down to you." He replied.

Frank was already climbing the ladder, reaching the platform just as Maj Hill finished hurriedly putting the gun back together, putting the butt onto the weapon upside down in his haste. Before he'd even dismounted the ladder, Frank began his rant.

"Boss, this fucking reporter thinks he's embedded with the platoon, apparently some prick has O.K.'d it with brigade HQ…"

CHAPTER FIVE

The Officer Commanding

Johnny Hill was a fourth generation Scots Guards officer from a very wealthy family that owned vast amounts of land and property that stretched across the coastline of Northern Scotland. His great-grandfather had served in France during World War One, his grandfather in North Africa during World War Two and his father the Falklands War in 1982, all serving with distinction and retiring as decorated Lieutenant Colonels after commanding their respective battalions. Johnny was the first male of the family to be born outside of Scotland, much to the disproval of the grandparents who were staunch Scottish nationalists. Although arrangements had been made for his mother to spend the last few weeks of her pregnancy at one of the country estates in Scotland, Johnny was born prematurely, and instead was born in a military hospital in London where his father was serving, only acknowledging his Scottish heritage when it was of benefit to him or helped him stand out from the crowd. Formal affairs were always a good opportunity for this and although he knew nothing of its history he would always make a point of dressing in full traditional Scottish Highland attire, donning his tartan kilt, with sporran, five-button waist coast and knee high socks. Despite this façade, johnny was a true

London socialite with no real knowledge or interest in his family's history or traditions. Attending boarding school in London, his early education had been excellent and at sixteen years old he moved into the MoD funded Welbeck Defence College in Leicestershire where he successfully completed his A-Levels, before moving on to the University of the Arts back in London. Unlike his predecessors Johnny had joined the military reluctantly, as a young man his ambition was to finish his time at boarding school as soon as possible and emigrate to the south of France where he could build a vineyard and produce fine wine. However, this dream had been destroyed by his aging grandfather, known affectionately by all his grandchildren as "The Colonel." He was the undisputed patriarch at the head of the family, and he controlled the fortunes it had amassed. The Colonel had written his will in intricate detail, dividing most of the family assets between his own two children, and his five grandchildren. His children's inheritance was unconditional, he was happy that they had achieved success in their own right and were both deserving. His grandchildren, as far as he was concerned, had not, and their inheritance was dependent on specific, individual factors. All would receive a substantial amount of money and heirlooms, but in order to receive a more generous bequeath, one that would afford them immediate retirement and a life of luxury, there were specific criteria for each. As the only male, Johnny's share, worth over £10 million would only be released after two key objectives had been achieved. The first he had already completed by obtaining his vocational degree in art. He had no passion for art but had been told it was a relatively easy degree to attain and managed it in two years, graduating at 20 years of age. The second condition was to reach the minimum rank of Major in the Scots Guards which he had almost done too. After graduation from university, Johnny had decided to take a "gap year" before enlisting in the army. He had already spent most of his life living in restrictive and regimented circumstances and wanted to take a break and enjoy himself a little before embarking on another year of formal education at the Royal

Military Academy Sandhurst for officer training. Johnny's gap year turned into two years as he enjoyed the London lifestyle of the upper class, driving nice cars, eating at the best restaurants and partying with the London elite until the early hours was an expensive lifestyle that his parents eventually tired of funding, forcing him to enrol at Sandhurst and do his duty just after his 22nd birthday. Welbeck College had prepared Johnny well for the Academy and he settled in quickly even though all of his friends from Welbeck had already been through the training the previous year as they had taken a single gap year, not two. Johnny's instructor was a Colour Sergeant from the Parachute Regiment called George Johnstone, a lean, muscular Falklands veteran from the Third Battalion the Parachute Regiment who had fixed bayonets and killed Argentine soldiers at close quarters as an eighteen year old in 1982. In 3 Para he was known as "JJ," a nickname awarded to him by his first platoon sergeant who was not particularly good at spelling. JJ had already been instructing officer recruits at Sandhurst for over a year, and during that time the students had given him another nickname, "The Gasket." This was due to his tendency to "blow a gasket" when his instructions weren't followed. Generally relaxed in his approach JJ interacted in an informal manner with his recruits, giving encouragement and praise as readily as advice and criticism. His students quickly learned though, that he had several pet hates, which if compromised would cause him to blow a gasket, with a drastic personality change. Such inexcusable infractions included, straps left flapping or dangling on equipment, dirty weapon parts, equipment that rattled during movement and the wearing of Gore-Tex clothing when it wasn't raining. These crimes would cause a disproportionate response from the instructor that would usually manifest in a loud verbal assault followed by physical punishment in the form of push ups, sprints or partner carries. One day while out on a loaded march on the training area JJ noticed that Johnny had failed to secure the adjustment straps on his rucksack, which flapped in the strong crosswind as the ran along a dirt track. Another officer cadet had failed to secure his knife, fork and spoon inside his pack, and they rattled together with every step. JJ quietly led them to the bottom of a steep hill in the forest before bringing them to a halt to explain the next part of the exercise. He began calmly, but his agitated pacing and clenched fists warned the recruits that the gasket was about to go.

"You lot seem to think it's alright to run around here like a bunch of Boy Scouts, with kit hanging off you like a Chinese laundry and clattering like a one-man band! Do that in war and you'll get people fucking killed! Not acceptable gentlemen." He was shouting now. "Bergans off!" He screamed. The recruits quickly removed their rucksacks, placing them on the ground at their feet.

Without looking JJ pointed behind him to the hill. "See that hill?" He yelled. "Well?"

"Yes Colour Sergeant!" Shouted the recruits in unison.

"You lot are going to run up and down that hill," He said still pointing. "Until it looks like *that* hill!" He said menacingly, raising his other hand to point at a knoll behind them.

The officer cadets turned to see the other hill to their rear. It was bare, nothing but mud, not even a single weed grew. A few seconds later they turned back to look at the first hill which was covered in ferns, weeds and a few small saplings. JJ could tell they were confused by their facial expressions. He explained to them that the bare hill was also once covered in foliage, until he found his previous recruit platoon asleep during an ambush and meted out the same punishment to them. That hill was thereafter affectionately known to staff and students at Sandhurst as "JJ's Highway"

For over an hour Johnny and the other 29 recruits ran up and slid / hurtled down the steep hill grabbing onto everything they could to help pull themselves up, simultaneously ripping it out from the ground as they did so. JJ stood at the top shouting at them the whole time using himself as the marker they had to go around before descending. As instructed, the men destroyed the surface of the hill, tearing and kicking out anything that wasn't dirt, until there was nothing but a pile of leaves and branches stacked at the bottom. The climbing up became harder and slower while the descent got faster and faster, with nothing to grab hold of. Once JJ was content, and to avoid injury, he ordered the men to stop with a few final words of encouragement.

"Good effort gents." He said dryly. "Don't fuck up your equipment again because there's plenty more hills around here." He paused to look at their faces, confident by their expressions that the lesson was learnt." Bergans on!" He barked and led them exhausted back to camp. This sort of punishment was exclusive to Johnny's platoon as JJ was by far the harshest instructor at the academy, but although he was strict, he was fair. Johnny respected JJ, but he did not like him, his unpredictability and aggressiveness was unnerving.

Johnny endured the year-long course, making some good friends on the way and passing with an above average grade. Being in the field was not his forte, although capable he did not enjoy roughing it outdoors, especially in the cold and wet of the army training areas where it always seemed to rain and he particularly hated wearing camouflage cream which felt like sticky slime on his skin and left a horrible grime on his clothing that always felt cold and wet. JJ would often reprimand him for insufficient camouflage cream, unimpressed by the minimalist tiger stripes he would apply and would remind him that if the enemy saw him, they would also see his men and they would all end up dead because of his slack attitude. JJ could associate any misdemeanour to somehow causing fatalities when making his point. One time he lost his temper during a lesson because a recruit used the letter "O" instead of saying "zero" when reading out an encoded message.

"Fucking phonetic alphabet!" He screamed in the soldiers' face. "Do that on ops and you'll get your blokes fucking killed! There's no time to piss about when people are trying to kill you! Attention to detail gents, it's not rocket science. O is a letter, zero is a number and it's not called O anyway, because you are in the army now, it's called fucking Oscar! Zero is a number. Zero!" Angrily he drew a zero on the blackboard with a piece of yellow chalk, over emphasising the line that scored through it diagonally to differentiate it from the letter O and snapping it in half. One hundred push ups later everyone got the message.

Other parts of military training were much more enjoyable for Johnny, especially the pomp and ceremony that came with the Officers Mess. Formal functions were held regularly, and the officer cadets were expected to display a good understanding and compliance of Mess etiquette. Any event that required Johnny to dress up in his smartest attire and enjoy a posh meal and alcoholic drinks was his favourite activity. As officers, in addition to their military studies the recruits would not only need to display a thorough knowledge of current affairs, politics and economics but also be competent in social skills such as silver service dining, public speaking and chess. For some of the young men and women, this was a steep learning curve but for Johnny this was second nature, socialising was something he excelled at.

After Sandhurst johnny was posted to the Scots Guards who were conveniently stationed in London, guarding Buckingham Palace and conducting ceremonial duties. For the soldiers it meant long days standing guard outside grand buildings with tourists taking photographs and trying to make them react as they stood perfectly still in doorways or gates. For officers there was little to do and Johnny filled his time between duties riding horses in Hyde Park and visiting his mates that had jobs in the city. After six years in the Guards Johnny was beginning to get bored of regimental life. He'd been a Captain for four years and fulfilled three different posts, two years as a platoon commander in London, two years as a recruit platoon commander at the Guards Depot and the last two years as a desk officer in Northern Ireland. Most of his peers had completed operational tours in Afghanistan or Iraq which held more weight than his Northern Ireland tour and he was keen to deploy to the Middle East as soon as possible so he could compete on the promotion boards.

One day during an equipment capability conference at Army Headquarters a unit that he'd never heard of gave a recruiting brief, during which they explained that they had been deployed on operations five times in the past seven years. They had been deployed as the advance force for 16 Air Assault Brigade on every major operation the British Army was involved in since Kosovo in 1999. The major delivering the brief described his personal experience at the unit, detailing the hardships of the six-week selection course, the excitement of the military freefall course and the nuances of working in small teams as a member of the Brigade Reconnaissance Force. As a major he seemed to have a great deal of autonomy and responsibility and Johnny was surprised to hear that the officer had joined the unit as a captain. After the conference Johnny sought him out and picked his brains over a drink in the Officers Mess. It turned out that the last three officers to command the BRF had passed the course as captains and all been promoted during their tenure in recognition of the high level of responsibility and operational successes of the unit. Learning that the next selection course was being conducted in five weeks' time Johnny decided to apply. He was injury free, in the best shape of his life and eligible for promotion in the next twelve months. It seemed fate was telling him to go for it.

The BRF selection course was renowned as being extremely difficult, both physically and mentally with a success rate of about 25%. On the first day thirty men lined up to conduct the first assessment, an eight-mile battle march carrying a 40lb rucksack and weapon, to be completed in two hours. This was a standard test throughout the army that was imposed on them as a kind of health and safety benchmark before more arduous training could commence. On day one, the eight-miler was the only event of the day and the course were dispersed afterwards to prepare themselves and their equipment for the real work, beginning at 0600hrs the next day. Day two began with another march, this time ten miles, carrying the same weight of 40lbs and their rifles. Johnny assumed that the time allowed for this would be 2hrs 30mins, based on the pace of normal tests but was surprised to be told the maximum time was actually 1 hour 45 minutes. Johnny was sure it was a bluff, courses like this always had psychological elements thrown in to dislocate expectations and keep them guessing. After all, how could they go 2 miles more in fifteen minutes less? He was about to find out.

The BRF sergeant addressed the course after their short warm-up as they waited on the start line, jogging on the spot and shaking their legs out in preparation. Most of them had done their research and knew what was about to come.

"Right gents, listen in!" He shouted. "Today the course starts proper. Yesterday was a token gesture, a walk in the park that my mum could pass, so if you struggled on that, this ten-miler is going to be a bit of a shock for you. Keep up with the instructor, do not fall back. Do not stop to help anyone else and do not argue if you are told to get on the ambulance!" As he spoke, he rubbed his hands together rapidly to keep them warm in the cold wind and rain. "Any questions? No? Good luck gents."

None of the BRF instructors wore badges of rank on their clothing and were addressed as "Staff" by the course. This was deliberate and avoided difficult situations if a course member outranked the instructor. Students were addressed by their surname.

One man had surprisingly failed the eight-miler, so the 29 remaining lined up in three ranks, ready to go.

The instructor at the font called out. "By the front, quick march." Setting off at a fast walk. Within a few strides he called out again. "Prepare to double!" That phrase was one the course would learn to dread, and they were all surprised to hear it so early-on in the test. "Double march!" He shouted, opening his stride and breaking into a run. Double time was usually a slow jog when load carrying, but he seemed to be running at a normal pace, as if he weren't even carrying a heavy rucksack. The sergeant was right, it was a shock, and the entire course quickly strung out along the dirt track of the training area as the running continued for almost a mile, returning to a fast walk only when they reached the bottom of a steep hill and started to ascend. Johnny was fit and one of the few that kept up with the instructor, but even he had never moved that fast with a rucksack before. The instructor crossed the finish line in 1 hour 43 minutes, allowing two minutes for stragglers to catch up and eleven members of the course managed to pass, including Johnny.

Over the next six weeks the course covered hundreds of miles, with reducing numbers every day as people left the course through injury, voluntary withdrawal or failure. The days were long, starting at 0600hrs and usually finishing after lessons in the evening at around 2100hrs and they worked weekends as well, only getting one day off throughout. Johnny's fitness impressed the instructors, and he passed every physical test including the solo navigation marches across the mountains, also proving his endurance and navigation skills. Although performing well, Johnny had managed to aggravate some of the instructors however, going out of his way to find out their rank and then address them as "Private" or "Corporal" instead of "Staff". This had come across as condescending, and it was obvious he was attempting to assert his authority over them.

After the first two weeks the emphasis of the course switched from fitness and navigation to tactics and military skills, where Johnny excelled in the classroom but began to show weakness in the field. The training area was always wet and cold, and he was caught short several times not pulling his weight when the going got tough. One day he was found asleep while on sentry duty but refused to admit it when confronted, and another day he argued with the instructor when his weapon was found to be rusty during a snap inspection. At the end of the course the BRF were split 50/50 whether to award him a pass or not, but in the end, he got it. The decision to give him the pass was influenced by several factors including the current boss was due to leave and they needed an officer to deal with the other officers in Brigade Headquarters and they could not guarantee a better officer would pass the next course. For some of the BRF soldiers, particularly those who had been directly involved with training him and seen him under pressure, that was a regrettable decision but it was made above their level between the boss, the brigade Chief of Staff and the Brigadier. Three months later, Johnny took over as the BRF commanding officer, arriving in plenty of time for a thorough hand over from the outgoing boss and to commence pre-deployment training for their next planned deployment to Afghanistan in a few months' time. Pre-deployment training was hectic, requiring a lot of work from the BRF boss and Johnny tried to avoid it by loading himself onto the high altitude, low opening, HALO parachuting course in the USA instead. Two days before he was due to fly out to California the Chief of Staff found out and ordered him to cancel, sending one of the junior soldiers in his place.

He and his platoon sergeant Frank had already clashed heads within the first week with different ideas about the command structure and responsibilities in the unit. The BRF was split into six patrols of six men, usually lead by a corporal who had spent several years in the unit and worked his way up to Patrol Commander. Johnny did not like the fact that some of the patrols had sergeants in the team but were still commanded by a corporal who was junior in rank, but that was how it had always been. Usually the sergeant was a new member of the BRF that had not yet gained the experience to be in command and the corporal was highly experienced, having completed the other roles in the patrol already. As far as the soldiers were concerned it made perfect sense and everyone was content but coming from the Guards where rank was all important and regularly abused,

Johnny suggested that should be amended. Frank had served in the BRF since the rank of Private and had been a patrol commander as a corporal on operations twice himself. The debate had ended when Johnny was told to leave the sergeants office after he had irritated him with his superior attitude and lack of humility.

"Boss, with all due respect, you've only been here five minutes and you want to change the standard operating procedures that we've used for twenty years, those SOP's have been proven on operations countless times, and you want to do that now, right before we go on tour.! He said.

"My job, as Officer Commanding is to make hard decisions Sergeant Cutler." Replied Johnny. "And your job is to implement them!" He stated boldly.

Johnny had overestimated his sergeant's subservience and was unnerved by his sinister response.

"Right now, your job, is to get out of my fucking office!" He was staring down to the ground and rubbing the sides of his head as he spoke. "And my job is to count to ten before I lose my shit!"

Johnny left, closing the door behind him. They were not going to get on.

Four months into the Afghan tour, their relationship was strictly professional and their dislike for one another was impossible to hide, despite their efforts. Johnny had created a new role, calling himself the "Ground Commander," and Frank was "Patrol Commander." Patrol planning and execution was Franks responsibility, leaving Johnny's responsibility rather unclear, but allowing the soldiers to conduct their work relatively unimpeded. Johnny was sat in his usual place up the tower, using a paintbrush to clean sand from his dismantled machine gun, when he heard a familiar angry voice.

"Boss, are you up there?"

CHAPTER SIX

His Bite Is Worse Than His Bark

Frank climbed the ladder quickly. "Boss, this fucking reporter thinks he's embedded with the platoon, apparently some prick has O.K.'d it with brigade HQ..." The sergeants' voice and expression left the startled major in no doubt as to how he felt about the situation and he knew that the best course of action to take was to plead ignorance, at least until Frank had calmed down. He continued. "What sort of complete idiot would have given the go ahead for that? We've got no space for passengers out here; you need to tell brigade HQ that we don't want him, and he'll be on the next flight back to Kandahar!" Frank was quickly working himself into a frenzy, walking round in a small circle like a caged animal as he spoke.

"Okay Frank, this is as much a surprise to me as it is to you." Lied Johnny. "Leave it with me, I will phone the Chief of Staff and see what I can do. He won't be going anywhere for at least two days though as there are no flights until Monday, he'll have to use the spare bed space in my accommodation until then."

Reece stood awkwardly at the top of the ladder, switching his gaze between the floor and the apparently uninformed Major.

"Monday and he's gone!" Frank conceded as he looked Reece in the eye with a face of rage. "You try and stitch up my blokes and

I'll fucking kill you and bury you in the desert. I don't trust you and I don't like you, so stay out of my way!" He warned. "And if I catch you taking photos of anything or anyone without permission, stand by, because I'll ram that camera so far up your arse, you'll have zoom lenses for eyes! Do you understand me?"

"Y y y yes sir." Spluttered Reece, who had shifted silently away from the edge of the platform for fear of being thrown off. Never having encountered this kind of reception before he didn't know what to do with himself. The soldiers he had worked with on previous jobs had always been keen to be interviewed and photographed and excited at the prospect of being in a national newspaper. He stepped to the side as Frank grasped hold of the ladder, swung his leg around and started his descent pausing on the second rung to say something to Johnny. "You might want to put that butt on the right way around if you want to use that gun.... And I'd put the spring back in as well if I was you, every little helps!" With that he made his way down the ladder and back towards the platoon compound, shaking his head as he cursed Johnny Hill under his breath. Frank had noticed his boss' error the moment he stepped onto the platform. No wonder he stripped and cleaned it in isolation, he didn't have a clue.

Johnny looked down slowly and to his embarrassment saw the return spring was indeed under his chair, rendering the gun useless. He removed the butt and replaced the spring into its housing. As he put the butt back on the right way up he realised that for the duration of the last patrol his gun was ineffective, he had been assembling it that way since the start of the tour, the fact that he was the only man not to have fired his weapon was the only reason this had not been discovered.

"Don't worry about him, his barks' worse than his bite." Johnny rose to his feet, wiping his oily hands on his trousers and approached a shell-shocked Reece with his hand extended.

The dejected reporter gratefully accepted the first friendly gesture he'd seen since arriving and breathed a huge sigh of relief as they shook hands.

"You must be Reece Carnell? I'm Johnny Hill, BRF commander. Tarquin told me you want to do a story on my platoon, and I think it's a bloody good idea. You can stay with me and I'll give you everything you need. I've already picked some of my best photos to go with your article." He knew the potential to elevate his social standing by appearing in a prestigious newspaper like the Daily Telegraph.

"You had me worried there for a minute, I thought you didn't know I was coming," Reece replied, a little confused.

Johnny reassured him, "Please forgive my Platoon Sergeant, it's really nothing personal, he hates everyone. I think he used to dislike me too. Anger issues! Give him a couple of days and he'll get used to the idea."

Although he wore the rank of major now, Johnny had not actually been promoted yet, he was temporarily awarded "acting rank" by the Brigade Commander for the Afghan tour. He hoped a strong performance on this deployment would persuade his superiors to award him "substantive rank" on return, at which point he would become a bona fide major, fulfilling the second condition of his inheritance and could retire a rich man.

CHAPTER SEVEN

The Sergeant

Frank Cutler the BRF platoon sergeant was a thirty-one-year-old paratrooper of thirteen years' service in his beloved Parachute Regiment, seven of these in the BRF. Well respected by his men he rarely had to ask twice for things to be done. Since joining the BRF he had deployed on six overseas operations and worked his way up from Private to Sergeant in the last six years. The nickname "Fallshirmjaeger Frank" had been given to him during his early days in 3 Para because of his passion for World War Two stories of the German paratroopers. His bed space was covered in memorabilia from the British, German and American Airborne forces of that period, and he proudly wore his German parachute wings on his smock chest since completing jumps with them at their airborne school. Looking like the archetypal paratrooper, he stood six feet tall with a muscular build, his blonde hair was shaved almost bald, and his face bore three scars. One scar, the most obvious, ran across his left cheekbone and was a result of a vicious firefight during a rebel attack in Sierra Leone in 2000, Frank had killed sixteen of the rebels during the battle which lasted five hours, three with his bayonet and one with his bare hands. His actions had prevented the BRF position from being overrun. Afterwards he had remained humble about his achievement, but the Platoon Commander was so impressed by his tenacity and bravery that he was nominated for a Military Cross, an award which he was presented by the Queen in 2001. Tattoos covered his body from his shoulders to his elbows and on his back was another in the shape of a totem pole with the battle honours of the Parachute Regiment scribed onto it.

Frank was what the army classed as "Old School". Fiercely proud of his unit he worked relentlessly to achieve and maintain the highest standards in himself and his men. His social circle was limited to "The Airborne Brotherhood", and outside of this the only people he chose to care for was his small family which consisted of his mother, brother and wife who was seven months pregnant with their first child. Interaction with anyone outside of this select community he limited by necessity. The remainder of the population was treated with indifference by the short-tempered sergeant and fell into two categories; "Hats", was the name given to all non-airborne soldiers and were considered inferior to the airborne. Their units had been polluted by the political correctness that was rife across the country allowing sub-standard soldiers to find employment in their ranks. Fitness tests had been scrapped and replaced by fitness assessments, positions of power previously filled by long service men were now filled by women in order to fill an equal opportunities quota and drugs were an ever-increasing problem. Frank had been let down by every "Hat" he ever made the mistake of befriending, including the last one in 1998 who stole his wallet during the Physical Training Instructors course they were both attending. The former Schoolboy Boxing Champion had broken the Coldstream Guards nose, jaw and two ribs when he found out and vowed never to trust a "hat" again. The other category was civilians or "Civvies". Civvy life held no interest for Frank, to him it was all too monotonous and unexciting and even though he still had nine years left to serve in the army the prospect of becoming one when he retired already bothered him. The friends he left behind when he joined up were either in prison or petty criminals reliant on drugs and booze. He hadn't spoken to any of them since leaving town for the Parachute Regiment Depot and had no wish to do so.

Frank was a big believer in bringing back national service as he thought it would solve a lot of the problems with the escalating juvenile crime and general lack of respect by youths these days. As a teenager he had been rapidly heading for prison himself until a judge gave him a second chance and he saw the error of his ways. Frank joined the Paras at eighteen years old, and for the first time in his life he was confronted by men that scared him. The instructors who introduced themselves to the sixty recruits at the Parachute Regiment Depot on day one of training were a menacing collection of four Corporals and a Sergeant. Three of the stern-faced instructors were veterans of the Falklands War, where the Paras had re-established their reputation as the world's elite fighting force by defeating Argentine troops at odds of 3–1 using bayonets and hand to hand fighting. This they had done after first marching fifty miles cross country. Frank although only sixteen years old had been in several fights with grown men and won them all but learned quickly that there was more to fighting than boxing when on his first afternoon he decided to pick a fight with his instructor. After lunch he took a lie down on his bed, a cardinal sin in Parachute Regiment Depot which infuriated the Corporal who entered the room as he was drifting off to sleep. The NCO rushed across the room screaming at Cutler to get up and, angered further by his lethargic response tipped the bed on its side with him still on it. Franks short fuse blew, and he quickly jumped to his feet and threw a right hook toward the raging Corporal who instinctively ducked the punch, simultaneously fish-hooking the young fighter and dragged him to the floor by his mouth. The highly trained Welshman then drove his knee into the flailing recruits back between his shoulder blades and put him into a choke hold, almost bending him in half at the same time. Gasping for air Frank was totally at the mercy of the NCO who calmly explained to the rest of the 10 man room who stood watching open mouthed that there was no such thing as a fair fight, just a winner and a loser, and paratroopers never lost. Just before Frank was about to pass out, he released his hold and walked out. Frank was deeply embarrassed but at the same time extremely impressed by the fighting skill of the man who had just dealt him his first defeat, the counter attack had been so fast that he had to ask his roommates what had happened.

From that moment on he decided that no matter what, he was going to become a Paratrooper and six months later, watched by his family he not only passed out of training, but was also awarded "Top Recruit" during the parade. The training had been relentless, harder than anything he had ever done or imagined but he had persevered and stood proud with the others that had also made it to the end of the process. Of the forty that started, twelve were left. Almost three quarters had failed, some through injury, some through lack of fitness or skills, one had gone AWOL. In the first month, on two separate occasions some-one had asked Frank and his roommates to help them kill them-selves. The first was after week 1 and he came into Franks room one evening while they were all sat around the table polishing their boots. Soaking wet and dripping water onto the highly buffed floor wearing just a pair of shorts he asked them if they could help him drown himself. Seemingly he had already filled one of the baths and tried several times, but failed, unable to stay submerged and instinctively coming up for air. He wanted the others to hold him under to prevent him coming up next time. They declined and one of them reported the incident to the duty corporal. A few days later he was gone, medically discharged. The other assisted suicide request came during week 4 when one of the recruits named Bufton received a letter from his girlfriend saying their relationship was over. He was already struggling to cope with the pressure and that was the final straw. That young man had persuaded Frank and one of the others, called Smith to follow him up to the 4th floor of the accommodation block and then asked them to throw him out of a window onto the concrete below. An unpopular member of the platoon that regularly angered the corporals, Bufton was responsible for the entire platoon being punished on many occasions. Frank and his room mate questioned his authenticity, guessing that it was a cry for help, to gain sympathy.

"Why don't you just jump?" Smith asked.

"I can't, I'm afraid of heights. I can't get to the edge." He replied. If I could, I would, but I can't get to the edge.

"Take a big run-up along the corridor." Smith suggested, pointing down the long corridor.

Frank interjected. "Plus, if we chuck you out, we'll be in the shit, we'd probably get thrown out of the regiment and have to join some non-ferocious regiment. Fuck that!"

"Or even worse we could be sent to .... the R.A.F!" Joked Smith. "Get a grip of yourself you mong." He continued. "And anyway, if you really wanted to kill yourself, you'd jump off the abseil tower, that's much higher. You'd probably only break your leg from here. Now the abseil tower, that'll definitely do the job, it's massive." He said. The following morning the Platoon Sergeant, Sergeant Johnstone broke the news to the recruits that Bufton had attempted suicide during the night by leaping from the abseil tower. He was found unconscious at the base of the tower in the morning by the security patrol and rushed to hospital with multiple injuries. After two weeks in an induced coma Bufton's life support was turned off. Frank and Smith never spoke of that night to anybody.

In the Paras, Frank had finally found a place where he belonged, a place where his mental and physical attributes could be nurtured and harnessed, a place where he could thrive and importantly, where he was surrounded by people like him. To many the Paras was a place for nut cases, but to Frank it was home. Since the age of eight Frank had wanted to be a paratrooper after he watched a documentary which followed a platoon of recruits through Depot Para, the training establishment solely dedicated to Parachute Regiment recruits. Every week he watched it with his mother and older brother on an old black and white television, mesmerised by the soldiers and the exciting activities they conducted, hanging on every word of the instructors as they pushed recruits to their limits in every episode. Before that programme aired, he fantasised about the typical careers boys his age dreamt of such as racing car driver or football player, but after the first instalment of the Paras documentary he made the decision, and never wavered since. Even after all these years he could still remember the theme tune that played at the beginning of the show, such was the impact it had on him. His plan was always to join the army at sixteen years old, as soon as he could after finishing school. Frank hated school and was expelled during his last year ending up attending a "naughty boys' school," officially the Secondary Support Centre. Because of its small size and strong teacher-to-student ratio the support centre could only cater for eight children per day which meant Frank only attended days per week. All the boys and girls were either on the brink of expulsion or already expelled from their original schools for various reasons, but mostly for aggressive or violent behaviour towards teachers or other pupils. Frank was there for both. A friend of his of Asian heritage had been getting bullied by some students and Frank had intervened, punching one of them to the ground. A teacher had heard the commotion and rushed to investigate, arriving in time to witness Frank sat on the other boys' chest, punching him repeatedly in the face. When the teacher, a short, fat, big eared science tutor nicknamed "Yoda" by the children aggressively wrested Frank from the fight, Frank had not realised who it was and assumed it was one of the other boys friends, instinctively lashing out and striking him also, knocking him to the floor with a bloody nose. With a record of fighting, absence and poor behaviour already behind him the Headteacher expelled Frank that day.

The support centre was much better for Frank. The teachers

were all trained in child welfare and counselling and worked in a much more relaxed and informal manner. Frank appreciated being spoken to as a person rather than a student and reflected the respect he was shown back towards the three regular tutors, two ladies and one man, who conversed with the kids on first name terms. Franks favourite teacher was Tom. Only thirty years old he appeared much older because of a full head of white hair that he wore brushed back in a flat top style, held in place by a copious amount of extra-hold hair gel. None of the kids knew, but Tom's hair had turned grey over night when he was only twenty-three years old, after he was caught in an IRA bomb attack in London in 1983. He had been Christmas shopping with his mother in Harrods when the bomb detonated. The blast ruptured both of his ear drums, rendering him completely deaf, but after a few months the hearing returned to his right ear. In his left ear he wore a hearing aid which served as a constant reminder of that day. His mother did not survive, her body mutilated by flying glass and debris was strewn across the first floor although strangely, her decapitated head which Tom discovered immediately after the blast was in pristine condition, her hair perfect and glasses still on her face. It was either the physiological shock of the bomb or the psychological shock of finding his mothers remains which caused his hair to go white. Tom had tried to join the army himself after the murder of his mother, also aspiring to be a paratrooper, he thought he would be able to avenge her death by deploying to Northern Ireland and killing members of the IRA. However, his deafness halted him at the first post when entering the army careers office wearing his hearing aid. Helping Frank get prepared for the army provided some consolation. Frank performed well while at the new school, attaining good grades for his work and building healthy relationships with the staff, particularly Tom who invested time into him and encouraged his military ambitions, even helping him with physical training advice and lending him some of his own weight training equipment.

Outside of school however, Frank had began mixing with an undesirable crowd. Attending the support centre three days a week, he was supposed to revise and study at home for the other two school days, but before long he got bored of that and sought stimulation outside. With all his friends at school Frank ended up wandering the streets of the town and was soon noticed and befriended by a group of older boys and young men that loitered in the town daily. Most times the gang numbered between four to six young men, some of them connected to the organised criminals of the town through older family members, and Frank slowly spent more and more time with them, gradually joining in with their criminal activities. It started with drinking alcohol, sometimes strong beer or cider, other times cheap spirits which were often stolen from supermarkets. This quickly escalated to Frank stealing the alcohol, then robbing bags, coats and purses that had been left unattended in shops, hotels and office buildings. Egged on by the older boys, Frank committed his first mugging a few weeks after joining the gang. The victim was a skinny young man who chose the wrong time to use a cash machine located in a poorly lit back street. The gang watched him withdraw what looked like a sizable amount of money which he placed in his wallet and into his back pocket and then followed him as he walked away. Frank had already been informed it was his turn to make some money for the nights drinks and caught up with the bespectacled man as he passed a disused petrol station. Frank called out. "Excuse me mate." He said. The man continued walking, pretending not to hear. Frank tried again, louder this time. "Excuse me mate." He said.

The man stopped and turned, and Frank walked up close to him, his three companions moving tactically to surround them.

"Can I help you?" The man asked nervously, looking around to see his escape routes blocked and pushing his glasses upwards with his index finger.

"Give us your money!" Demanded Frank.

"I haven't got any." Said the man convincingly, showing the palms of his empty hands as if to prove it.

"Hit him Frank!" Shouted one of the thugs impatiently.

"We saw you at the cash machine mate! Give me your fucking wallet or you are going to get battered!" Frank said, adopting a more sinister tone.

"I haven't got any money. I just got a statement printout. Now leave me alone or I'll call the police! Go on, fuck off!" The frightened man hoped his words would deter an attack.

"Hit the prick!" Ordered another of the assailants.

Frank had already made that decision and cracked the young man with a big right hand to the chin, knocking him to the floor unconscious. Kneeling beside him Frank quickly found his wallet in the back pocket and stuffed it into his own trouser pocket before standing up and walking away briskly. The others followed closely behind but one of the gang members stopped and stood over the flattened victim. Frank noticed.

"I've got the money here." He called out.

"Yeah I know, I'm coming." Said the thug calmly, before swinging his foot rearwards and then kicking the helpless victim in the head as hard as he could, before running to catch up with the others. Laughing hysterically, he jumped in the air and high-fived one of the others who was also laughing like a deranged lunatic. The only person not laughing was Frank and as they walked away back slapping and congratulating him, he felt ashamed. The unprovoked attack on a defenceless man weighed heavily on Frank and for the next couple of weeks he only got involved with the theft jobs, he knew it was wrong but he enjoyed the drinking and socialising it paid for so carried on. One day, while drinking in the town bus station a stranger walked past the group minding his own business when one of them launched an empty beer can at him. The stranger casually bent down to pick it up and turned towards them. "No thanks lads,

I'm driving." He said, continuing on his way and depositing it in the next bin he walked past. For some reason this enraged the young men who immediately leapt to their feet and went after him, following him out of the station into a rear courtyard, where a couple of them ran ahead to block his route. That day there were six of them and they circled him menacingly as he stood still in the centre.

"I don't want any trouble lads." He said.

"Too late smart arse!" One boy replied.

Frank spoke up. "Why don't you apologise and get out of here while you still can?" He proposed, trying to save the man a beating.

"Yeah, say sorry and we'll all pretend you didn't just take the piss back there, and let you go on your way." Agreed another.

The man looked like he could handle himself, standing about six feet tall, he had broad shoulders and muscular arms with veins showing and he didn't appear afraid. But he knew as well as they did, he couldn't win a fight against all six of them.

"Lads." He conceded. "I apologise if I offended you, I don't want any trouble and I'll be on my way now."

"Apology accepted, now piss off and don't come back!" Said Frank. Happy that violence had been averted.

The man nodded towards Frank to acknowledge his command and turned to leave only to be met as he pivoted by a piece of broken paving slab smashing into his face. One of the thugs was not content with the truce that had been negotiated on his behalf and had taken matters into his own hands, picking up the lump of concrete and swinging it sidewards into his face, shattering his orbital and cheek bone. As soon as he fell two of the others waded in, kicking and stomping on him while he curled up, semi-conscious, in the foetal position to protect himself. A woman screaming at them to stop from an adjacent office window saved him from further damage when they ran away.

That incident resulted in Frank and his five friends getting arrested, one was sent to prison for grievous bodily harm, two were handed suspended sentences and the others, including Frank were fined. The lady who had shouted from the window had provided a witness statement that they had not delivered any of the blows to the victim. During Franks case his teacher Tom had given an excellent character reference and his solicitor had appealed to the Juvenile Court judge for leniency, stating that he wanted to join the army and a heavy sentence would prevent any possibility of that. The judge, himself an ex-army officer who had served in the Korean war took this into account and awarded the lowest conviction available to him, which meant Frank would be eligible to apply for the army after two years, telling him in the courtroom. "I have no desire to deny you a career in her majesty's armed forces if that is indeed your intention. But be under no illusion young man, if I see you here before me in this court again within the next two years, I will not be so lenient, and you will go to prison! Is that clear?"

"Yes, your honour." Frank replied solemnly.

"Be assured that I am a man of my word Mr Cutler. I hope that you are also." He warned sternly.

"Yes, your honour." Repeated Frank.

The whole arrest and prosecution had scared Frank, at one point thinking he was going to prison, but surprisingly that was not the last time he got involved with crime. That came a couple of weeks later when he was in town one evening with one of his delinquent friends. Walking down a road, they were looking inside the windows of cars parked by the kerb when Frank noticed some money on the passenger seat of one. On closer inspection he could see it was a five-pound note and decided he should take it. Nominating his friend to keep lookout he searched for something to smash the window with, picking up a rock from a garden nearby and returning to the car. The lookout gave him the nod and Frank quickly used the rock to shatter the glass with one hard strike, discarding it on the pavement. After another quick check to see if anyone was coming, in one fluid action, he punched through the shattered window, reached into the car and grabbed the cash, removing it from the vehicle and taking it with him as he left the scene in a brisk walk. His friend followed on the opposite side of the road and they both began to run once they turned a corner ahead, getting as far away from the crime scene as quickly as they could. Stopping after a couple of minutes they sat down at a bus stop.

"How much did we get?" His accomplice asked.

Frank held up the haul. "Five quid." He said.

"Nice one mate. Easy money." The young man reached into his pocket and pulled out some change, picking out a few coins before offering them to Frank. "Here you go mate, two pounds fifty. I give you this, you give me that, and we're even. Don't spend it all at once."

Frank watched glumly as his mate took the five-pound note and replaced it with the coins for a 50/50 split. Shortly afterwards he made his excuses, took his money and made his way home. That night he decided that was the last crime he would commit. He realised that he had just risked everything for two pounds and fifty pence. The walk home and the next few days were tense and every time he heard a knock at the door or saw a police officer he was filled with dread that he might be arrested. The judge's words echoed in his mind. Imagine appearing in front of him again, being sent to prison and ruining the chance of joining the paratroopers for such a pathetic amount of money. He was ashamed of himself.

Returning to the support centre he sat down with the staff to apologise for his behaviour and to thank Tom, promising to commit to studying. Six months later his schooling came to an end. He had knuckled down as promised and passed all the exams he took, although they were not the GCSE's he would have taken at a normal school, instead a less recognised award used by specialist training centres like his school, young offenders prisons and the military. With 18 months of his sentence remaining before he could apply for the army Frank sought work, rarely lasting more than a few months before moving on to something else. Every job he took, from labouring on a building site, to meat packing in a warehouse quickly got boring, but they all strengthened his desire to join the army and they all motivated him to get fit and strong enough for the paratrooper training he wanted to undertake.

A year and a half later, having kept out of trouble and prepared himself physically and mentally Frank walked through the Armed Forces Careers Office to apply for the Parachute Regiment. The office was manned by two serving servicemen and Frank was approached by one of them as soon as he entered.

"Hello young man, how can I help you?" He asked.

Frank was a little puzzled, the man was not what he had expected. About the same height as Frank, he wore a bright white shirt and trousers with razor sharp creases pressed into the legs and sleeves, shiny black shoes and sported a beard. His immaculate shirt was tucked into his trousers and his belly hung over his belt slightly.

"I want to join the army." Frank said hesitantly.

"Are you sure I can't interest you in joining the senior service?" Replied the officer.

"What's that?" Frank asked.

"The Royal Navy!" He responded pointing to a large poster of a ship on the wall. "The senior service of the British Armed Forces, founded by King Henry the Eighth in 1546, a hundred and fifty years before the British Army." He stated proudly.

Frank looked him up and down, he was not selling it. "I want to join the paratroopers." He clarified.

"How about the Royal Marines?" Persisted the officer. "You could be a soldier *and* a sailor. Travel the world, make a man of you. Get to wear this uniform, the chicks love it!"

Frank could think of nothing worse, to him he looked like an ice cream salesman.

"I really want the paratroopers." He reiterated.

"Okay, young man, your loss. Personally, I'll never understand why someone would want to jump out of a perfectly good airplane." He said condescendingly.

"To catch the enemy by surprise and kill them!" Frank answered quickly.

The sailor shook his head disapprovingly. "Another one for you Andy." He shouted.

Another man appeared behind the counter, this time clean shaven and dressed in camouflage clothing and boots.

"Hello mate, my name is Colour Sergeant Randall, what can I do for you?" He said.

Frank sat down with the Infantry Colour Sergeant for over an hour listening intently about what the army had to offer and how the joining process worked and was honest about his criminal conviction and violent background when answering questions. The soldier liked Frank and was impressed by both his attitude and his physical performance when asked to do 10 chinups, 25 sit ups and 25 press ups in the office, which he did easily.

"Why don't you join your local regiment and become a Royal Green Jacket like me?" He asked.

Frank had never even heard of them before but was surprised and interested to learn he had a local regiment.

The soldier went on. "The Green Jackets have been around since the 18th century, we invented camouflage, we are world renowned for our shooting skills, we march faster than anyone else in the army and we've got a lot more battle honours than the Parachute Regiment." He was using his fingers to count out the plus-points as he spoke. "Plus." He added, leaning towards Frank.

"We get sent to Northern Ireland all the time! In twelve years, I've been there nine times." He said proudly.

Frank was not sure if that was a good thing. The only time he'd heard about Northern Ireland in the news was when soldiers were killed or injured in terrorist attacks. The Colour Sergeant continued with his awful sales pitch. "We've lost more soldiers in Northern Ireland than any other regiment and we've got more Victoria Crosses than any other regiment too!" He stated.

Frank promised to consider the offer but hoped he had made it clear that his first choice was the paras and left the office feeling proud. The first hurdle was overcome. He never saw Colour Sergeant Randall again, so never had the awkward conversation of why he wasn't joining his regiment, and after several interviews and medical assessments he received an invite to attend a two-day Potential Recruit Aptitude Course ran by the Parachute Regiment to weed out the time wasters before recruit training even started.

The course was conducted at the Parachute Regiment Depot, where regular recruits completed 26 weeks of training and selection. Arriving at the camp, Frank was mesmerised by the frenetic energy inside. Recruits ran everywhere at full speed and instructors followed barking orders incessantly. His course was made up of twenty-one applicants who were all met at the guardroom on arrival and escorted to the course building where they were introduced to their instructor and allocated a number. He was one of the first to arrive and for the next two days became "Number Five." Numbers One to Four were already sat on their designated beds when he walked into the bunk room. Noticing a large number 5 printed on the headboard he also sat on his bed and filled out the paperwork he'd been given, while they waited for the remaining sixteen applicants to arrive. Everyone was nervous, engaging in small talk quietly after a few minutes and Frank sized up the others as they filtered through, slowly filling the accommodation. The young men varied in appearance ranging from about 17 to 22 years old, one looked older than the rest. About 24 years old, he was extremely muscular and covered in tattoos with a clean-shaven head. Frank felt inferior, someone like that would definitely pass. As he looked around, he couldn't help but judge the others by their appearance too, silently assessing their chances of success. He wasn't the only one doing it, they all were.

The first event on the course was a two-mile run in shorts and T-shirt. Running down a footpath beside a dual carriageway it was impossible to get lost and the corporal explained that he would be standing at the turn around point and they would go around him in a clockwise direction and back to the start as fast as they could. The corporal, a rather small, skinny Scotsman explained that they had 15 minutes to complete the two miles but should be aiming to do it in under 12 if they wanted to become paratroopers. "Are there any questions?" He bellowed. The tattooed man raised his hand. Checking the number pinned to his T-shirt the corporal responded. "Yes, number eleven, what is it?" He asked.

"What if I get to the turning point before you?" He said cockily. "Is it marked?"

Frank noticed two of the other instructors look at each other with raised eyebrows.

"If you get there before me, you've passed the course number eleven!" Replied the corporal, who like the other instructors was wearing a pair of khaki trousers, boots and a maroon T-shirt. Frank thought it unlikely that he could run that fast in boots and assumed there must be a catch. Maybe they would all be made to crawl on the way back or something else to slow them down. The race started with an order that would become familiar throughout his career.

"Standby......GO!!" Shouted the Scot setting off at the front at a fast pace.

The course jostled for position on the narrow footpath and chased after him, with the tattooed man catching him quickly. Speeding up slightly the corporal edged ahead taking his follower with him as they increased the gap from the remainder who spread out along the tarmac path behind them. The corporal ran smoothly and efficiently, wasting no energy as he deliberately maintained a short distance ahead, listening to the breathing rate of the young man behind him increasing and his heavy gait pounding off the ground. After half a mile Number Eleven was slowing down, his legs heavy with lactic acid from sprinting. Gradually some of the others started to catch and overtake him, including Frank who was in fourth place. At the one-mile point, as briefed the corporal was stood waiting, shouting encouragement at the runners and as Frank ran around him, he gave him a slap on the back. "Good effort Number Five. Catch the man in front." He said. Frank was made up and put on a burst of speed to close the distance. Running back towards the start point Frank's confidence was given a massive boost as he passed people still on the outward leg. Some of them had looked super fit at the start, but he was way ahead of them. With the finish line in sight and the first two runners already forming an orderly, line Frank heard footsteps behind him and pushed as hard as he could, not wanting to be overtaken so close to the end.

"Good work Number Five, work hard, drive on." Said the Scottish corporal as he went past, not even breathing heavily. "Stay with me." He shouted, pointing to the ground beside him. Frank tried his best but couldn't keep up, finishing a few seconds behind the instructor, who happened to be an army cross country champion.

The rest of that day was filled with a busy schedule where they were introduced to the rifle and taught how to strip and assemble it, visited the Airborne Museum and shown how to march as a squad. Everywhere they went was at the double, but the corporals did not scream and shout at them like they did the recruits who seemed to be under constant pressure. At dinner time

Frank's course were taken into the canteen and he was shocked at how the recruits ate their food. None of them spoke, they just concentrated on consuming as many calories as possible in the short time allocated and he watched as one young soldier rammed food into his mouth like he hadn't eaten for a week. The recruit was eating his main meal of sausages and mash at the same time as mouthfuls of his dessert and bites of bread, stopping only to wash it down with a quick gulp of water. He knew that was the only way to ensure he got a bit of everything. After a few frantic minutes, a voice called out from behind a lattice wall divider.

"Bruneval Platoon! Outside!" The hungry recruits' instructors had finished eating and stood up to leave. They responded immediately, standing up and making their way to the exit via the plate wash where they binned any leftovers and dropped off their cutlery, cups and plates, still stuffing food into their mouths as they hurried through the door. If they weren't ready and waiting when the corporals got outside, they would get punished. It was no wonder they all looked so thin.

The second day was equally frantic, and, in the morning, they were taken to the Assault Course. Frank did well, finishing in the top five again but realised that was an area he needed to work on, it was the hardest thing he'd ever done, and his legs were exhausted at the end. The last physical test of the course was an aerial assault course called the Trainasium and when he saw it Frank immediately recognised it from the TV show he'd watched as a young boy. One of the corporals demonstrated what to do and fearlesslessly ran, jumped and climbed the scaffold structure that stood 45 feet high, with no safety nets or ropes in sight. Every obstacle was initiated by an instructor yelling "Standby.. GO!!" and Frank completed it without a glitch, even though it was scary, but a few of the others did not do so well, freezing with fear on the jumps or refusing to walk across the high obstacles that rattled and swayed beneath their feet.

On completion of the course the applicants were called in to see the officer in charge one at a time. Of the twenty-one that started, seven had passed and were offered a place at recruit training, the remainder sent home with a recommendation to try another less demanding unit. Frank was happy to be one of the seven. It was the hardest thing he'd ever done and all the way home on the train he felt proud of himself for the first time ever. One month later his real training began, along with 39 other young men who wanted to be paratroopers.

CHAPTER EIGHT

Settling In

Still standing on the tower platform a little shell shocked, Johnny's efforts to reassure Reece after their explosive introduction by Frank had settled his nerves a little. The observant reporter had noticed that the officer was also intimidated by Franks' strong personality and was obviously wary of his volatile temperament. He gave Reece some encouraging news that filled him with cautious optimism. "Our next patrol is deploying in four days, and you will ride with me in my vehicle. Best seat in the house. Until then, let's get you settled in." Pausing briefly Johnny reached for the chin strap on Reece's helmet and undone the quick-release buckle that secured it to his head. "First things first." He said. "You can take that body armour and helmet off now, there's no need to wear that stuff when you don't need it, you'll be sweating like a Royal Marine in a maths test! This camp is pretty safe, in fact it hasn't been hit for nearly seven days now."

"A whole seven days eh?" "Safe as houses then!" His sarcasm was lost on the major who was determined to make a good first impression on the reporter.

"Here, let me carry that for you, I'll take you to the accommodation, and then we'll go get a nice cup of tea." Johnny led the way, weaving his way through a complex series of blast walls, tunnels and makeshift doors before they came to his room. By the time they stopped, Reece was completely disorientated. There was zero chance of him finding his own way back. Johnny pushed open the wooden door that had been repaired using wood from broken down pallets and duct tape and held it open for Reece who followed him closely, the door closing itself behind them under the tension of some rubber from an old bicycle inner tube. The cold air inside, blasting in from a clattering air conditioning unit was in stark contrast to the already hot and dry atmosphere outside and it felt refreshing as it immediately cooled him down. Reece shivered, to be honest it was probably a bit too cold.

As part of a welfare package the BRF had been allocated one air conditioning unit, which was intended for the rest room. That was where the men went to relax and watch the satellite T.V which had also been recently purchased and installed by a trusted local shop owner. They had amassed an impressive collection of pirate DVD's from the small bazaar close to the camp which they watched every night at 8 O'clock when it was cool enough. Inside, soldiers from the Royal Engineers had fabricated six rather impressive wooden benches in exchange for two bottles of Jack Daniels whiskey. They were lined up one behind the other with just enough space down one side for the men to walk and the seats were padded with sturdy black foam, taken from the inside of ammunition boxes. A large projector was affixed to the ceiling, secured inside a red plastic Coca-Cola crate with paracord then cable tied to a metal pipe that ran from wall to wall. A black lead hung down to a makeshift shelf, where the men would connect it to a laptop to watch their films. The room was also used for holding briefings and issuing patrol orders before deploying on missions.

On the day that the air con unit was fitted the BRF soldiers were test firing their weapons on the shooting range outside of camp, except for their commander who opted out, claiming he was too busy writing a report, but actually couldn't be bothered with the weapon cleaning that would follow the firing. The workmen had been just about to start knocking a hole in the wall of the rest room when Major Hill had walked in and, seizing the opportunity, explained to them there was a change of plan and it was now to be installed in his quarters. He had been having terrible trouble sleeping at night due to the heat and refused to leave his door open, because of an irrational fear of bats, and the air con would ensure him some quality sleep as well as a place to escape the midday heat. Luckily the soldiers never knew what he'd done as there would have been outrage. Despite the irritating noises it made, Johnny was sleeping better.

The room itself was about 12 feet squared, there were two camp cots in opposite corners and a red rug on the floor that had been bought from a local trader. In the middle of the room at head height hung a bare light bulb, which acted as a magnet to the insects outside if the door was left open at night. In Johnny's corner the grey concrete walls were decorated with posters of pin up girls from magazines, maps of the area and several photos of himself in various poses with a variety of weapons and equipment. Next to his cot was a small table that he'd made from scrap wood. It had four legs but only three were in contact with the floor as one had been cut half an inch too short and he used it to hold his alarm clock, book, pistol and framed photograph of his fiancée which he kissed every night before he went to sleep. Johnny placed Reece's kit onto the cot in the other corner. "This is your bed, make yourself at home." He said enthusiastically-. "I've got a meeting, but I will be back in about half an hour. Why don't you unpack your stuff, then I'll take you for a tour of camp when I get back?" With that he walked to the door, taking his pistol from its holster and removing the magazine to check the rounds before dramatically slamming it back into position before re-holstering it. He opened the door and stepped outside, pausing momentarily to put on his Oakley sunglasses with one fluid movement and stepped back outside into the bright sunshine.

Reece couldn't help but be impressed. Johnny had put on a good show and he was being very hospitable. If he could convince Frank to get on side, he might be able to get the exclusive story he wanted. He sat on his cot and opened the zip on his dust covered bag which had slowly changed colour from its' original black, to a dirty brown. Undoing the zip had got increasingly difficult over the weeks as it got clogged up with dust and the tab had snapped off making it hard to grip. He unpacked slowly, refolding his clothes as he pulled them out and placed them in neat piles either side of him on his cot, every move he made creating a loud creak from the stretched material of the temporary bed. Socks, t-shirts, underpants and cigarettes were laid out until he was surrounded by his belongings. Standing up, he quickly realised that there was absolutely nowhere for him to put his things, not a shelf or drawer in sight. In a way it reminded him of his first night in his old room in Shepherds Bush. He looked at Johnny's ramshackle table with a new-found envy, maybe he'd find some wood and make one for himself, only better! In the meantime, he'd have to live out of his bag, so he re-packed it, placing the items he would need first nearest the top, his cigarettes and toothbrush. Waiting half an hour for Johnny in that room seemed like a waste of valuable time, so he decided to go back outside for a look around, taking his camera with him as always.

As soon as he stepped through the door Reece realised, he could remember absolutely nothing of the route he'd taken to get there, deciding to turn left and see where he ended up. At the next junction he turned right thinking that if he alternated left then right it would kind of keep him going forwards and would also make it easy to retrace his steps when he wanted to go back. He passed several people in the rat-runs, some acknowledging him, others eying him up and down suspiciously. Some of the rooms had people sleeping inside, laying half naked on top of camp cots with folded clothes or bags for pillows and no bedding, some rooms had small groups of soldiers inside quietly chatting or playing music loudly, sometimes, rather inconsiderately, next door to those asleep. Clothes were hung out to dry on lengths of cord and bungee all over the place, others lay draped over walls and doors. Some of the clothes were wet because they had been washed, some were soaked with sweat because they had been worn for physical exercise and would be dried out and worn again without even being cleaned, the salty sweat crystallising in the material, making the fabric stiffer and more abrasive each time. Maroon T-Shirts were obviously the clothing item of choice as they were everywhere, most of them emblazoned with a Parachute Regiment cap-badge and some with gung-ho writing on or pictures of the devil or guns or something else sinister. Portable solar panel chargers that had been purchased from the American Base Exchange store in Kandahar sat on top of walls in between radio antennas, re-charging mobile phones, MP3 players and cameras. Every bit of space was being utilised. Reece stuck to his alternating turn method as much as he could, sometimes having no choice because of a locked gate and felt confident he could find his way back.

Ducking through one last gate he found himself in an open courtyard with a large white domed tent in the middle. He noticed a soldier exit the tent holding a paper plate with what looked like a burrito on it and a polystyrene cup full of an orange coloured drink. Feeling thirsty, he entered the tent, hoping to acquire himself a refreshing drink. He took one step inside the tent before a deep voice barked. "Out!"

Reece looked up to see a tall, burly chef, standing behind a hot plate in his white shirt and chef's hat with black and white chequered chef trousers. On his chest was a silver badge of rank showing three chevrons.

"Out!" The sergeant repeated abruptly, pointing his outstretched finger behind the stunned reporter. "That is the exit! Come in through the entrance!" He ordered, pointing to the door at the opposite side of the tent. "Handwashing facilities are over there."

"Sorry Chef." Said Reece. "I'm new here, first time."

The chef relaxed slightly. "OK mate, so it's a one-way circuit. In through there, dhobi your hands there, diggers there, hot scoff there, cold scoff there, screech and brews there, gash there, exit there."

Reece was like a rabbit in the headlights, trying to follow the chef's directions and decipher the terminology at the same time as he rapidly pointed out the things he was saying with a chopping motion of his hand, arm bending at the elbow and body rotating robotically.

"Okay, thanks Chef." He said, backing out through the exit and walking around the tent to the entrance way. He entered nervously, anticipating another telling off as the chef watched him closely, arms folded high on his chest. After washing his hands, he entered the self-service area.

"Excuse me Chef, is there anywhere I could get some squash please?" He asked timidly.

"Screech and brews are there." The grumpy chef repeated, pointing again to a bank of large silver cylinders stood side by side on an old 6ft wooden table which bowed slightly under the weight. Reece knew that a brew could mean tea or coffee, which must have meant "Screech" meant juice. He was right and sure enough, written on one of the cylinders on a sheet of white A4 paper was "Oringe." He took a cup and held it underneath the tap as he filled it to the top, drinking it down in one thirsty go. The orange cordial had been made strong, really strong and he grimaced slightly as the aftertaste hit, sucking on his back teeth involuntarily. He refilled his cup and carried it slowly towards the exit, taking his time to drink this one. Stood next to the bin his took the final mouthful then thanked the chef as he disposed of the empty cup.

"Thanks for the screech Chef." He said gratefully. For a second, he contemplated pointing out the spelling mistake on the drinks dispenser but decided to leave it.

"Not having some scoff?" Queried the sergeant, proudly gesturing to the food on display with a sweeping motion of his upturned hand.

"Not right now thank you. I'll have some scoff later if that's alright." Replied Reece, embracing the lingo. Goodbye."

Looking at his watch he saw that he'd been out and about for over ten minutes already, so Reece thought it best to return to his and Johnny's room.

Retracing his steps, he stepped up and ducked awkwardly at the same time to get back through the home-made gate he'd previously used. Sticking to his alternating turns faltered at the first junction as he couldn't remember which turn he'd made last on the outward leg. It was 50/50. He noticed a pair of battered Nike running shoes that looked familiar hanging from the wall by their laces which had been tied together and decided that must have been the way he'd come from, heading down the narrow alley. He'd chosen wrong and was heading in the opposite direction to his room, toward the tower. By sheer bad luck the Nike shoes he'd seen were the most popular running shoe in the entire Airborne Brigade. They were designated Nike Pegasus, and Pegasus was a historical mythical figure adopted by the British Paratroopers during World War Two, worn proudly by the elite soldiers until it was replaced by the Screaming Eagle of 16 Air Assault Brigade when 5 Airborne Brigade was remodelled in 1999. The soldiers had never accepted the new insignia with many retaining their old Pegasus badges, secreting them on the inside of their para-smocks or floppy hats. The Eagle was commonly referred to with contempt as the "Screaming Budgie" by the men. Along with the maroon T-shirts and maroon regimental towels, those trainers were the least distinguishable reference points to aid his navigation. After a few minutes Reece conceded that he was lost and stopped a pair of passing soldiers for guidance.

"Excuse me." He said, rather embarrassed. "Could you point me in the right direction to Johnny Hill's room please?"

"Johnny who?" The taller man replied.

"Hill. Johnny Hill." Repeated Reece.

"Big John?" The shorter soldier said, adopting a pose to demonstrate a fat man, cheeks puffed out, arms bent out by his sides.

"No, I don't think so. He's about my size." Said Reece.

"Little John?" Said the soldier, adjusting his posture and holding his hand at waist height as if to display Johnny's height.

"No, not little either. About my height. Dark hair." Reece clarified, pointing to his own head.

"You mean Geordie John?" Said the tall soldier, looking puzzled, gripping his chin with his thumb and forefinger.

"No, I don't think so." Reece replied. "Major Johnny Hill, the BRF Commanding Officer."

"Ah, Major Hill?" One of the soldiers said knowingly

"Yes." Said Reece, nodding enthusiastically.

"Wears a maroon beret, like mine?" The smaller soldier said pointing to his beret.

"Yes." Said Reece. "Same as yours."

"Wears a crown on his shirt.? The taller man confirmed, pointing to his shoulder, where officers wore their rank badges.

"Yes, that's him gents." Said Reece, relieved to be progressing. "Do you guys know him?"

"Never heard of him mate!" Came the dry reply. The soldiers had been stringing him along, with no idea of who Johnny was the whole time.

"Why don't you come with us instead?" The taller man spoke. "Come and meet our friends, they'll like you."

The tall man grabbed Reece around the shoulders, hugging him tightly in the small alley. "We haven't had a new toy for ages." He said.

Suddenly Reece felt very nervous as the two men began to usher him in the direction from where they'd come from. The atmosphere had very quickly turned quite sinister. He struggled to free himself but the taller man, who now looked extremely angry and intimidating grabbed him by the jaw and spoke to him menacingly face to face, noses touching.

"Listen to me Mr Photographer, you are coming with us. Stop wriggling about and we won't have to hurt you. You'll look pretty in the nice little dress we've got for you, but not if you've got no fucking teeth in your mouth!"

Reece was terrified. He stopped resisting and began to cooperate.

"Okay, Okay." He said nervously. "I don't want any trouble."

Suddenly he heard a familiar voice, and the grips on his arms immediately relaxed.

"Good afternoon gentlemen."

The soldiers braced up allowing Reece to also straighten up from his head-down position. It was Johnny, striding confidently towards them through the alleyway.

One of the soldiers threw up a salute, which Johnny reciprocated.

"Hello Sir, both men said in unison."

Johnny recognised Reece. "Ah, got restless, did we? I see you're making friends." He hadn't noticed the angst on Reece's face or the nervousness of the compromised soldiers. "Well I'm all yours now. Shall we head back?"

Reece extracted himself from between the two would-be abductors. "Yes, absolutely." He replied. "Let's go!"

Johnny looked at the two soldiers. "Gentlemen." He said, bidding the farewell as he stepped away.

"Sir." They replied, heading the opposite way at a brisk walk, then running after they turned the first corner.

Reece followed close behind Johnny, not daring to look back.

"Where were you going with those lads?" Asked Johnny. "You know about 3 Para Mortars, don't you?"

"No, not really." Said Reece. "But I'm guessing it's bad!"

As they walked Johnny explained the infamy of the battalions Mortar Platoon, known throughout the British Army for its antics. Many tales had done the rounds throughout the army over the years, some true, some not, but none ever confirmed or denied by the alleged perpetrators. Often the stories were mistakenly attributed to other units of similar notoriety, some even appropriated them as their own to inflate their own status. Almost all were at least based on true events, that had been regurgitated and recycled during alcohol fuelled gatherings, gaining and losing details by the narrator each time to make for a better story.

Johnny told his version of one such story. "A couple of years ago..." He said quietly, quickly checking over his shoulder to check nobody was following them before starting again, already with an amendment. "A few years ago, one of the contract cleaners went missing from 3 PARA's camp. No-one knew his name, but they all called him Rain Man because he was a bit retarded and used to carry a scrap book wherever he went. Anyway, after a few days his parents reported him missing and the police got involved and everything. About a week later the coppers came onto camp and spoke to the RSM but nobody said anything and because he was a known crackhead, they just assumed he'd just gone on a bender and pretty much forgot about him. Turned out, the last place he'd been seen was going into the Mortar Platoon Block with his mop and bucket. Nobody saw him come back out but his cleaners' trolley was last seen abandoned outside the Red Lion pub in town after some of the blokes rode it down the hill to go drinking. About three weeks later there was a power cut, or a flood or something like that and a civvy contractor went into the

Mortars Block to fix it. When he opened the utility cupboard, the missing cleaner jumped out. Apparently, he was all wrapped up, like an Egyptian Mummy with black gaffer tape, with gaps over his eyes, mouth and private parts!" Johnny pointed to the accompanying parts of his body as he spoke. "On his head was his mop bucket and stuck up his rear end was the handle of the mop, dragging behind him as he hopped down the corridor, bouncing off the walls."

Reece was shocked. "This can't be true, surely, I mean surely not!" He exclaimed.

"Well there's a lot of people that say it is true, including the guy who told me, and he is very reliable." Johnny replied before continuing. "So, this guy has been locked up for three weeks, he can't see where he's going, just desperate to escape and hops his way straight to the top of the stairs, falls all the way down, breaks his neck!" Johnny tilted his head to the side sharply, sticking out his tongue out to one side and rolling his eyes upwards, at the same time doing his best attempt at producing a cracking sound from the side of his mouth.

"Jesus Christ!" Reece reeled backwards, putting a hand over his mouth in disbelief. "Did he die?" He asked.

"Nope." Johnny said. "Ambulance came. Straight to Intensive Care. Coma for two weeks. Hospital and physio for a couple of months. Released."

"So, what had happened to him, where had he been for three weeks?" Reece asked, totally absorbed in the story.

Johnny continued. "Well apparently, when he was supposed to be cleaning, he used to go round the accommodation stealing from the blokes. Took thousands so they say, and nobody had a clue who was doing it, there were all sorts of theories and accusations going on, until one day, one of the soldiers caught Rain Man stealing some cash from his locker and gave him a bit of a kicking. They say he thought he'd killed him because he was unconscious for so long. In a flap, the soldier then wrapped his body in a bed sheet and hid him in his wardrobe. Later that night, there was a party in the accommodation and the young lad confessed what had happened to the others and took them to his room where it had all happened. Expecting to find a corpse, they went to get him out of the locker, but he was awake and in a right state. Then he started shouting and saying he was going to the police, so they decided to keep him."

"Decided to keep him? Why?" Asked Reece.

"Because they knew they were in the shit. And the last thing the Mortars need, is the police searching their block! There's rumours that there's all sorts of stuff hidden away in there."

"What kind of stuff?" Reece was intrigued.

"Guns, ammunition, explosives, pyrotechnics, that kind of stuff. Also, they reckon there's the skull of an Argentinian P.O.W from the Falklands War in there, all hidden in the walls and ceiling space." Johnny explained.

"Holy shit!" Said Reece. "So, what did they do with the bloke?"

"Well there are a lot of different stories. Some say he was used as a table for three weeks, some say he was kept as a slave to do all the blokes ironing, cleaning and read them bedtime stories at night, and others say he was pimped out to smack-heads that were smuggled into camp for £10 a time. It all kind of gets a bit hazy after that to be honest. Either way it was pretty bloody bad." Johnny chuckled.

"Pretty bad!" Reece snapped. "Kidnap, slavery and forced prostitution is well beyond pretty bad! I take it those soldiers are now in prison?"

"Evidently not. You were just talking to one of them back there!" Johnny replied.

"What!? How the hell did they get away with that?" Reece queried, with a glance behind, now even more concerned for his safety.

"Apparently the cleaner didn't want to press charges and the police said there was a lack of evidence."

"Jesus Christ! That is outrageous!" Said Reece. "He was probably too scared to press charges. Absolutely shocking! What ever happened to the poor bloke?"

Johnny continued the anecdote. "Well after he came out of his coma, he was in a wheelchair for a few months but he's alright again now, healthier than ever. And do you know the best bit about all of it?" He posed the question.

"The best bit?" Said Reece. "There's a best bit? I give up, tell me."

"He's clean!" Said Johnny triumphantly. "Hasn't touched heroin ever since. Went through cold turkey whilst in his coma and intensive care. Every cloud has a silver lining eh?"

"Hmmm, not sure about that, but at least he's ok I guess." Reece said, somewhat uncomfortable with the whole story. "I wonder what he does now?"

"He's back in his old cleaning job on camp. They kept it open for him. He loves it" Johnny stated cheerfully.

Reece frowned, shaking his head slightly. That was the most bizarre story he'd ever heard. Regardless, true or not, he knew he'd one day be telling it to someone else, in his case considering the likely audience, probably with a few details omitted.

They continued their walk, in silence, Reece wondering how much truth was in the tale and Johnny wondering retrospectively if he should have told that story to a reporter he'd only just met.

For the next few days, following Johnny around became Reece's full-time occupation and he quickly learned his way around the camp, which was actually quite small and not that difficult to navigate once he got used to it. Anytime he was on his own he ensured to give a wide berth to the Mortar Platoon area. The day would usually involve three visits a day to the cookhouse for breakfast, lunch and dinner, at least one visit to Headquarters where Reece would have to wait outside because of security clearance and several visits to the BRF compound. The compound was the place he liked to visit the most but being with Johnny was making it difficult to engage with the soldiers as the majority obviously did not like him and kept their distance. Sensing their cynicism towards his motives, Reece kept a low profile whilst in the compound, respecting the personal space of the soldiers. After a couple of days, he had established which of the men were introverts and which were more open to having photos taken or talking to him, but he still always sought permission before using his camera. Any conversations that he'd had were initiated by the soldiers as he did not want to come across as pushy. He'd just loiter innocently until one of the men felt He hoped that this approach would work, and they would soon accept him as friendly forces.

By the third day a lot of the BRF had got used to Reece's presence, some actively encouraging him to photograph them, performing for the camera then sitting down with him to view and critique the pictures. Reece was genuinely keen to learn about the men, their backgrounds and experiences as well as the equipment they carried and trained with in preparation for the forthcoming patrol. The third morning also marked the first dialogue between him and Frank beyond the scowls he'd received up until then. After looking him in the eye for a few uncomfortable seconds Frank had actually acknowledged him at breakfast.

"Alright Grease?" He said dryly. Deliberately mispronouncing his name.

"Morning Frank, I'm good thank you. How are you?" He replied happily, pretending not to notice the little dig.

Frank had exhausted his civilian interaction capacity already and walked away without further response. Despite his best efforts Frank had been unable to reverse the decision to let Reece join their patrol, the decision had been made well above his pay scale and resistance was futile. Instead he decided to roll with it and exploit the opportunity to get some recognition for the men and the unit while retaining integrity. Frank had noticed the way Reece had been conducting himself and as far as reporters went, he seemed not too bad. That day the men went about their usual business of exercising, conducting rehearsals on weapons and equipment and socialising, however there was definitely a change in atmosphere as everything was done with more purpose in preparation for the deployment the following morning. The soldiers were good at hiding their nerves or apprehension, but some were definitely more withdrawn or excited as they not only prepared physically, but also psychologically. One of the soldiers re-wrote a letter to his parents that they would receive in the event of his death. All the soldiers were encouraged to do it and most did, knowing that it might bring comfort to those left behind if the worst was to happen. Others chose not to for their own reasons, some found it too morbid, some thought it was tempting fate. This soldier had written one earlier in the tour and not put a great deal of effort into it, but since then several people had been seriously injured or killed and he himself had experienced a couple of near misses. The updated letter was much more considered and personal to his parents that he missed so much. He actually felt a strong sense of guilt for putting them through so much stress and worry by being away, especially his mother who had never wanted him to join the army, instead encouraging him to train as a plumber.

CHAPTER NINE

The Patrol

Reece woke abruptly to the sound of a slamming door as Maj Hill left the room and headed for the kitchen for a cup of coffee. It was 2 o'clock in the morning, two hours before they were due to leave. The major had been noisily unpacking and repacking his equipment until after midnight and Reece had managed little sleep. He closed his eyes hoping to get another hour, when his roommate returned, opening the door with a kick and shouting "Wakey, wakey, hands off snakey," simultaneously turning the light on with his elbow as he carried in two plastic cups of hot coffee.

He sat up bleary eyed and accepted the drink Johnny presented him. This had become morning routine over the last four days and was beginning to wear a bit thin on Reece, who wasn't a morning person at the best of times.

"Thanks Johnny, but why are we up so early, have timings changed?" The bright light caused him to squint as he lit up his first cigarette of the day.

"The early bird catches the worm Reece, got to do a final kit check before we go, make sure we haven't forgotten anything."

"I checked last night; everything Sgt Cutler told me to bring is in my rucksack. Except for a gumshield, but I can't see why I would need that anyway."

"That's his way of telling you he'll knock your teeth out if you piss him off," chuckled Johnny.

Reece had written down everything that Frank told him to bring to ensure he forgot nothing and had also packed some extra items that some of the other paras recommended he take. Into the rucksack issued to him by the Quartermaster Sergeant he'd packed a sleeping bag, sleeping mat, warm jacket, spare socks, five days rations, six litres of water, a book, emergency spare camera and two hundred cigarettes. He got dressed and made his way to the canteen or "cookhouse" as the paras called it, for some toast. An hour later the BRF soldiers started to filter through, an early breakfast had been booked and the chefs had put on a good spread with plenty of sausages, bacon, beans and even pancakes which the men made the most of, knowing a long day was ahead of them. Some of the men still kept their distance from Reece, choosing to ignore him but others sat with him at the table and chatted happily. He hoped that the next few days would enable him to bond more with the BRF and earn their trust, especially Frank who was such a big influence on the others. At 0330hrs everyone left the cookhouse and headed for the vehicle park where the drivers carried out their vehicle checks, and the machine gunners removed the gun covers and oiled their weapons. This preparation was carried out silently in the darkness, the last thing they wanted to do was alert anyone that they were about to leave camp. Once everyone was ready Frank called them in for a brief.

"Right lads, you all know the score, if you see anything that is a threat to any of us, neutralise it, get the drop on them before they take the initiative. Anyone gets in your way and puts your life in danger, one way or another, get the fucker out of the way, by whatever means. If that means run them over, do it, and if they happen to be women and kids, well I'm sorry but one of us is worth more than one thousand of them fuckers. Do not hesitate,

I want maximum fucking violence if it goes noisy and if we fuck up, we'll deal with it when we get back and I will back you up all the way. That doesn't mean you can shoot anyone that looks a bit anti but use common sense and clear judgment. At the end of the day it's better to be tried by twelve than carried by six! Let's have a good patrol, we have got the firepower to deal with anything they might throw at us and they know that. We are in fucking charge round here, this is our area. Airborne."

"Airborne," came the subdued reply.

Frank always reminded the men what he expected of them and what they could expect from him before starting a patrol. Other units had suffered casualties as a result of young soldiers' hesitation to engage the enemy. He blamed this on the commanders' failure to instil confidence in their men who had become well aware of collateral damage and litigation claims. The BRF knew that they could count on him to stand by their decision, he trusted their judgment and they thrived on the responsibility that gave them.

The men took their places in their respective vehicles and waited silently for Franks call over the radio.

"Engines on three…one, two, three"

Simultaneously all ten vehicle engines kicked into life, this was done so as not to alert anyone within earshot of how many vehicles there were and was standard operating procedure "SOP" for the BRF. Masked by the low drone of the engines the men cocked their array of weapons under control and applied safety catches.

Only one member of the patrol was unarmed. Looking increasingly worried and craving a cigarette, Reece was sat on top of the fuel jerrycans stored at the back of the Land Rover commanded by Johnny. The soldier manning the machine gun in the back of Johnny's' vehicle was the patrol signaller, Jim, responsible for maintaining communications with Brigade Headquarters back in Kandahar Airfield, a great responsibility. A sociable man, he was quite pleased to have the company of Reece in the back of the vehicle with him and had re arranged the equipment in the back in order to make him as comfortable as possible. He had even managed to find an old car seat to tie to the top of the jerry cans which would be Reece's seat for the next few days. The vehicles drove slowly through the compound gates toward the camp entrance, jostling into their order of march in single file. The drivers kept the engines revving low to minimize sound and together they made a low drone as they trundled through camp, passing by tents that housed dozens of men still sleeping. Frank led the patrol as always, he had diligently planned the route and would be using his vehicle mounted GPS to navigate from one waypoint to another, cross checking with his map and compass along the way. His driver was a formidable soldier called Danny who had joined the BRF from the Grenadier Guards in 2004. After an outstanding performance on the selection course he had been encouraged by Frank and the previous boss to transfer to the Parachute Regiment and had gladly done so, preferring to focus on pure soldiering, without the distraction of ceremonial duties. Frank and Danny enjoyed each other's company, sharing a dry sense of humour and a passion for soldiering and Frank had made sure to get him in his team as soon as he could. The convoy snaked its way through the gates and barriers of the inner perimeter, exchanging waves with the British soldiers who guarded them and then past the outer perimeter, guarded by soldiers from the Afghan National Army (ANA). The BRF had removed the light fuses from their vehicles and covered them with sandbags to avoid the possibility of accidental initiation or reflection and all night-time driving was conducted on night vision goggles or as the soldiers called them "NVG's" so they soon disappeared into the darkness.

After a couple of minutes Johnny was becoming restless, repeatedly checking his GPS and compass.

"We're going east, we should be going north!" He muttered. "Jim, get on the net and ask Frank why he's going east when we should be going north." He demanded of the signaller.

Jim did not want to be second guessing Frank. "It would be easier if you asked him yourself boss. Use Channel 1."

Johnny paused to think, then spoke into his microphone "Frank, this is Zero Alpha, do you know you are heading east over?"

There was a delay in Franks response but then came the reply "Roger that boss, like I said during Orders, we'll head east 3 clicks as deception, in case our ANA friends decide to broadcast our movement to the Taliban." "We'll be swinging north once we get over this ridge, over."

"Copy that, roger, over and out." Johnny had spent most of the orders talking to Reece so was unaware of the deception leg they were conducting. Frank did not trust the ANA at all and would always depart the base in a different direction to mislead the gate guard on his intended route. Reece sat, facing rearwards and watched the other vehicles exit the gate one at a time, the darkness of the night gradually enveloped him as they moved away from the lights of camp and the silence of the desert replaced the noise of generators and chatter. Before long the camp was merely a small orange glow in the distance behind them as they embarked on their journey.

The convoy moved slowly and deliberately across the uneven ground, testing the driving skills of the men and the endurance of the vehicles as they negotiated steep climbs and descents, large divots and boulders. The engines barely exceeded idling speed as the overstressed chassis shook violently from side to side, suspension squeaking as it coped with a weight well beyond its intended design. The Land Rover was a firm favourite and trusted workhorse of the British Army, but the demands of this operation were compromising the fleet, with vehicle chassis cracking, clutches breaking, and suspension being wrecked on a daily basis. The BRF were reliant on their vehicles, so treated them with respect. Reece sat quietly looking into the darkness, the vehicle ahead visible intermittently when they drove up a hill and became silhouetted by the clear starlit sky. Every few minutes he would catch the eye of Jim as he checked behind, who'd occasionally give him a nod or thumbs-up. The soldiers all wore night vision goggles which enabled them to see each other quite clearly at close distances, the ambient light from the moon and stars enhancing the picture. Technology meant that night became day for the BRF which gave them a huge advantage over the enemy. Every so often the patrol would stop, sometimes to observe the way ahead with thermal imagers, scanning for a safe route or investigating a light source, other times to study the map.

During one of these short stops Jim called across to Reece "Come here quick, I need to piss."

Reece ducked under the roll cage and stood next to Jim in the turret. Jim hastily removed his headset and placed it on Reece's head. "Listen out for me for a second mate, if anyone asks for Zero Alpha, that's me, just say "Wait out." With that Jim vaulted up through the turret and jumped down beside the vehicle to relieve himself. Reece didn't get the opportunity to decline and suddenly found himself stood next to a machine gun, manning a radio. Immediately he felt a massive weight of responsibility fall upon him, his senses were heightened and he felt super-alert, scanning the darkness, listening intently to the radio and his surroundings, dreading the thought of the radio bursting into life with army-speak. Every sound drew his attention, every movement drew his gaze, he could hear his breathing and the light pressure of the headset against his ear seemed to amplify his heartbeat to an audible pulse. He glanced down as he heard the sound of Jim's urine splashing on the floor, then quickly averted his eyes upwards as a shooting star momentarily lit up the sky above him, he noticed a red light flashing on top of a hill behind him and fixed his eyes on it as it continued to flash, wondering what it could be, maybe it was the Taliban signalling to each other, alerting their comrades of the BRF approach, instigating an ambush! Jim climbed back into the turret after what seemed like an eternity, but was only a couple of minutes, and took the headset from Reece's head, placing it back onto his.

"Cheers mate. Any messages?" he asked cheerfully.

"No messages, but I have seen a light flashing over there from the hillside. It might be someone signalling, maybe Morse code or something!" Reece pointed toward the light source excitedly, a sense of pride washing over him. In that moment he felt like part of the team, one of the boys.

Jim immediately recognised the flashing red light as a mast that they had passed earlier in the night but decided to play along.

"I think you might be right mate! The Taliban are well known for their Morse code skills. Have you got a pen and paper? Let's see what these sneaky bastards are saying."

"I've got a pencil and paper." Reece replied naively.

"That'll do mate, quick, I'll decode, you scribe." Jim could see the excitement on Reece's face and felt the smallest amount of guilt as he continued his prank.

"Ready." Said Reece.

Jim was proficient at Morse code, but that skill was not required. He screwed his eyes into a squint as he stared at the light, placing his left hand against the side of his face, forefinger resting on his temple as if concentrating hard.

"Okay mate it's Tango............Tango...............Tango."

"Roger. Tango, Tango, Tango. Reece repeated, suddenly adopting a military persona.

Jim continued. "Tango..................Tango...............wait...... Tango." "Read that back mate.

Reece was now beginning to question the authenticity of their decoding mission, cautiously reading back; "Tango, Tango......... Are you pulling my pisser?" He looked up from his notebook at Jim.

Stifled laughter erupted from the front of the vehicle at the same time as Jim slapped Reece on the shoulder, chuckling. "Sorry mate, I'm winding you up, it's just a red light on top of a mast. All masts have got them so aircraft can see them. That one's been visible all-night mate, but you've been too busy monging it with your thumb up your arse to notice."

Johnny stood up on his seat in the front and turned to face Reece, pointing at him as he spoke. "You're going to have to eat that page in your notebook now! We don't want the enemy getting their hands onto sensitive information!"

Reece sat down, embarrassed but also relieved, his short stint at soldiering had been exhausting. Jim spoke quietly into his microphone "Zero Alpha roger, out." He leaned forward to relay a message to Johnny. "Frank's got eyes on a heat source up ahead, there's a lot of movement to our west he's checking out."

Johnny promptly issued his direction before returning to his seat. "Tell everyone to go firm and I will move up to Frank to make my estimate."

Jim dutifully informed the patrol over the radio as the driver pulled away, slowly making his way to the vehicle ahead.

Johnny twisted in his seat to face rearward. "Reece!" He called urgently. "Reece!"

"What?" replied Reece, raising his own voice as much as he thought acceptable.

"Frank needs me at the front, so we're going to link up with him. As the commander I have to make all the kinetic decisions."

"Sure, okay." Said Reece raising his eyes to the heavens. In the cover of darkness, the driver and Jim were also shaking their heads, eyes rolling. Everyone knew who the real commander was.

Kinetic was a word very popular with the army, Reece had noticed, especially the officers who seemed to use it at every opportunity, often out of context. Any activity, either by the enemy, or friendly forces would be described as "going kinetic", "getting kinetic", "be kinetic" etc. It was the latest buzz word in the Officers' Mess and had replaced less in-vogue words amongst the well-educated officers.

"Kinetic battlespace." - Area with a lot of enemy activity.

"If it goes kinetic."   - If people start shooting.

"Be kinetic."   - Be fast / aggressive.

"Kinetic engagement."- Intense / violent contact.

The soldiers had their own buzz words too, normally less complex, and during this tour it was "smash!" "Smash!" had also replaced several other words in the men's relatively simple vocabulary:

"Smash a chick!"   - Have sex with a girl.

"Smash some scoff!"   - Eat some food.

"Smashed it!"   - Done a good job.

"Smash some PT!"   - Go to the gym.

As they approached the vehicle ahead of them Johnny took control of the machine gun mounted to his front, pulling the butt firmly into his shoulder, slowly moving it from side to side, feigning keenness for his soldiers to witness. He pulled alongside, stopping parallel with the driver, inches from his face.

"Everything okay guys?"

The driver sat motionless, staring ahead. "All good thanks Boss." He replied politely, not wishing to engage in conversation.

"Good-o. I'm just pushing up to the front to assess the situation." Johnny informed them, reinforcing the importance of his command.

"H" was sat in the commanders' seat. "We know Boss, we're all on comms." He said, pointing to his earpiece. "Frank has just dismounted to get a better look from the high ground."

H was the senior Corporal in the BRF who had passed the Selection Cadre with his good friend Frank. Both from A Company, 3 Para, they had known one another for over ten years and served as each other's trusted confidante. H was the first choice as Franks successor as Platoon Sergeant. During his early days in 3 Para, H was given his nickname by his section commander who mistakenly thought his name was "Hetherington" and decided that was too long.

"Far too long! Sounds like royalty." He barked at the fresh faced private. "Do you think you are royalty? Do you think you are special or something?"

"No Corporal! " Replied H obediently.

"Good, neither does anyone else! From now on you are "H" He told him.

"Yes Corporal." H replied obediently. And, so it was, for the rest of his career he was called H. His actual name was in fact Jon Etheringson.

Johnny turned to his driver. "Let's go!" he snapped. As they neared the next vehicle, he made a rapid forward chopping motion with his right hand, signalling to his driver to keep going, they trundled past, not stopping this time. Once past the vehicle Johnny relaxed, resting the machine gun in its mount and sitting back in his seat until the next vehicle came into clear view and he put on his performance again. Franks vehicle was now in sight through the night vision goggles, a black squarish mass in the green display that slowly appeared as something more recognisable as they drew closer. Revealing more detail with every second, Johnny could make out the gunner in the turret, the machine gun, the rucksacks tied to the side of the Land Rover and then the wheels. Judging distances through the goggles was difficult but once they were within a few metres he could make out the faces of the 2 remaining men in the vehicle. Leon was manning the machine gun. "Frank is over there Boss.11 o'clock, 25 metres" He said to Johnny as his vehicle halted beside him, and he heard the distinct sound of a handbrake being applied.

Leon was the machine gunner on Frank's Land Rover, at 19 years old, the paratrooper was the youngest soldier to ever pass the BRF course and Frank had been highly impressed by his skills and tenacity. Almost failed on his fitness during the first week, he was given a chance because of the sheer aggression and determination he had showed. That decision was justified when he got the chance to showcase his soldiering skills during the tactics phase.

Johnny reached into the space between the two front seats and grabbed his rifle before debussing onto the soft sandy ground, realising as he did so that his legs had gone quite numb from the prolonged period sat down. He stood on one leg and shook out the other vigorously, encouraging the blood flow to resume, then swapped legs. His toes tingled as the circulation resumed. Scanning the ground to his front he could not see Frank so again reached across into the space between the seats, this time retrieving the thermal imaging camera, called a SOPHIE sight. He flicked up his night vision goggles, rotating them through 180 degrees so they sat high on his head in their mount, the built-in sensor switching them off automatically to avoid any light escaping. He then pressed the SOPHIE sight to his eyes before turning it on, again not wanting any light escaping and potentially alerting the enemy to their position. The thermal imager was much bulkier than the NVG's resembling a portable PowerPoint projector and it was extremely inefficient with battery usage providing about 30 minutes' worth of usage before requiring a recharge. Half of the vehicles carried one of the cameras as well as a charger for the batteries which was continuously rotating the two batteries they had. A relatively new piece of equipment the BRF were fortunate to possess the SOPHIE's and other units in the Brigade were envious of the capability. During the tour the camera had proved to be an awesome piece of kit able to identify heat sources well beyond the range of the other night viewing aids, alerting the BRF to Taliban fighters up to two kilometres away on previous patrols. The thermal picture flickered as it started up, but immediately he could see Frank lying in the prone position ahead of him, showing as a ghost like white figure. The thermal camera detected heat signatures and displayed them as a black and white picture, similar to an old television, white for hot, and black for cold. Franks head, which was uncovered, produced a bright white picture, the equipment he wore on his body was a shade of grey, and his clothing a duller white where the heat was insulated, his boots were black. As Johnny watched him Frank lowered the SOPHIE sight he was also using and turned around, his expressionless face looking him square in the eyes. Frank used the hand signal for "on me" or "come here" over-exaggerating his movements so he could be understood in the darkness. Johnny turned off, then lowered the thermal camera slowly, frowning as he tried to work out how it was possible that Frank could see him with a naked eye, when he couldn't even see him through NVG's. He slung the SOPHIE sight around his neck, flipped down his NVG's and walked over to Franks vantage point in a crouched position. He crawled the last few metres on his belt buckle until he was by Franks side in a small divot amongst some rocks.

"What have we got Frank?" He asked.

"Not sure Boss, there's something up ahead that's not right." He whispered in his gruff voice.

Frank had halted the patrol when he was alerted by numerous heat sources earlier on. As he crested a small ridge, he'd noticed erratic movements ahead, white heat sources shifting about frantically in all directions that had aroused his suspicions.

Johnny raised his SOPHIE sight, pressing the rubber eyepieces tightly to his eyes. "Jesus Christ!" he exclaimed. "What the hell is that?" Head shaped heat sources were scurrying about in the distance, maybe 1 kilometre away, ducking in and out of view. "Is it an ambush?" "Let's call in an air strike!"

Frank responded calmly. "I don't know what it is Boss, but it can't be an ambush with that many people running around. Not even the Guards are that bad at ambushes!" He joked.

"How many?" Asked Johnny.

Frank had been trying to count the number of people he could see, but with the constant movement it was impossible to accurately tell.

"Twenty to thirty." He replied.

"Can we get air assets to have a look?" Johnny enquired. Most aircraft were equipped with sophisticated cameras, capable of identifying accurate detail on targets from high altitude without alerting them to their presence.

"There's nothing overhead Boss, everything is dedicated down south for the 3 PARA offensive." Frank stated. 3 PARA were launching an attack in the south of Helmand Province to clear a small town of Taliban. The town was a staging post for fighters transiting north across the border from Pakistan and thought to have a bomb factory amongst its buildings.

Both men lay still in silence, elbows on the ground, eyes pressed firmly against their cameras, watching. The only sounds were the idling engines of the Land Rovers and the occasional whirring of the small motors in the cameras when they were zoomed in or out.

Minutes passed. "Hang on, what's this?" Frank broke the silence.

A white heat source was rising above the others, moving towards them, gaining in elevation. As Franks eyes focussed on the figure it gradually became clearer as a human form, a man, draped in a shroud, moving slowly, laboriously up a slope. In one hand he held a large staff or cane, his other hand resting on his thigh, pushing down on it with every step to aid him in his ascent. The white and grey figure came to a halt by a large rock which showed as black through the thermal imager as it had cooled through the night, collapsing sideways to rest against it. He carried no obvious weapons as he stood still, catching his breath from the climb. After a few seconds, he bent down into a low squat. Both Frank and Johnny had guessed what was about to happen but were involuntarily unable to avert their gaze. The man stood back up, using both hand on his cane to support his weight. After fidgeting with his clothing, he slowly wandered off again in the direction he'd come from, leaving behind a small deposit on the ground that glowed white hot through the thermal camera.

"Dirty bastard didn't even wash his fucking hands!" Grumbled Frank.

They continued to observe the man as he walked down the hill, stopping after a few paces and waving his arms erratically. Although they could not hear him, it looked as if he was shouting at someone as he raised his cane above his head, swinging it from side to side.

"I think he's seen us!" Said Johnny anxiously. "We should definitely call an air strike, or artillery!"

It was difficult to tell which way the old man was facing through the image intensifiers at such a long range, but Frank was positive they had not been compromised.

"I tell you what Boss, if he can see us, then I'll give him a job as Lead Scout for the rest of the tour, cos he must have eyes like a fucking shithouse rat!" Frank quipped. Suddenly, a short distance from the old man two odd shaped heat sources appeared. Moving quickly, they darted away from the gesticulating man as he pursued them, disappearing out of sight once more.

"Goats." Said Frank. "Fucking goats."

Now that he had seen the two goats it became obvious to Frank that the other heat-sources he'd been watching for the last ten minutes were all goats too, and the man, their herder.

"Johnny could also recognise the shape of the animals now it had been brought to his attention. "I guess we won't need that air strike now then!" He chuckled. "I reckon we can take those buggers all by ourselves!"

"Funny!" Replied Frank dryly. "Let's mount up, still got a couple of hours before first light."

"Are you sure you don't want to do a full-frontal assault while we've still got surprise on our side?" Johnny continued. "Or maybe a left flanking assault."

"That'll do Boss." Frank was tiring of the wise cracks. "You're welcome to take over as lead wagon any time you want, I could do with a break."

Johnny crawled backwards a few feet before standing up and walking to his vehicle, avoiding Franks offer of responsibility, unsure whether it was genuine or not. He needn't have worried, it wasn't. Frank knew Johnny wouldn't accept and besides, he would never voluntarily relinquish his position at the front anyway. They both resumed their seats in their respective vehicles before Frank updated the others on what he'd seen over the radio.

Frank set off into the darkness once again, the others following in order. Johnny waited for three vehicles to pass him before slotting into his place as the 5th vehicle. A few hundred metres later, Frank could clearly see a Bedouin camp in the small valley he'd been observing. Four tents shaped like circus big tops stood lonely in the desert surrounded by wandering goats. Smoke rose from the centre of two of them as the herders gathered inside to eat and socialise. The allegiances of the herders were unknown, but it was highly likely they were armed. Uninvited guests would likely be greeted with suspicion at best, gunfire at worst. The patrol gave them a wide berth, observing as they went past. The Bedouin would never know the angst they had caused as the patrol disappeared into the next valley, leaving only tyre tracks behind as evidence they were ever there. The patrol continued for another couple of hours over the undulating desert, the slow, deliberate movement only ever pausing briefly to investigate any heat sources, shapes, sounds or movements, before continuing. As the driver Danny had the freedom to choose his route as he did his best to avoid boulders, divets and the occasional thorny bush. Danny kept roughly on heading by picking a feature in the distance and moving towards it as best he could. Sometimes it would be a piece of high ground on the horizon, sometimes a star. Inevitably, at some point he'd lose sight of it as they all looked very similar, so he'd just follow his nose until Frank corrected him. Danny had lost sight of what initially seemed an unmistakable, prominent hilltop after driving down a hill, and had been slowly veering left for about a minute. Frank had noticed, but only ever corrected him once the adjustment was substantial, otherwise they would be constantly zig zagging across the desert.

"One o'clock mate." Frank turned his head towards Danny as he spoke, but his eyes remained looking forward.

"Roger." Replied Danny as he turned the steering wheel slightly to the right, slowly moving through 30 degrees.

"12 o'clock." Frank's simple directions told Danny to straighten up, so he immediately found a new reference point on the horizon and continued towards it.

Frank checked his watch, pulling the green sweatband he used to keep it covered to the side to reveal the luminous hands glowing brightly in the dark. It was almost first light. He radioed the order for the patrol to switch their night vision kit over to daylight kit, as the sun would soon be breaching the horizon. The patrol halted. If a firefight broke out now, as it got light, the last thing Frank wanted was for the patrol to be messing about with equipment when they should be shooting. Taking turns, the soldiers removed their night vision goggles, returning them to their backpacks and swapped the telescopic night sights on their weapons for the much smaller daytime ones. This was carried out quickly and quietly and within minutes the patrol was ready to move again, carrying on into the unknown.

"Can you hear that?" Danny whispered, pulling himself forward by the steering wheel, listening intently.

Frank looked puzzled. "What....The engine? .I can..."

"Shhh." Danny interrupted, holding up his left hand, index finger pointing skywards.

"I can hear it." Leon said grumpily from the rear. "The most annoying sound ever!"

"What, your mum?" said Frank. "Begging me to shag her...again?"

"No... That!" said Danny, pointing into the distance ahead.

"Fucking what!?" Frank snapped impatiently.

At that point, before anyone could reply the radio kicked into life. It was Johnny. "Frank, this is Zero Alpha, can you identify where that sound is coming from? Over."

Danny and Leon both started to laugh, and Frank saw the funny side too. Even Johnny had heard it, and he was a quarter of a mile further away than them.

Leon gestured as if he was shouting but spoke quietly "Too much live firing Frank! Turn your hearing aid up mate!"

Danny drove forward slowly as he spoke "It's a call to prayer you deaf fucker, sounds like it's coming from over there. His hand was still pointing to their forward, left. After a couple of hundred metres he stopped again, this time turning off the engine.

"Surely you can hear that now old man?" He said grinning. The look of intense concentration on Frank's face was a picture.

Just then a favourable breeze carried the sound of the Muslim call to prayer just enough for Frank to hear it.

"Yeah yeah, of course I can hear it, now you two have stopped gobbing off. Call to prayer. I can hear it you pricks!" Everyone knew Franks hearing was bad, but he was in denial and would never admit to it. Frank spoke into his radio. "All callsigns, this is Frank, we've got some noise coming from the north west, moving closer to take a look. Zero Alpha acknowledge, over."

"Zero Alpha, roger, shall I move to your location to conduct an estimate, over?" Johnny replied.

"Negative Boss, stay in formation, I'll call if we need you, out." Said Frank.

The patrol continued towards the sound of the Islamic call to prayer, passing a small hill on their left side. Once past the hill a cluster of flickering orange lights became visible in the distance, and the sound of the singing Imam became clearer, as a small town woke up and went about its morning routine.

Frank decided to investigate the town closer and exploit the opportunity of arriving unannounced while the people were still half asleep. He briefed the patrol over the radio to move closer together as they approached cautiously, trundling along a dirt track at a speed barely faster than walking pace. As they neared the village its topography slowly became more visible. Frank could make out some of the compound walls, a few parked cars and the minarets of the Mosque in the first light of day. The patrol halted about half a mile short of the village. Their position was slightly elevated, affording them good observation over some of the compound walls. All together there were only about thirty compounds visible, with a disorganised web of vehicle tracks leading into and out of the centre from all directions. After a few minutes of observation through their numerous viewing aids they once again approached cautiously.

CHAPTER TEN

We Are Not Russians

Frank noticed some movement ahead. "Leon, keep an eye on that compound, six-hundred metres, ten o'clock." he said.

"Roger that." Leon was already traversing the gun onto the large mud walled compound to his left. Along the top of the wall he could make out several small shapes silhouetted by the sun as it ascended behind the village. When the shapes started to hurriedly move around as the patrol neared, it confirmed them as people peering over the wall at the approaching convoy.

"There's at least eight pax Frank, no weapons seen," Leon said watching the people through the telescopic sight of his weapon.

"Keep watching mate." Frank quickly but calmly rested the butt of his GPMG down and reached into the dashboard pulling out a pair of issue desert camouflage, leather gloves. The gloves had the fingers cut off and were blackened with oil and dirt. He put them on in the same way as always, left glove first, followed by the right. Then he interlocked his fingers and outstretched his arms making his knuckles click and punched each hand with the other. This ritual was picked up on by the other men in the vehicle which triggered them to conduct rituals of their own. Danny the driver sat up and leaned forward into the basket on the bonnet to retrieve his helmet which was covered in dust. Without taking his eyes off the track he blew on it in vain to remove some dust and put it on his head, pulling the chin strap under his chin. Leon donned a similar pair of gloves to Frank and quickly reached down inside the turret to pull the lid off a box of GPMG ammo by his feet. The men had learned through experience that Frank only put his gloves on when he was expecting a contact because he didn't want to cut his fingers on the gun mount while carrying out his weapon drills.

"Go firm mate, let's see what these fuckers are up to."

Danny slowed the vehicle to a stop as requested and applied the parking brake, the engine idling quietly as the soldiers observed their surroundings. "I don't remember a village here on the map." He said as he reached under his seat and pulled out a folded-up map with a production date of 1983.

"Well remembered mate, that's because it's not on the map. The maps are so old, it could have been here for years." Frank replied.

"All call signs be aware, there is a motorbike approaching from the rear. Passenger on back, no weapons seen, the driver is waving and smiling." The gunner in the rear vehicle had his weapon trained on the motorbike as it approached slowly but tried to portray a non-threatening posture as he warned off the rest of the patrol over the radio. When the motorbike got close the driver stopped, dismounted and gestured with his hands as he spoke, apparently wanting to come closer to talk. A young child remained seated on the motorbike, holding onto the seat behind them. The soldier waved the rider forward then halted him again about 25m from the vehicle. "H" the vehicle commander got out and walked back down the dirt track to the afghan, all the while covered by his gunner and driver who had debussed with his rifle. When he got to the old, bearded afghan man, he quickly established that his Arabic was not up to the task and called for the interpreter Mohamed who had been relegated from Johnny's vehicle to one of the others to make room for Reece. Within seconds Mohamed dutifully came running down the track to translate.

"Roose? Roose?" The old man was pointing at the convoy and

shrugging his shoulders.

"What's he saying?" H asked.

Mohamed grinned. "He's asking if you are Russians."

"What? Where the hells he been for the last 20 years? Tell him who we are and ask him if there's any Taliban here." To be respectful H looked at the old man as Mohamed spoke, surprised at how long it took to translate so few words.

The old man listened with a stony-faced expression then replied quietly, gesturing with his hands towards the village and towards the vehicles.

H continued to look him in the eye as he listened and took out his notebook and pen, ready to write down the information that seemed to be getting volunteered.

After about a minute of rambling the man stopped and looked at H.

"What did he say?" H asked Mohamed.

"He says the Taliban were here, but now they've gone?" He replied promptly.

H paused, waiting for more.......... "What else?"

"He says they have left now to go to the mountains." Mohamed added.

H was tiring of the laborious trickle of information. "That can't be it, I know he said more than that! Listen, you're the translator, so I need you to translate...Everything!"

Mohamed relayed the information in more detail. "He says the Taliban have lived in the village for the last year but moved on in the last few weeks to go and fight in the north." "He says that there were about 50 fighters but only one or two stayed behind to work on their farms, now it's just farmers and their families."

"Take his name and get the name of the village elder."

Mohamed spoke again to the old man and wrote down some

notes in his British Army issue notebook.

"And ask him if there are any mines around here." H was always on the lookout for signs of old Russian mines since the BRF had struck one on a previous patrol injuring 3 of their men but luckily not killing any of them.

Mohamed posed the question and the old man shook his head as he spoke.

"He says there are no mines, it is safe here." Mohamed reassured H. "He asks if he can go home now."

"Tell him thanks, and he can go." H replied.

Mohamed told the old man he could go on his way, which seemed to make him happy. The old man extended his hand to H and he reluctantly shook it, then watched as he walked slowly back to his motorbike which had been left with the engine idling noisily. He grabbed the handle bars and swung his leg over the seat in one fluid motion with surprising agility for a man of his age, kicking the stand backwards and rocking the bike forwards in a well-rehearsed sequence before revving the engine and heading off toward the village at speed, a trail of swirling sand left in his wake. On returning to his vehicle H quickly retrieved his small bottle of hand sanitizer from his kit and squirted a generous amount onto his palm, rubbing it into his hands vigorously, the old man's hands were filthy, with long dirty nails. He rinsed them with a small amount of water before applying a second helping of the lotion and waving his arms back and forth to dry them in the arid air. H informed Frank and the others over the radio on what the old man had said.

At the front of the patrol Frank and Danny were surprised by the sudden appearance of two men heading towards them from the middle of nowhere.

"Where the fuck did they come from?" Said Frank.

"I have absolutely no idea?" Replied Danny, equally bemused. "Looks like they've just been down to Tesco to get the milk."

The two men walked slowly, rising out from a small gulley. Arms swinging, they held hands by just their interlocked pinky fingers. They wore immaculate traditional white dish-dash suits, beige pakol hats and sandals, one with a brown waistcoat, the other a black one. Both had well-groomed thick, dark beards and each carried a carrier bag in their free hand. Frank got on his radio "Send the Interrupter to the front."

"Roger, he's on his way." Came the prompt reply as Mohamed was despatched for the second time.

Frank had nicknamed the interpreter the "Interrupter" since their first encounter when Mohamed was talking when he should have been listening.

The 2 men nervously walked up to Franks vehicle, giggling like naughty schoolgirls and holding each other closely as Mohamed arrived, breathing heavily from his short dash. The men acknowledged him in Arabic and began talking excitedly, often looking across to the soldiers and giggling effeminately as they spoke.

Frank, Danny and Reece greeted them in their best Arabic. "Salaam aylakum." they said almost simultaneously.

"Who are these fine gentlemen?" asked Frank

"They are from the village." Said Mohamed, pointing to the compounds in the distance. "They want to know if you are Russians. I explained to them who you are."

"Ask them if there's any Taliban here." Requested Frank.

"The other guy already told me they've all left. There are no Taliban here Frank, just farmers." Mohamed replied.

"I know but ask them anyway please mate." Frank insisted.

Mohamed took out his notebook and pen and wrote as he conversed with the men before briefing Frank.

"They say there are five hundred Taliban in the village." He said without a hint of surprise or wonder.

"Five hundred!" Queried Frank. "In the village? Right now? Double check that for me please mate!"

Mohamed once again spoke to the two men, all three of them gesturing and speaking loudly as if in an argument. He turned back to Frank.

"Five hundred." He confirmed confidently, showing him the number he had just written in his notebook, pointing at it with his pen. "Five hundred Taliban."

"Well that changes things!" Frank said.

Frank spent the next ten minutes conversing with the two local men, using his map to identify the whereabouts of the Taliban in the village. The information was very inconsistent and lacking in detail, but he made notes and drew sketches to try and make sense of it. After ten minutes he said thankyou and goodbye to the men in his best Arabic and sent them on their way.

"Tashakur." He said in his best afghan accent. "Huda hafez."

The men giggled, obviously amused by his attempt at their language and returned the farewell, turning towards the village and walking away, glancing over their shoulders regularly as they went.

At the rear of the convoy, a car approached slowly, seemingly following the same route that the patrol had taken. The wheel arches were almost touching the tyres, either because of a heavy load or shot-out suspension. The headlights, or at least the one that worked was held in place by a piece of string, hanging pathetically and shining directly down in front of the car but was no longer necessary as the light of dawn increased, the sun now just below the horizon.

H debussed and waved the white Toyota Corolla forward. The car slowly crept towards him, eventually stopping about twenty metres to the right of his vehicle. The car was white with orange front doors and H quickly guessed it was a taxi. The driver sat with his window down, his left arm resting on the outside of the door casually.

Before H got the chance to speak the taxi driver initiated the conversation.

"Hello my friend." He bellowed cheerfully. "How are you?"

H made his way over "I'm good mate. How are you?" he replied equally cheerfully, pleasantly surprised by the man's good English.

"Why are the British here my friend?" He asked, rolling his "R's" like many of the Afghans who spoke English as a second language.

"We come in peace mate." H reassured him. "We are here to help you."

As he reached the taxi, he bent down to look inside the car. Eight passengers were squeezed into the space designed for four. On the back seat were four women, all dressed in sky-blue full burkas, with even their eyes covered by a lacy mesh. Three children aged between 4-5 years old were awkwardly sprawled across the women's laps, all fast asleep in contorted positions, supported around their waists by presumably their mothers to stop them slumping further. In the front passenger seat, a middle-aged man sat comfortably alone, smoking a hand rolled cigarette that filled the car with a foul-smelling smoke. H noticed that the passenger seat wasn't even pulled forward to afford leg room to those behind. The driver extended his hand toward H, a broad smile on his face.

"Welcome to my country." He said.

H accepted his handshake "Thanks."

"Do you like Afghanistan?" "It is beautiful yes?"

"It's very nice mate, yes." H lied. Like most soldiers he hated the place, and this was his second tour there.

"Do you like football my friend?" asked the driver randomly.

"Football?" Repeated H. "Yeah I like football. Why?"

"Manchester!" He declared proudly. "The greatest team! My team!"

"Happy days mate, that's my team too." H replied happily. "Good man."

Excitedly, the taxi driver unzipped his jacket to show off his favourite football shirt underneath. H recognised it immediately as a Manchester United top as worn in the 1999-2000 season.

The driver pointed at the number 7 printed on the shirt, blurting out once more. "David Beckham!"

H, a staunch, lifelong Manchester City supporter was repulsed. United were the sworn enemy! This time he would have to wash his hands at least 3 times!

"Are you fucking kidding me?" Well that's the end of that friendship!" He muttered dryly. "Down to business." He took out his notebook and asked the usual questions of the taxi driver, who was returning from a trip to the nearest hospital over 100km away where all four of the women had undergone pregnancy check-ups. The man's English was very good, so Mohamed was not required, and H finished with his questions after a few minutes. Anticipating another handshake H prepared by withdrawing a water bottle from its pouch with one hand before wrapping up, notepad in the other.

"Nice to meet you mate, have a good day."

The driver extended his hand once more, but H's hands were full, and he gestured awkwardly to make that clear.

"Goodbye my friend. Peace be upon you." He said as he drove away slowly.

"Fuck off you United bastard!" Snarled H through gritted teeth as he turned away. There was no way in hell he was going to shake his hand again! H rubbed the sanitiser into his hands again, wiping the excess on the seat of his trousers then called Frank and

Johnny on his radio straight to update them. Frank arranged for them all to rendezvous at Johnny's vehicle to exchange information, which they did immediately.

When they arrived, Johnny informed them that the village Police Chief had been contacted through an Afghan liaison officer and he would be coming out to meet them shortly which was promising news. After talking through their various interactions and comparing notes for a few minutes Frank summarised.

"Okay, this is what we know so far:

1. The village is either called Al Haz, Al Farz or Namad.

2. There are between two hundred and ten thousand people here.

3. There are no landmines, except for the ones that are everywhere.

4. There are somewhere between one to five hundred Taliban fighters here, unless they've gone somewhere else.

5. And the village elder is either called Mr. Mohammed, Dr. Muhamad or Mr. Doctor."

"Right, happy with that. Mission accomplished. What the fuck!?"

"Here comes the cavalry." Said Johnny suddenly, raising the binoculars he wore around his neck to observe the two vehicles speeding towards them from the village.

The two Toyota Hilux's drove extremely fast across the uneven ground, bouncing and swerving erratically, each with passengers stood in the back, holding on tightly to whatever was available with one hand, the other hand holding their AK47 rifles, muzzles pointing skyward.

"Now we can get some honest answers about this place." He continued.

Frank and H looked at each other knowingly and nodded sarcastically.

To avoid a blue-on-blue, Frank informed the rest of the patrol on what was happening over the radio and soon the police were parking their vehicles alongside Johnny who had climbed on top of his vehicle to wave them in.

The police chief was in the front vehicle and opened the door before the vehicle had even stopped. His feet dangled out of the car momentarily before he jumped out. A short man, his face was obscured by the door until he slammed it shut. His belly overhung his trousers as he adjusted his belt before donning his dark blue police hat and walking towards Johnny. Johnny had also donned his headdress, checking himself out in a small mirror quickly to ensure his maroon beret sat neatly on his head. As Johnny got close the police chief extended his arms out to the side.

"Salaam alaykum, welcome to Al Haz." He said.

Frank and H looked at each other and nodded. Frank drew his pencil and circled the words in his notes. "Al Haz it is." He said quietly.

Johnny mirrored the chiefs' posture and they embraced, patting each other's backs vigorously.

"Thanks for meeting us Chief." Johnny said. "I'm Major Hill. We did not know that Al Haz was even here. What a beautiful village." He spoke loudly and slowly as if talking to a hard-of-hearing infant.

"My friend, please." The chief shrugged his shoulders and gestured toward the village. "Al Haz is…. how you say…… a fucking shit hole, not good! There is no food, no school, no water, no nothing, maybe you give some money to helping us?"

"Yes, maybe." Answered Johnny. "Can we go to your police station and take a look around?"

The police chief turned to his men, who were milling around by their vehicles and spoke something in Arabic. In response they all laughed. He looked back at Johnny. "I tell them that you want to visit police station."

"Why do they laugh?" Asked Johnny.

"Because we do not have." Replied the Chief. "Taliban blow it up, many men killed, very bad!"

"Oh, sorry to hear that Chief. When did that happen"? Johnny asked solemnly.

"Three days." The Chief said matter-of-factly.

"Three days ago?" Johnny said in a heightened pitch. "When did the Taliban leave?"

The Chief twisted his torso to look over his shoulder and again spoke to his men, who chuckled some more, shaking their heads.

"Taliban have not gone away. Still here!" Himself chuckling at the question.

"How many?" Frank called out.

The police chief looked at Frank disapprovingly. In his mind Johnny was the only one that should be talking to him, officer to officer. He looked back at Johnny, ignoring Franks interruption. Johnny asked the same question, this time warranting a response.

"Maybe fifty Taliban here." He said nonchalantly.

Frank glanced at H once again as he picked up his pencil, this time scoring out his writing and replacing the numbers with new figures. "Fifty Taliban." He muttered as he wrote.

"You come with me, I show you village, no problem." The Chief offered. "Follow my tracks. Many, many mines from Russians all around. Tracks good. No tracks, no good. Very bad."

Frank amended his notes accordingly. "No track equals No Go!!" He wrote

"Okay, just give me a few minutes to speak to my men." Johnny replied.

Johnny called in the vehicle commanders and conducted a briefing while the signaller sent a Situation Report to HQ. Frank was suspicious of the Chiefs motives but agreed to enter the village as they needed to promote their presence and gather intelligence as this place had somehow evaded detection until now. After the briefing, the commanders returned to their vehicles and passed on the information to their respective crews. Frank did the same and opted to keep his battle-ready gloves on, anticipating trouble. His team followed suit and prepared to take the lead behind the police.

Once everyone was ready, Johnny gave a thumbs-up to the Chief who immediately accelerated at full throttle toward the village, followed closely by the second police car. The dust cloud they created rose high in the air, engulfing Johnny and the men close by, before it started to settle.

Danny looked at Frank. "What's this, Wacky Racers?"

"Don't worry mate, let them go." Frank said calmly. "We'll take it steady, just follow the dust cloud as it clears. And stick to the tracks"

As instructed Danny followed on, well behind the police who had covered about 300 metres before he even moved. The police were waiting at the edge of the village when the patrol arrived a couple of minutes behind them. The Chief was revelling in the attention they were receiving from the locals as they stood in the streets and on their roof tops to investigate the procession of military hardware approaching. This open show of force would massively reinforce his authority and credibility, since it had been undermined by the Taliban.

The convoy entered the unmapped village and trundled steadily through the dirt tracks between compound walls. Stray dogs ran wild, barking at the intruders while the people stood still, looking on in silence. Women, who wore headscarves covered their faces as the men got closer and children ran alongside the vehicles, staring at the white-faced soldiers and their unfamiliar equipment in wonder.

For Reece, this was a journalistic paradise. Here he would capture genuine authentic images of a place no outsider had ever photographed, raw emotion, innocence of youth and reality of war in one place. He didn't know it yet, but these pictures would not only establish him as a world class photographer, they would change his life. He snapped away excitedly. The convoy turned left at a street corner where a small group of men sat in the back of a pick-up truck. Between the five men seated, four AK47's were clearly visible and at least one RPG but the police did not react and continued past. Leon raised his hand to wave to the stern-faced men, assuming they were also police, but none responded as they passed. The remaining vehicles received a similar response as they continued down the street which was obviously a local marketplace. Makeshift stalls lined one side of the road selling fruit and vegetables, bread, cigarettes etc. Every so often someone would acknowledge the soldiers with a slow, nervous wave or nod of the head as they stared in stunned silence.

Danny watched in disgust as a fruit seller pulled a large bag of bananas from the sewer drain where they'd been stored overnight to keep them cool. The trader then carefully poured a bucket of water over them before hanging them out on display from his stall ceiling by a piece of dirty rope.

"That's alright then, they're clean now!" Said Frank sarcastically, who'd also witnessed it.

"Yum. Not for me thanks chef, I'm full!" Joked Danny.

The convoy drove all the way through the village, weaving its way down the tracks that were wide enough, passing the main mosque, some smaller mosques, a derelict school, a pharmacy, shops, a factory and several water wells emblazoned with Red Cross signage. Overall, the village seemed to be in pretty good order with few visible signs of battle damage except for the odd hole in a wall that may have been created by a bullet strike. The only exception was the old police station, which had clearly suffered a substantial attack. The internal walls were peppered with bullet holes and the exterior front wall was almost obliterated where a suicide bomber had detonated their device in the foyer. Bloodstains could still be seen on the walls and floor and the entire interior was littered with paperwork, glass and broken furnishings where it had been blasted then subsequently looted for anything of value. Surprisingly the adjacent buildings were not damaged, but the station itself was beyond repair and stood as a stark reminder of the Taliban threat.

The convoy drove past the station, each vehicle in turn slowing down to take a close look at the site. Reece asked his driver to stop momentarily so he could get some detailed shots of the scene. He desperately wanted to go inside to get some more photos but was told he couldn't for his and the others safety which he knew was the right call. After a brief pause and some frantic photographing from standing, squatting, kneeling, and prone positions his vehicle also drove on.

As they exited the village the police cars once again sped off ahead towards some parked vehicles a few hundred metres away in the open ground. When Frank and the others caught up with them the police had already taken up position around a small gathering of men. There were roughly ten vehicles and twenty people gathered together. On the ground a huge embroidered rug was placed, weighed down on the edges by rocks to prevent the wind from blowing it away. Most of the men were sat on the rug, legs folded, talking quietly amongst themselves. Some were sipping tea or eating food from a generous buffet that was laid out in the centre. There was rice, meat, cakes and biscuits as well as several intricately decorated urns and teapots. All the men looked elderly, many with long grey beards. Well dressed, they had all removed their shoes which were neatly lined up down one side of the blanket. One man was sat in a wheelchair, his left leg amputated above the knee, his left arm below the elbow and a black patch over his empty left eye socket, all wounds sustained from his time in the Mujahedeen, fighting the Soviets. His single shoe was placed on the edge of the rug along with the others.

Frank instinctively organised the patrol into an all-round-defence formation, pushing the vehicles and weapon systems into the best positions for arcs of fire and view to best provide early warning and protection for the group.

Johnny had dismounted from his vehicle and purposefully made his way towards the gathering. His driver had also dismounted and followed closely to act as close protection during the apparent impending meeting. Mohamed, realising that his interpreting skills would be needed, also urgently joined them as Johnny stopped at Franks vehicle for a quick chat.

"I guess we're having a shura then!" He said.

"I reckon you're right Boss." Replied Frank. "I take it you didn't know either?"

"Nope! Wish I did though. Would have been nice to do some prep!" Johnny sighed.

"Keep an eye on that little fucker Boss. He'll use this to make himself look like the big man." Frank warned, suspicious of the police chiefs' motives. "And keep your boots on!"

"Won't that offend them?" Queried Johnny, looking at all the boots lined up beside the carpet.

"Yep!" said Frank unapologetically. If violence erupted, Frank wanted everyone ready to move.

A shura was a formal setting for a consultation or council involving all key stakeholders.

The Chief came across to collect Johnny with another man. "Major, the Council want to speak to you. This is Dr. Mohamed Ahmed, he is the village elder. He has brought everyone together for shura."

"Salaam alaykum Dr Ahmed, my name is Major Hill."

Frank updated his notes one more time "Doctor Ahmed." He mouthed as he quickly scribbled.

The village elder shook Johnny's hand, his frail old fingers forming a gentle grip. Johnny looked him in the eye as the old man spoke slowly in Arabic, nodding when it seemed appropriate. The old man's speech was laboured and as he spoke, he revealed a mouth deficient of most of its teeth. Stringy saliva trails connected his top and bottom lip and they expanded and contracted as his mouth opened and closed. His breath smelled strongly of coffee which he breathed into Johnny's face as he talked in close proximity, straining to speak with any volume. His eyes were almost completely grey with a small ring of their original dark brown remaining, probably riddled with cataracts, and they sat in deep sunken sockets in his withered face. Long hairs protruded from his ears and nostrils, but he did not have a beard like the others, just a few wispy stray hairs on his chin. Also, unlike the others he did not wear the traditional dish-dash outfit. He instead wore a western style tan, three-piece suit and well-polished, brown leather brogues. A neatly folded handkerchief sat in his blazer breast pocket and a yellow-gold watch adorned his wrist. Aside from the pakol hat on his head he looked like any other doctor you might see back home, albeit in the 1970's.

They exchanged pleasantries through Mohamed, the interpreter, and the elder offered Johnny some food and drink, which he accepted politely.

A young boy who was busy running back and forth with food and drinks for everyone fetched a teapot and some cups and brought them to the old man who gestured toward Johnny. The old man spoke, and Mohamed translated.

"He says please, you are our guest, you must take first."

Johnny bowed forward slightly as he nodded to the old man. "Thank you, erm, tashakur." He said as he took a cup from the young boys outstretched hands. The elder then took his cup, followed by the Chief and lastly, at the bottom of the pecking order, Mohamed. Everything was based on hierarchy and tradition here. Johnny held his cup as the boy poured some black coffee, filling all of the cups in the same order as they were issued before returning to the buffet and coming back with biscuits which were distributed the same way.

The old man spoke again as Johnny took a sip of the hot, pungent brew which was surprisingly sweet and refreshing. Johnny waited for him to finish before looking at Mohamed for the translation.

"He says we will start soon. We just wait for the Taliban now." Mohamed explained.

Johnny almost spat his coffee out. "Taliban!?" "The Taliban are coming here?" He asked.

"Yes of course." Said Mohamed. "All of the leaders will attend the shura."

Johnny's hand had instinctively reached for his pistol. He gripped it within its holster.

The elder noticed and spoke urgently to Mohamed.

Mohamed translated. "It is no problem Major. The shura is a place of peace. There can not be a shura without the Taliban, do not worry."

The elder placed a hand on Johnny's forearm. "Okay, okay." He said reassuringly.

The police chief reinforced the elder's words. "My men are here to protect, there will be no trouble. Very good." He said with confidence, proudly gesturing towards his men who sat around disinterested, weapons slung behind their backs, hands in pockets.

In contrast, the BRF were on high alert, weapons at the ready, scanning the surroundings.

Johnny's radio crackled in his ear. "All call signs, this is Jim, be aware we have a vehicle approaching from the south. Zero Alpha acknowledge."

Johnny replied. "Zero Alpha roger out." He turned back towards the village to see a pick-up heading their way. As it neared, he recognised it as the one from the village which had the armed men in.

"More of your men?" He said to the police Chief.

The Chief shook his head. "Taliban." He replied. "Very bad men!"

Johnny quickly relayed the surreal situation to his men via the radio and Frank then gave some new direction. "Ginge and Danny, get yourselves in position with your sniper rifles, everyone else stand-to until this meeting is over. All commanders acknowledge, over."

In order, the commanders acknowledged the instruction and Franks two most trusted snipers deployed with their Long-Range Rifles to optimum positions.

As the Taliban pick-up entered the parking area, the soldiers watched them closely, noting their weapon systems, their equipment and their physical appearance. Reece was tasked to take photographs, so he fitted a large telescopic lens to take pictures in detail, zooming in on faces, the number plate and ammunition containers secured in the back of the vehicle. The Taliban fighters wore black dish-dash suits and black turbans wrapped around their heads. The hatred in their eyes as they stared at the soldiers was intensified by the mascara that some of them wore, but this was evenly matched by the glares of the soldiers who held them in equal contempt. You could cut the atmosphere with a knife but for now the truce was to be respected.

The Talib commander and his driver stepped out of the vehicle, while the remainder remained seated in the back. The commander walked towards the elder, his gait very graceful, almost gliding along the ground. Bolt upright his arms swung a small amount from the elbow down. A tall man, no more than 40 years old, his skin was dark, his beard jet black, as if dyed and oiled and his large brown eyes accentuated by a thin line of mascara. The elder greeted him, shaking his hand before they both removed their shoes and entered the shura. The Taliban commander was obviously well known to the group as many more of the men greeted him with a wave or handshake. Even the police chief shook his hand, but he deliberately avoided Johnny, which saved him the dilemma of shaking his hand or not. That set the scene for the meeting, the commander avoided eye contact or any kind of interaction with Johnny throughout. To him he was and infidel and a foreign invader who had no right to even be there.

The meeting lasted nearly four hours, with all in attendance contributing. At times it seemed as though things were getting heated, but it was just their way of communicating and although there were disagreements, conflict was avoided by early intervention from the elder who's presiding authority they all respected. There were also moments of laughter amongst the old men as they shared anecdotes which resonated to the men outside the meeting too, lifting their spirits momentarily from the boredom of their security taskings. Johnny realised that the presence of the patrol had already caused a great deal of anxiety among the villagers, even though they had only been there a few hours. The people worried that fighting would follow, and they would be dragged into a conflict that had mostly not affected them so far. Many of the locals were not even aware of the foreign presence in their country, they lived so far away from the fighting. Most attempted to portray a position of neutrality during the shura, knowing that openly supporting one side or the other could jeopardise the safety and security of their families and livelihoods. At some point they knew they would be forced to choose a side, either the Taliban, the Police, the Elders Council or the Foreign led Army. Johnny understood the complexities of the situation and ensured he said nothing that could compromise anybody. He also made sure he did not make any promises to the many requests for help, which came at him from all directions. The people wanted to know what the foreigners could offer. Some of the more educated men knew of projects in other parts of the country that had been funded by the U.S or NATO and saw an opportunity for their village to receive similar support. Johnny took many notes, filling several pages with their list of demands. Infrastructure, clean water, food, medicine, sanitation, petrol, mobile communications... the list went on. What he was also able to do was take note of the personalities in attendance. Whenever someone talked, he ensured he got their name and profession and throughout the meeting he tried to connect the people together through common interests and agendas. This information would form part of his patrol report on return to base and help in the greater effort of determining the hierarchy of the Province.

When the shura concluded, the Taliban commander was first to leave, politely announcing his departure to the Elder before collecting his shoes and returning to his waiting posse. As he drove off the tension in the air subsided immediately, although for many of the soldiers it was quite the anti-climax. Being so close to the enemy but unable to engage had been frustrating. Both snipers had set their crosshairs on the fighters several times, rehearsing a shot to the head or body, wanting them to do something rash, daring them to draw weapons or display a threat. Coming down from such a heightened state of psychological arousal would always make them feel very tired later in the day. Maybe next time.

Johnny however was not tired. He'd drank several cups of coffee during the meeting and was feeling the effects of the local brew which unbeknown to him was fortified with opiates from the poppy harvest. After a lengthy farewell process, he walked over to Frank, who had stayed next to his vehicle studying his map and programming his GPS.

"That seemed to go well." Johnny said excitedly, grinning broadly.

Franks eyes widened and he jerked backwards in shock. "What

the fuck have you taken Boss?" He exclaimed. "Your eyes are like fucking saucers!"

Johnny knew there was something foreign in his bloodstream, and although it felt amazing, he knew it probably wasn't legal. "Might have to volunteer myself for a drug test when we get back. I think that was more than an espresso!" He said, still smiling.

Frank laughed. "Good job you're not driving! You're off you're bloody nut!"

Danny was also enjoying the sight of the strait-laced officer high as a kite. "Yeah, cos that would be dangerous, luckily he's only gonna be sat behind a machine gun! What could possibly go wrong?" He joked.

"That's actually a good point Dan, we better stay here for a bit until he comes down a bit." Frank said, still chuckling to himself. "Boss go grab a few minutes rest in your wagon. We'll all have a scoff and a brew, then you can brief me and the blokes on the meeting in about an hour."

"Roger, over." Said Johnny. Within two minutes he was sat in his seat fast asleep.

While Johnny slept the men took turns to prepare and eat their rations, always ensuring at least one of them per vehicle remained on sentry behind the turret mounted machine gun. Five of them were 7.62mm GPMG's and the other five were .50cal Heavy Machine Guns, a devastating amount of firepower in its own right. Some of the men liked to cook their food individually, others preferred an "all-in" where they would all put into one big bowl, then share it out, often supplemented with curry powders and hot sauces. Most drank tea from the rations or their own supply of Tetleys or PG tips tea bags from the UK. Some used small foldable gas burners to cook on, others stuck with the issued Hexamine fuel tablets and the stoves they came with. One used three nails knocked into the ground instead of the issue stove and balanced his metal mug on top of those with the fuel blocks burning underneath. A few of the men opted to just eat the rations cold, straight from the packet and drink water although nothing was ever truly cold in the desert heat. A few of the soldiers sat with the police who were very interested in the ration packs, swapping their home-made bread for packets of biscuits and sweets. The young boy who'd been serving the buffet at the shura also distributed the remaining cakes and biscuits among the soldiers and police before departing with the last of the guests. All in all, it was somewhat of a feast.

Frank gave the men adequate time to eat and drink before waking Johnny and rallying the patrol together. Johnny's eyes had returned to normal and he seemed to be back on planet earth. Jim had made him a cup of sweet tea and he gratefully drank it.

The vehicle commanders were waiting for their orders, all keen to find out about the meeting so Johnny gathered himself together, read through his notes, then made his way, brew in hand, to where they were seated in a semi-circle. The police chief was also there, his appearance seeming to rapidly decline with every passing minute. Within a few hours he'd transformed from being reasonably smart and presentable to an absolute mess. His shirt now partially untucked, had large sweat patches in the armpits and back and the laces on one of his boots hung down where they had come undone. He'd somehow gone from clean shaven, apart from a moustache, to a substantial beard growth and his hat sat askew at a 45-degree angle on top of his head.

Johnny and Frank briefed the men on the outcomes of the meeting and the plan for the rest of the day before they dispersed back to their own teams to brief them.

The police chief was keen for the BRF to stay as long as possible so he could exploit their influence as much as possible and offered to show them the parts of town they had not seen including some abandoned Taliban defensive positions on the village outskirts. Also, he wanted to show them the disused sports ground where the Taliban had carried out their public executions. Johnny and Frank thought that this was good intelligence to collect and worthy of staying for, so agreed.

The BRF followed the police back into the village where they completed the tour. For some of the older soldiers, driving through the streets was reminiscent of Northern Ireland, not in appearance but in the way they were received. News travels fast, people were now aware of who they were, and many had already chosen sides. Trundling down one street they might find the people welcoming, waving, smiling etc. Turn a corner and the contrast in atmospherics was palpable with looks of hate and people slamming window shutters closed as they passed.

The soldiers remained alert but made a conscious effort to adopt a non-aggressive posture as they drove, pointing the vehicle mounted machine guns skywards and waving at the people who were out in the streets. One of the soldiers threw fruit flavoured boiled sweets from the ration packs to excited children who ran alongside his vehicle, but stopped after he saw one young boy receive a nasty slap around the face from an adult male, clearly not happy with their presence. The boy had caught a sweet and triumphantly returned to his father to share it with him, but the black clad man was a Taliban supporter and the child's overt display of gratitude to the soldiers angered him greatly. The boy would receive a beating and the sweet would lay on the ground until a dog found it and hungrily wolfed it down, wrapper and all.

Arriving at a small knoll on the edge of the village, the police chief debussed and encouraged Frank to join him as he brushed off a well concealed wooden trap door with his foot before lifting it up and dropping into the hole up to his waist. The patrol was already positioning themselves into a defensive perimeter, so Frank stepped out. Within a few seconds Johnny was also on the ground and made his way to the entrance.

"Hold on Boss!" Said Frank. "Let the police go first."

Frank wasn't about to let the men go into an unknown underground defensive position without checking it out first. Two more police officers followed their commander into the trench, ducking down and disappearing into the bunker on all fours. Frank called Danny over.

"Let's have a look around before we go into that hole." He said cautiously.

"I was hoping you'd say that." Danny replied.

The two men accompanied by Johnny, walked cautiously to the entrance, mindful that there could be booby traps or munitions left behind, then continued over ground in the direction that the tunnel headed. Up ahead they noticed several recesses cut into the rock facing out towards the valley below and went to investigate. Peering into them they saw the police peering out from the inside.

"All okay?" Asked Frank.

"All okay." Replied the chief. "Very good."

Further along a police officer appeared, rising from the ground.

"Yes please." He shouted, ushering Frank forwards. A second entrance to the tunnel system had been opened. "Come, come." He said.

Frank knew that if there were any booby traps, they would have been detonated by the police so decided to have a closer look himself.

Inside was cramped with barely enough space for two men to walk past each other. A couple of sleeping platforms and a small kitchen area had been excavated into the rock for the inhabitants but apart from that it was simply a fortified firing position to observe from and shoot from. Several structures of similar proportions were shown to the BRF that afternoon and the police chief explained that they had all, at one time or another been occupied by the Police, the Army or the Taliban. Frank ensured that photographs were taken, and sketches made of the positions as well as recording their locations on the map. Once all the defensive positions were visited the Police Chief offered to take them to the Sports Ground. Frank and Johnny agreed, if they could get that done before darkness fell, they would be able to move on from the village, rest up overnight in the open desert and continue the patrol North in the morning.

The Sports Ground was underwhelming, resembling a poorly maintained open-air car park that you might find at the coast back in the UK rather than a pitch where you'd play a game of football. Granted, it was fairly flat and there were a couple of benches made of concrete for spectators and evidence of an old fence around the boundary but apart from that it was just more dirt and sand. The police chief showed them where people had been stoned to death, crucified and flogged in a very matter-of-fact manner, using Mohamed to translate when his English was not up to the task.

Again, the soldiers recorded everything for the patrol report.

While they were talking an old man walked across the pitch, holding his arms out to the side in a non-threatening posture as he got closer. Frank had been warned of his approach over the radio after the man had been stopped by one of the teams. A policeman intercepted him and after a brief conversation escorted him to where Frank, Johnny and the police chief stood.

The old man spoke to the chief in Arabic and Mohamed translated for Frank and Johnny.

"He is saying that there are missiles in an old Taliban compound over there." Mohamed pointed in the direction from where the old man came from. "He is worried for his family, because his house is also over there. He wants to know if we will take away the missiles so he can be safe?"

"Ask him what sort of missiles." Johnny requested.

Mohamed spoke to the chief and the old man for some time before reporting back. "He says there are two hundred multiple launch missiles inside a compound 300 metres that way." He said pointing again in the same direction. "He says children are playing in the compound right now, climbing all over the missiles. He says Taliban leave them there when they go to fight in the mountains."

The police chief backed up what Mohamed had said. "Very bad. Many bombs. Not good!"

Johnny saw the potential catastrophe. "Okay, let's go and take a look. Lead the way Chief."

The old man sat in the back of the chiefs' truck and they sped off, followed by the BRF who were keeping up to date with proceedings over the radio. The compound in question stood isolated, quarter of a mile from the village like a ranch from a Spaghetti Western. A low 3-foot mud wall encircled the high main wall of the compound at a distance of 100 metres, with breaks where tracks entered from all four sides. A few outbuildings stood outside of the perimeter, used as stables for goats and cows when the place was occupied. The patrol drove through an opening of the low wall, towards the single entrance to the inner compound. Arriving at a half open gate there were several motorbikes parked outside heavily laden with what looked like pallet wood, balanced across their seats horizontally. The wood was skilfully stacked high and secured by tatty pieces of old rope, somehow not flipping the bikes front wheels in the air with the weight. Inside the compound was a large shed type building with its own heavy wooden gates which were held wide open by some rocks placed on the ground. A broken padlock lay on the floor suggesting that entry had been forced into the abandoned building, along with a huge discarded tarpaulin, which had been pulled away to reveal the scavengers find.

"Tell them to stop, NOW!" ordered Frank sharply, his eyes widening to take in the sight before him. "NOW!"

The police chief, joined by his men ran into the shed shouting at the young men who were clambering all over the wooden boxes, hurriedly smashing them open and breaking them apart so they could liberate the timber. Two of the men were using sledge-hammers while another used a boulder to break up the transit boxes while others collected the wood and ferried it back to the motorbikes. The wood was top quality and would be fetch a good price, so they worked fast before others found out about it. Not interested in the contents, the young men had already broken down many of the boxes, which were now flat packed onto the motorbikes outside. However, inside the boxes were live munitions, rockets for a vehicle mounted multiple launch rocket system that was stored in a separate compound in the village. Swinging metal sledgehammers at them was not good for anyone's health. About twenty rockets had already been piled to one side haphazardly after being lowered to two men who clambered over broken bits of wood and stacked them precariously on top of each other, seemingly ignorant to the obvious danger of the situation.

The men were reluctant to stop their pillage, so the police used more forceful tactics, hitting them with pieces of wood from the floor, swinging them wildly, striking whatever part of the body they could reach. Desperate to acquire as much of the wood as possible the young men continued to gather up whatever they could as they retreated back to the motorbikes, repeatedly being hit as they scurried through the barn clutching the valuable resource. One man bled profusely from a wound on the top of his head, the blood dripping onto the wood in his hands and then the ground, leaving a red trail in the dirt and staining his white shirt. After a couple of minutes, the melee was over, the sound of the motorbikes' engines fading into the distance.

Frank worked out roughly how many rockets were there, assuming that the remaining boxes were all full and including those already unboxed.

"There's about 170 rockets in there Boss." He informed Johnny. "Better call this in, we can't leave it here, it's an accident waiting to happen!"

"Roger that!" Said Johnny, immediately striding towards his vehicle where he could call HQ on the radio. Jim had already relayed what he knew over the command net and handed Johnny a handset as he sat down in the front seat of the Land Rover.

While Johnny reported the find, Frank directed the patrol into new positions so that they could secure the compound to stop anyone else gaining entry. He pushed them out to the low wall which would provide good protection if they needed to defend the compound and also some separation if there was a blast. It also kept them close enough that they could still communicate and support each other.

Johnny finished his radio conversation and called Frank over to his vehicle.

"Brigade are sending the Royal Engineers to deal with this lot." He informed him. "It's too big for us to deal with."

"Too right, let the big boys have this one." Said Frank. The BRF had soldiers from the Royal Engineers in its ranks, who were highly qualified in dealing with explosives, but this task was well beyond their capability with the limited resources they carried. Usually they would blow up ammunition finds in situ, but to do that here would cause way too much collateral damage, wiping out half the village.

"Problem is." Johnny continued. "They can't get them here until tomorrow afternoon."

"Thought as much. Those boys are busy." Frank acknowledged. "Looks like we're here for the night. Could be worse, at least we're not in the middle of the village. That would have been a drama. At least we've got half decent arcs here, and the police can help with the security.

"I'll speak to the chief to see where he wants to put his men." Volunteered Johnny.

Johnny spoke to the chief briefly before returning to speak with Frank.

"What's the plan then Boss?" Asked Frank.

Before Johnny could answer, the two police cars rapidly accelerated away from the compound and disappeared down a track into the distance, in the opposite direction to the village.

Johnny smirked. "Well, his plan is to go home for the night and come back tomorrow. They don't like driving in the dark, and where they live is a thirty-minute drive from here."

"I thought they lived here." Frank stated.

"So did I." Replied Johnny. "But apparently not. Too dangerous! He had no intentions of staying here tonight!"

"Cracking police force!" Frank laughed, joined by Johnny and Jim. "Useless twats!"

The BRF were already in good positions as Frank had anticipated a delay, so he called in the commanders for a brief from him and Johnny to keep everybody up to date. Each vehicle would be manned throughout the night by one man on sentry duty, the others would rest or carry out administration tasks. The only exception was Johnny's vehicle who did not take part in sentry duty, instead one of them would maintain a radio listening watch, rotating every 2 hours like the others. The men quickly settled into routine making the most of the last of the daylight by cooking rations, cleaning weapons and taking care of their feet which had been sweltering all day. Feet were aired and powdered one at a time, with a change of clean socks every few days as a morale booster. Both feet were never undressed at the same time in case of a contact with the enemy.

As night fell, Frank made his way around the perimeter, visiting each vehicle and ensuring he spoke to each of the men in turn. He liked to see for himself how the soldiers were getting on both physically and mentally, and it was good for them to see him too, it showed them that they were all going through the same thing and if he made it look like everything was under control, that made them feel confident too. Doing the rounds took him a couple of hours during which time he'd shared several brews, heard a few jokes and enjoyed a couple of impressions of the Platoon Commander. Before getting back to his vehicle for his turn on sentry duty he paid a visit to Johnny's position, to let him know all was ok and check to see if there was any news from Brigade HQ.

CHAPTER ELEVEN

Missing In Action

J im, the signaller was sat in the back of the Land Rover wearing his headset. On his lap was a week-old copy of a newspaper that he was attempting the crossword puzzle in.

"Where's the Boss?" Frank asked him.

"He went for a dump" Jim replied casually.

Frank quickly scanned the area, noticing Johnny's driver was sleeping, then with urgency in his voice quizzed "Well who the fucks gone with him and where did they go?"

"He doesn't like crapping in front of people Frank, he always goes off by himself, he went over there." Jim pointed towards one of the stables 100m away, a small building made of concrete blocks with a gaping hole in the roof. Frank walked over to his vehicle where the sentry was facing towards the building, his machine gun locked off in the horizontal position.

"Where's the Boss Leon?" His voice was shaking a little as he tried to control his emotions, a mixture of anger and anxiety. Nobody was ever allowed to stray from the relative safety of the Harbour without a cover man to watch his back.

"He's still taking a crap Frank, I can see his webbing at the top of the ditch. In fact he might be knocking one out because he's taking ages!" Looking through his night vision goggles Leon pointed to the webbing belt that Johnny had removed before squatting in the steep sided irrigation ditch which ran past the small building. He hated keeping it on during a call of nature, so he'd always place it to one side and rest his rifle across the top.

"Prick!" Snapped Frank as he raised his rifle and looked through his telescopic night-sight towards Johnny's unattended equipment. "Prepare to move Leon," Frank jumped into the drivers' seat and started the engine, placing his rifle on the passenger seat. Leon unlocked the gun, pulled the butt into his shoulder and braced himself in the turret. Frank accelerated hard towards the stable hoping that his concerns would be for nothing. Within seconds he was there, skidding to a halt and leaping from the vehicle. "Cover me," he shouted to Leon who had already taken up his fire position on the machine gun, pointing it ahead of Frank's path. Frank had his rifle in the shoulder, a finger on the safety catch and another on the trigger as he reached the top of the ditch. "Johnny!" he shouted, "Johnny!" There was no rifle on top of the webbing and no sign of Johnny, he was gone.

A second vehicle arrived as hurriedly as the first, "What's going on Frank?" asked a puzzled H.

Frank shouted. "It's the Boss, he's gone!" Frank and H quickly ran into and around the old stable, meeting at the other side, both calling for Johnny as they searched. Leon was scanning along the ditch and surrounding area with the thermal camera while simultaneously trying to raise Johnny on the radio.

Frank bent down and picked something up from the floor. "He's not going to answer mate." He said. Holding Johnny's discarded radio in the air.

"The bastards have got him, they've literally caught him with his pants down, the silly fucker!" Said Frank angrily. "Leon, get on the net and tell Jim to call HQ and let them know the boss is MIA.

"Oh shit! murmured Leon. He took a deep breath and gathered

his thoughts before speaking into his radio to alert the other sentries who in turn quickly passed on the bad news to the remainder. Within a couple of minutes, the whole group was awake, equipment loaded, rifles reassembled and mounted in their vehicles ready to move.

Frank was using the Thermal Imaging camera to scan the area, hoping to catch a glimpse of a fleeting enemy, a vehicle, a group of men, anything that might give him a clue as to where Johnny had been taken. There was no way he had walked off without his equipment by his own free will. But the night was silent apart from the barking of a distant dog. Frank caught sight of a heat source on a small hill to the north and zoomed in the camera to investigate but soon realized it was the barking dog when it stood up and walked around. From such a distance there was a delay of a couple of seconds from watching the dog sit down and raise its head upwards, to hearing the sound of its eerie howl. This caused other dogs in the area to start their own howling, adding to the sinister atmosphere. Frank lowered the scope, there was nobody to be seen. He turned to Leon.

"Leon, get Tonto in here to work out what happened." Frank had purposely not gone right into the area that Johnny had been taken from because he did not want to contaminate any ground sign that might explain what had happened. Nobody goes into the ditch until Tonto says so.

Tonto was an experienced tracking instructor who'd completed his Jungle Warfare Instructors and Tracking Instructors courses in Brunei back to back. His love of the jungle environment made him a natural on both and after his courses he was asked to come back as an instructor. This he did, and he spent 2 years teaching tracking and tactics to the army earning himself such a renowned reputation that he was regularly used by several police forces in the UK to assist in missing persons search missions after he returned. He was given his nickname during his courses because of his amazing ability to read ground sign, like the character in the Lone Ranger movies.

Tonto arrived with the remainder of the group who took up an all-round defence position, weapons at the ready, scanning for the enemy. He carried a large Dragon light torch which he shone into the ditch.

They caught him by surprise, sneaked up from behind while he was crapping. Three blokes, wearing boots. Tonto pointed to the ground. They've dragged him backwards while he was still doing a shit, look how the crap is spread to over there. They've put him on his back and bashed his head in here using this rock and whatever else they had. Tonto held up a white rock the size of a baseball, it had blood on it and several black hairs, a spattering of blood was visible on the floor, this had been a vicious attack, Johnny would be in a bad way. Tonto reached down and picked something out of the dirt, "What the fuck?" He reeled slightly when he realized what he was inspecting.

"What you got?" asked Frank.

Tonto walked up close to Frank and held up what he'd discovered but whispered so as not to alert the others. "It's a fucking front tooth mate, they've beaten the shit out of him!"

"We've got to find him Tonto. Do your magic mate, where's he gone?"

"This way, stay behind me but cover my front." Tonto set off at a fast walk, stopping every few meters to confirm he was heading in the right direction. Frank followed closely with two of the others for support. The vehicles provided fire support as the four men moved off and trundled slowly behind off to a flank. Johnny had been carried and dragged across the hard-baked ground, making it easy for Tonto to find a trail. After negotiating their way through the ditch and across a dirt track the trail was heading in a straight line for a compound two hundred metres away. "Chances are they've taken him there Frank." Tonto shone an infra-red beam onto the compound wall. "Send the wagons there and we'll follow the sign to make sure."

"Okay mate, good work." Frank informed "H" what was going on and the vehicles could be heard driving toward the compound immediately.

Tonto and his close support team continued to follow the ground sign which carried on towards the compound.

H arrived at the compound first and debussed. No heat sources, light or movement had been seen during the approach, but the men had to assume there were hostiles inside. A large metal gate lay wide open and the compound appeared deserted. "H" took three men and moved to the wall. Getting a lift up he popped his head over to look inside, it was empty. The compound had no internal rooms or walls, just a perimeter. "Get the wagon lights in there," he shouted to his driver who quickly pulled the vehicle up to the entrance and turned on the lights.

H spoke into his radio. "It's empty Frank, there's nobody here but we'll have a good look around."

Tonto was still following the sign, and now only one hundred metres from the compound. "This is the way they came mate, I'm positive."

"Stay with it mate, I trust you." Frank reassured him.

H noticed something on the floor in the compound and moved closer to investigate. "You beauty!" he said. "Frank," he spoke into his radio. "I've found the boss's pen, he's been here."

"Over here," called one of the men. "Looks like there's a tunnel."

A piece of wood painted the same colour as the ground lay on the floor in the compound corner, partially covering a hole beneath it. The hole was about a metre wide, easily big enough for a man to climb into. As H arrived to take a look the soldier lifted the lid with his foot and shone his torch inside, discarding the lid with a kick.

"No, no, no H tried to stop him, but as the lid was lifted it was too late and they both heard the distinct sound of a hand grenade fly-off lever as the booby trap was triggered.

"Take cover." They both instinctively shouted simultaneously.

Everybody hit the deck, most not knowing why, but expecting something to go bang. And it did. The tunnel entrance was booby trapped with an improvised bomb and hundreds of nails, nuts, and bolts were blasted in all directions, embedding themselves into the compound walls and shooting indiscriminately into the distance. The pursuit would end there, it would be too dangerous to enter the tunnel, knowing that there would likely be more to follow.

The patrol was over. Now the focus was entirely on the recovery of Johnny, but despite the best efforts of the BRF and a company of paratroopers with helicopter support, he was nowhere to be found. During the search, a large cache of heroin, several weapons and $10,000 U.S in cash were discovered, but nothing to indicate the whereabouts of the unfortunate officer. The tunnel system was found to be heavily booby trapped and destroyed by engineers using explosives, after several other exits were identified. After exhausting all options and hitting a wall of silence from the locals, the BRF reluctantly called the search off after 24hrs and began the drive back to camp, once again driving through the night across the undulating broken terrain of the desert. The journey back was much different to the way out. The sense of urgency was obvious, with less frequent stops and a faster pace across the terrain. For Reece this made for an uncomfortable journey, holding on tight to the roll cage as he bounced around. His forearms and wrists straining with the effort and filling with lactic acid. Even his jaw was aching from clenching his teeth tightly together after he'd face planted into a water jerry can whilst crossing a particularly bumpy field. The small cut he'd sustained on his eyebrow caused a trickle of blood to run down his cheek to the corner of his mouth and into his helmet chin strap. Instinctively his tongue licked at it, the salty liquid mixed with the sand which covered him from head to foot giving a unpleasant gritty taste. He turned his head quickly to the right and spat it out, the slipstream carrying it away from the vehicle. He only licked it once. Under normal circumstances he would seek medical attention but this time it would have to wait. The treatment that Johnny was probably enduring at the hands of the Taliban made his laceration insignificant. He shuddered at the thought.

Frank took the most direct route back to camp possible without compromising the security of the patrol, stopping less and investigating distant heat sources and movements faster. His main effort was to return to base as quickly as possible where he could utilise all the resources and agencies available there to locate and plan how to rescue Johnny. The abduction had hit him hard, withdrawing into himself and becoming very quiet. Although Johnny was the boss, Frank felt responsible, he was as angry with himself as he was with Johnny. During the search, he'd been instrumental in the thoroughness of the operation, coordinating with the Afghan Police, Royal Engineers, the dog handlers, Apache helicopter crews and village elders to ensure every possibility was exhausted before moving on to the next. He had not slept for 48hrs but was not tired, his mind was racing. The men were all feeling it too, this was unchartered territory for the BRF, never having to deal with a man-away before on any operation. The role of Platoon Sergeant was in some ways an isolating one. Frank had found he'd slowly drifted away from many of the men, especially the newer members who had never known him as anything other than their Sergeant, having to enforce the rules and discipline soldiers meant that the dynamics of his relationships had inevitably changed. A couple of his old mates had initially struggled with the change, but it didn't take long for everyone to settle into it, Frank was a natural fit for the job.

CHAPTER TWELVE

My Old Boots

Johnny's abduction was big news, not only in the military, but also in the media and despite the MoD's best efforts to keep it under wraps, the British Press had quickly learned of the situation and were already about to publish the story along with pictures of Johnny the day the BRF returned to Kurzak Camp. However, before they got the chance, the Taliban released their own story and broadcast a propaganda video over the internet which showed Johnny, dressed in a set of bright orange coveralls, kneeling in front of a large black and white flag. Behind him stood five masked men, all dressed in black, brandishing a variety of weapons from knives to a grenade launcher. One of the men, stood in the middle directly behind Johnny did all of the speaking as Johnny knelt slumped forward. He spoke calmly, casually waving a large kitchen knife around the whole time. At one point he grabbed Johnny by the hair and pulled his head backwards. Despite the swelling and black eyes, it was unmistakeably Johnny, who remained passive throughout, his body language dejected, defeated. The increasingly agitated man held the knife to Johnny's throat as he made his demands, which were subtitled at the bottom of the screen. He demanded the immediate release of all Taliban prisoners and the unconditional withdrawal of the foreign invaders or Johnny would be executed during the next live broadcast in 48 hours. Johnny's head flopped forward when the man released his grip, his blood-soaked hair, matted together visible on screen.

It was hard to watch but, just like every intelligence agency in the UK, Frank and his men watched the footage repeatedly, searching for clues. They studied Johnny's every move in detail to see if he might be trying to covertly communicate, pausing the video, zooming in on his eyes and mouth for any sign, but there was nothing. The men did not know it but, Johnny had endured a dozen rehearsals of that video before that version was recorded. On some he had indeed tried to communicate by blinking and mouthing words, but the Taliban had noticed and punished him with beatings to his already broken body. During the first rehearsal he had even attempted to escape, launching his own attack onto the captors but was quickly overpowered and subdued. For that he was brutally beaten on the soles of his feet with a walking stick, breaking several toes and metatarsals. Each time the scene was rehearsed he thought it was for real and each time the knife would be held to his throat. By the time the broadcast version was made Johnny was psychologic-ally exhausted, no longer caring, part of him hoped it was the end. The pain throughout his body was unbearable, he was tired, thirsty and hungry and could see no chance of getting out of the awful mess.The resistance-to-interrogation course he'd under-gone was hard, pushing the boundaries of realistic training, and at the time seemed brutal, but nothing could have prepared him for this hellish torture.

Leon was sat in his converted prison cell scrutinising the footage in slow motion on his laptop computer when Reece walked past the doorway, stopping suddenly as he noticed something famil-iar on the screen that he had not seen previously.

"Stop!" He blurted out. "Rewind!"

Leon twisted his body around on his camp cot to see Reece stood in the doorway pointing at the screen. "You what." He said.

"Go back a few seconds!" Demanded Reece, moving into the cell and stooping closer to the computer.

Leon hit the rewind button.

"There! Play....Pause!" Reece instructed. "Fuck my old boots! They're my old boots!" he exclaimed, one hand covering his mouth, the other pointing excitedly at the screen, he could hardly believe his eyes. "They're my old boots!" He repeated, the pitch getting higher each time.

"What are you talking about you lunatic?" Asked Leon, looking back and forth between Reece and the screen.

Reece moved even closer to the computer, his head almost resting on Leon's shoulder as he touched the screen with an outstretched index finger. "See those boots?" He pressed on the screen, blurring a small portion of the picture with the pressure, highlighting the feet of one of the captors who stood, menacingly brandishing a machete.

"What about them?" Leon moved his head closer to investigate.

Reece continued "I gave those boots to one of the Taliban when I was doing my story up in the mountains."

"There the same as any other brown boots mate, what makes you think they're yours?" Queried Leon.

"They are mine! I'm telling you. Look at the laces, they're different colours. I snapped one and replaced it with some white paracord, and then I snapped the other one and could only find a black lace to replace that. Plus, I always miss out the bottom inside eyelet when I lace up my boots, look" He pointed down to the boots on his feet and then to the ones on the screen that were configured in the same way. "It stops the seam digging into my high arches."

Leon's frown turned into a smile as he compared the boots. "You've got to be fucking kidding me. Let's get Frank."

There was no denying it, the boots were laced just like Reece's and he was certain that they were his. This was the first and only lead they had, the Taliban had been very careful not to leave any clues in the video as to where Johnny was being held captive. Without Reece's personal knowledge, nobody would have ever realized the significance of those boots, even the intelligence agencies had drawn a blank.

Frank called in Tonto and together they spread several maps and satellite photographs across the table which they hoped contained the mountainous area where Reece had lived with the Taliban for five days during the making of his special report, to try and ascertain exactly where he'd been taken. From the moment he was picked up by the Afghan fighters he was unaware of his location. Adhering to the conditions laid down by the Taliban he carried no means of communication or navigation. Even his camera was left behind, replaced by a disposable point and shoot type supplied by his escort. The Daily Telegraph had secured unprecedented access to a key commander in the area called Fahruk who had guaranteed his safety in return for an unbiased story that he hoped would portray the local fighters as martyrs against the western invaders. Reece had shown a draft version of the story to Fahruk through a well-educated Talib who spoke good English and after a few small changes was given the go-ahead and escorted back to his original pick up point. During his stay the English speaker and Reece had struck up an unexpected friendship. The young man's name was Zahir, Zar for short and he loved to practice his English by speaking to Reece for hours on end. Zar was Pakistani but had left his wealthy family and home to join the Jihad in Afghanistan in 2004 after the Taliban were overthrown by the U.S and British the previous year. Reece found it ironic that this young man of 19 years old professed to hate the west but wore a Manchester United shirt under his dish dash and spoke constantly about western music, T.V and American celebrities. Through all the propaganda Reece saw a vulnerable young idealist whose mind had been warped by the idea of Jihad and martyrdom. He hoped that he would be able to change his mind and somehow save him from his path of inevitable self-destruction. The Taliban base where Reece had stayed was a small village of only a few compounds high in the mountains and only accessible by an arduous three-hour trek up a mountain path. To get to the base of the mountain path Reece had, in one day, travelled by car, donkey and on foot, stopping every hour for a brief rest while he and the Talibs smoked a cigarette. Reece studied the satellite photograph looking for something that he could recognize, the map was of no use to him, just a confusing mass of brown lines which he could not interpret. "Think of your route, did you go up and down, or just up? Did you cross any bridges, streams, wadi's? Were there any signs of habitation?" Tonto needed something to narrow down the search.

"The drive was only for about an hour, then I got bounced around on the donkey for a couple of hours until we headed up the mountain path on foot for about three hours. There was nothing really mate, it was just desert and rocks and all I remember about that journey is getting sunburnt to death all down the left side of my body and on my calves and neck. In fact, my right arm was the only part of me that wasn't burnt. I just wanted it to end, I have never been so knackered!"

"That's good mate, an hour's drive would get you 60 – 80km, two hours on a donkey, another 15km, so we're looking for a mountain 75-100km from your start point and there's not that many places where you can walk up hill constantly for three hours, that would give you an elevation of about three thousand feet so we're narrowing it down."

"What time did they pick you up from here?" Tonto pointed to the track junction on the map where Reece had first nervously surrendered himself to the three Talibs that had collected him in their white and red Toyota Hilux.

"It was about eleven-thirty that morning. I remember thinking that I should eat my lunch early before the Afghans arrived so I wouldn't have to share it with them."

"Tight fucker!" Muttered Frank.

Reece continued. "They were supposed to pick me up at 9 o'clock but were late."

"They weren't late, they were watching you, making sure you weren't setting them up, they're not stupid." Despite his hatred for the enemy, Tonto had learned to respect their employment of good basic tactics. "What part of the day did you get sunburnt?"

"My arm and leg were while I was on the donkey, I remember getting off and my left leg was on fire and when I put my backpack on, I scraped my arm and it hurt like hell." Reece recalled.

"Okay, so you must have been heading westerly, that puts you roughly here." Tonto drew a circle on an air chart, centred roughly 85km west of his start point and went across to the pile of maps that littered the floor, quickly finding the one that corresponded to the area of interest. "So, the sunburn on your calves and neck, that occurred during the ascent up the mountain, right?"

"That's right, in fact I remember turning round when the sun dropped behind another mountain behind me and thinking "Thank Christ for that" as I got my first bit of shade that day."

"That means you were heading easterly" Calculated Frank, based on the movement of the Sun throughout the day.

"Why would they head West, then East?" Queried Frank. "Some sort of deception plan maybe?"

Frank and Tonto studied the map.

"There." Tonto said excitedly. He pointed to a place on the map at the base of a mountain. "This mountain is inaccessible from the south and east because of the cliff face but this spur from the west could offer a good route up through that saddle and along that ridgeline." He was using the tip of his pencil to point out the features on the map to Frank, but the terminology meant nothing to Reece.

"The distances are about right." Frank could see the logic in Tonto's appraisal "About 80km from the pickup point, with another mountain to the West. Let's get the satellite imagery of this area and take a good look."

"Trouble is Frank, how are we going to get there without being compromised?" Asked H. Everybody knew that the Taliban would have sentries overlooking the approach routes and that a helicopter insertion would give the enemy forewarning.

"Well I can't see how there's going to be anywhere big enough to parachute into, so we'll have to risk walking in."

"How big do you need?" Reece queried.

"Ideally, at least 50m by 50m."

Reece shrugged his shoulders to signal his ignorance of metric measurements.

"About half a football pitch." clarified Frank.

"What about a full-size football pitch? There's one beside the village. I played a game on it with the Taliban."

"At what point were you going to tell us about the football pitch you absolute fucking twat?" Snapped Frank. "How many mountain villages do you think there are with football pitches in them? Not fucking many! Right, we need some satellite imagery, I'm going to the Int Cell to see what I can find, Captain Compass come with me."

Reece had just earned another derogatory nickname from his favourite critic in recognition of his lack of navigational skills, but he could tell that it was in jest. Ever since the patrol Frank's attitude towards him had changed. Sure, there was still a lot of testosterone, but Reece got the impression that he was slowly earning his trust. He smiled wryly as he followed Frank out of the Ops Room and into the searing desert heat outside. Was it conceivable that they could one day be friends? Maybe it was.

The young reporter felt a sense of optimism. Everything might just work out.

Frank had a natural presence about him like nothing Reece had ever experienced, he unconsciously exuded confidence and professionalism which became infectious to those around him, and if he ever did have doubts, he made sure not to let the men know. This aura and reputation that he had inadvertently created was not only a great achievement, but was also a heavy burden that he carried on his shoulders, a huge pressure to perform to the highest standard, to lead from the front and get the job done at all times, without compromise. He knew that his men trusted him with their lives and would never question his decision, but he also knew the realities of war and that a wrong decision would result in casualties. Thankfully the BRF had not taken any casualties and Frank hoped that if they ever did, he would be able to deal with it. A good friend of his was a Platoon Sergeant in 3 PARA and had lost two of his young soldiers. Frank had been disturbed by the marked change to this extremely tough man's personality. He wrongly blamed himself for their deaths and was obviously finding it difficult to cope. In their short meeting between patrols Frank had tried to reassure his friend but knew it had been to no avail, the damage was irreparable and the only way to ease the pain was by taking revenge on the Taliban, although this too would only provide a short respite.

On arrival at the Intelligence Section, Frank spoke to the Sergeant who he knew from previous exercises and tours. After a brief chat the Sergeant walked off, returning quickly with some rolled up black and white satellite imagery maps. Frank shook his hand and briskly turned around, gesturing for Reece to follow him with a sideways nod of his head. Reece followed closely behind as they stepped out of the cool air-conditioned tent into the midday heat of the Afghan sun. With the maps under his arm Frank broke into a jog as they went quickly back to the BRF Ops Room and unfolded them on the big briefing table.

"Holy fucking dog shit, it's a football pitch!" Frank exclaimed. He was studying the satellite image with a magnifying glass, scrutinising every detail. "Tonto, go round up the blokes, we need to get a plan together."

Tonto left immediately to gather the men. Frank wanted to brainstorm a couple of ideas before he took the information to the HQ. They had 48 hours before Johnny would be executed and he wanted to be part of any rescue mission.

After a couple of hours, the BRF had produced a couple of plans that Frank could present to Brigade HQ. Unlike most units, BRF planning was an all-inclusive process where everybody's ideas and opinions were valued and taken into consideration, regardless of rank or time served. Experience had taught them that even the youngest or least experienced soldier might pick up on a mistake or an oversight by a senior member. Frank took the footage, the photographs, and his plans to the Operations Centre where he found the Chief of Staff sitting outside smoking a cigarette. The COS was the Brigade Commanders right-hand-man and the perfect person to endorse the proposal. Frank updated him on the latest intelligence before presenting an overview of his plan. The COS's body language seemed quite negative as Frank spoke, arms folded, downturned mouth etc. but he carried on confidently.

"Good work Frank, but unfortunately that's not in your remit, that's a Special Forces task." Said the Major, himself an ex-SAS officer.

"I know that Sir." Frank replied respectfully. "But you said it yourself, the SF are fully committed to another task."

"We can have another team out here in 3 days, they will need minimal time from when they arrive in theatre to executing the rescue mission." The officer persisted.

"We haven't got three days Sir, we've got less than two. Me and my blokes are ready to go now. If we wait for the SF it'll be too late."

"Sergeant Cutler stand down!" The Chief of Staff said abruptly, asserting his authority. "You are not part of special forces, you are reconnaissance, not hostage rescue. Do I make myself clear?" The Chief of Staff was not a fan of the BRF and resented their reputation as an elite unit and regular comparisons to the special forces that he had served with.

"Loud and clear Sir." Frank reluctantly conceded, there was no use in arguing, the Major was one of the most influential officers in the Brigade. "But for the record, I never said we were special forces."

CHAPTER THIRTEEN

Friends In High Places

F rank snapped as he closed the door behind him. "Fucking prick!" he growled. Most of the men were sat in the TV Room waiting expectantly for his return.

"What happened?" H asked, anticipating bad news.

"Well there's good news and bad news." Frank replied, looking across to the waiting audience. "The good news is, the Special Forces are flying a team in to do the rescue."

The men relaxed briefly, some sitting upright on their chairs, exchanging glances and relieved expressions.

"Awesome!" Said H. "That's great news. What's the bad?"

"Bad news is, they won't be here for another five fucking days!" Frank went on. "Which is no use to anyone, especially the Boss, because he'll be already dead by then!"

"What are we going to do then Frank?" Danny asked.

"We're going to do it our fucking selves!" Frank replied. In that moment, with his men looking at him for an answer, for inspiration, he had made up his mind. "We get a plane to get us overhead, we go kill those mother fuckers and we bring Johnny back."

"Yes!" Said H. "Let's smash this shit up!"

Frank turned to look at Danny, one of the BRF's Forward Air Controllers. The FAC's were trained to call in air strikes and had access to all planned flight information to aid their planning for air support during missions.

"Danny, I need you to get hold of the flight information for all UK C130 operations over the next couple of nights, including crew names."

"On it." Replied Danny, immediately standing up and heading out of the room towards the Ops Room.

Frank shifted his gaze to H. "Mate, I need you to speak to the RAF Equipment Section and see how many freefall parachutes are out here, plus oxygen equipment."

"Done." H Said, also promptly exiting the building.

"How are we going to get anyone to take us up in the air though Frank?" Asked Leon. "If Brigade have said no, how can we get an aircraft?"

"Leave that to me mate." Frank said reassuringly. "I'll get us up. Even if I have to fly it myself."

"Or we could just hijack one!" Leon suggested, jokingly.

Frank frowned, turning his head slightly as he contemplated the suggestion, his eyes moving quickly from side to side as he thought it through. "I hadn't thought of that, but yes, that is another option. Good call." He nodded to himself as he spoke. "But that's a last resort." He confirmed.

Leon looked across to the others worriedly. They all knew he was only joking but Frank had taken him literally. They knew he would do it too.

The rest of the day was made very busy for all the BRF soldiers. Danny had obtained printed copies of the Air Tasking Orders which detailed every flight in the operational theatre, including drones, helicopters and airplanes and was compiling a list of all that had the potential to conduct their insertion. H had been liaising with the RAF Equipment Specialists to ascertain the quantities and location of parachutes and oxygen equipment for a High Altitude Low Opening (HALO) parachute insertion and Frank had been talking to the RAF Liaison Officer about the possibility of conducting joint continuation training between the BRF and the RAF crews.

The RAF were very strict on currency and competency training when it came to parachuting, so Frank used the angle of carrying out a jump rehearsal to keep everyone in date. Not only were some of the soldiers about to fall beyond their six-month currency requirement, but so were some of the Pilots, Loadmasters and Parachute Jump Instructors that were deployed. In order to keep in-date, the sortie would need to go as far as the "Red Light" being turned on while the paratroopers stood on the open ramp at the back of the plane. This was the penultimate event before the "Green Light" which was the order to jump. Up to that point, during a rehearsal, everything would be conducted as per the real thing, with soldiers and crew breathing from oxygen tanks as the plane climbed to jump height. All equipment checks and actions would be carried out in accordance with standard operating procedures, the only difference being that they would not actually exit the aircraft.

The BRF met up at the Ops Room at 1600hrs that same day to discuss progress.

H started off. "Good news Frank, there's twenty freefall rigs in Kandahar right now."

"What about tandem?" Frank replied.

"Two tandem rigs as well." H stated.

"Oxygen?" Said Frank.

"Plenty of O2 mate, no dramas there." H responded with a thumbs-up.

"Mega. Good job." Frank Said. "Danny, what about flights, what have we got out of Kandahar?"

Danny referred to his notes before answering. "There's four RAF flights tonight...." He stopped to check his watch before continuing. "Wrong, three RAF flights tonight and two tomorrow night."

"Write off tonight. There's no way we'll make it in time." Frank stated. "Are there any lifts to Kandahar?"

"There's a Chinook coming in tonight at 2300hrs with some stores. Dropping off and going back to KAF direct." Danny said.

"That's our chance. We'll get on that." Frank addressed the group. "Get your kit together, we're leaving for KAF tonight and we'll be on one of those planes out of there tomorrow night to go smash some fuckers. Light scales. Bullets and water! Any questions?... No?...... Good. Let's get going then.

The soldiers left, all making their way to their equipment to pack. All that was required was weapons, viewing aids, radios, rations, water, ammo, and more ammo.

Reece stayed behind to ask Frank a question.

"Is there anything you want me to do while you guys get ready?" He asked.

"Yep. Get yourself ready. You're coming with us mate." Frank replied.

"To Kandahar?" Quizzed Reece. Unsure what use he would be there.

"To get Johnny." Said Frank with a glint in his eye. "Ever jumped out of a plane before?"

"Are you serious!?" Reece squeaked, his mouth and throat suddenly very dry. "I don't know how to use a bloody parachute!"

"No, you don't. Luckily for you though, I do, and I can strap you to me." Frank stated calmly.

"What!?" Reece was part excited, part terrified by the proposal.

"Is that even allowed?"

"Sometimes it's better to ask forgiveness than to ask permission." Frank said, deliberately avoiding the question.

"What!?" Repeated Reece. "Are you crazy?"

Frank considered the question for a second before replying sincerely. "Potentially, yes, but I'm no psychiatrist. I'd say, officially, no. Potentially, yes." He said without a trace of sarcasm or jest in his voice. "To be honest, you're not the first person to ask me that question."

Reece's question had been rhetorical, but Frank was a very literal man, and very honest. Reece digested what had just been said, staring blankly at him. If he was crazy, did it make any difference? Maybe it actually made him a better paratrooper. Maybe they were all crazy, that would explain a lot!

"Do I get a gun?" Reece asked.

"Fuck off!" Scoffed Frank. "I might be crazy, but I'm not stupid! Anyway, the pen is mightier than the sword apparently, so bring your pen. Better still, bring a pencil, sharpened at both ends!"

"Got a pen right here." Said Reece, pulling one from his pocket and offering it to Frank. "Swap for your gun?"

Frank offered nothing in the way of a reply and turned to walk away. Reece's humour was actually quite similar to his own. He paid a visit to the RAF Liaison Officer before walking back to the BRF compound to pack his own equipment.

The Chinook helicopter arrived exactly on time to deliver its load of stores including mail, rations, ammunition and medical supplies and the BRF were there to help unload it as the pilot kept the rotors turning, ready for a quick turn-around. The soldiers got on board with their equipment after Frank had a short discussion with the Loadmaster to confirm who they were and where they were going, taking alternate seats on the port and starboard sides as directed to evenly distribute the load. Frank had hastily organised for the soldiers to be manifested onto the flight under the guise of 2 days R+R in Kandahar. Reece recognised the Loadmaster from the flight he'd taken into Kurzak, it was the same crewman that had helped him undo his safety belt on the Landing Site. Reece returned the thumbs up he gave him, feeling surprised, and a little embarrassed that he could remember his fumbling incident, before realising that everyone was receiving the thumbs up as a check before take-off. The loadmaster could not remember Reece, he was one of hundreds of faces that he had seen over the last few weeks. The Chinooks were the workhorses of the RAF, ferrying personnel and equipment throughout the country all day and night, pushing the crews and machines to their limits. The loadmaster looked out of the windows on both sides, turning his head awkwardly to fit his oversized helmet into the small windows, before moving to the tail gate and checking rearwards. Once happy that it was safe, he informed the pilot through the radio intercom, holding his microphone close to his mouth so he would be heard over the noise of the two engines above them. Adopting the prone position, he hung his head over the tail gate to continue checking as the pilot began the ascent, the volume of the engines intensifying as power was increased. Reece was passed a box from the soldier sat next to him and took out a set of small, yellow ear defenders, passing the box along the line to the next soldier. Mimicking the others, he withdrew them from their small cardboard box, then rolled the foam between his thumb and forefinger to squash them down, before pushing them into his ear canal. As the spongy foam expanded the feeling was quite soothing as it gently applied pressure inside his ear and drowned out the sound of the engines and hydraulics to a much more bearable dull rhythmic beat. The helicopter tilted forwards then accelerated hard out of the camp towards Kandahar Airfield. Within a couple of minutes every one of the soldiers were asleep, they knew a busy couple of days were ahead. Reece knew there was no way he would be able to sleep, instead he took a few photos of the scene and gazed into the darkness outside, occasionally catching a glimpse of light from a car or building below.

The morning was filled with frenetic activity as the men went about the base convincing people that they were conducting some low-level continuation training. Luckily, because their role was very niche, most people didn't really question what they were asking for and complacently facilitated their requests. Parachutes were drawn and the Oxygen Bay prepared the breathing apparatus. Frank engaged with the crew and Parachute Jump Instructors who had all been briefed on the sortie and were actually pleased that they could maintain their competence levels with the training flight. The only thing that would stop the mission now, was if the aircraft were taken for a higher priority task and that was unlikely as the primary task for the sortie was to conduct communications monitoring and frequency jamming to disrupt the enemy communications network. The military parachuting world was a small one and most of the people involved, from parachute packers to pilots, knew each other from various deployments and training exercises. Frank felt conflicted deceiving people he'd known for a long time but knew that telling the truth would not only risk the mission, but also force people into an impossible position.

Everyone went about their business as if preparing for a real parachute descent into the desert. A realistic piece of ground was chosen as the notional drop zone, parachute and equipment inspections were carried out and orders were delivered as per a full dress-rehearsal. The turn-around had been extremely fast with the RAF liaison team buying into the idea wholeheartedly and using the opportunity to test their deployment readiness capability. There was one man however, that was not convinced by the narrative and had been watching closely how the BRF had conducted themselves. The pilot sat in the shade of his aircrafts wing, quietly observing the unusually quiet and serious way the soldiers conducted themselves. Normally there would be banter between the paratroopers, or between the soldiers and the RAF, but they were uncharacteristically well behaved. All of them seemed to be keeping their heads down, playing the grey man.

Something was going on, he thought. He waited for Frank to separate from the others and followed him when he walked across to a pallet of water bottles to replenish his almost empty bottle.

"What are you lot up to Frank?" He said to the surprised sergeant.

"Hello Sir. I heard you were the pilot tonight." Frank stuck out his hand and they shook.

"Give me some credit Frank, I wasn't born yesterday. What are you up to? You might be fooling these young lads with this little pantomime but I'm not buying it!" The Squadron Leader spoke with authority but quietly enough as not to alert anyone within earshot.

"Beg your pardon Sir? Not sure what you mean." Frank replied innocently.

"I've known you for seven years Frank and one thing I know is that you tell it straight, so I'm going to tell you straight. I think you are trying to use my plane to do something you are not supposed to. I think it is very strange how you've asked to do this parachute rehearsal during my flight, and I know Johnny has been captured. Now you tell me what the hell is going on or I will turn the whole thing off. And I'm sure you don't want me to start asking questions to Brigade HQ."

Squadron Leader Hudson had been the pilot on several parachuting exercises with Frank over the years and had always been a good man. He had even completed a tandem parachute jump with one of the BRF in 2004 and had always been impressed with the way the BRF had conducted themselves. He was an intelligent man, always asking questions and had a real passion for flying. Frank decided to put his cards on the table. The game was up. If the Squadron Leader reacted badly it could ruin Franks career, potentially his plan could be seen as attempted mutiny. He hoped that he could appeal to his better nature not to report him. He beckoned him over towards a noisy generator where his voice would be drowned out to anybody nearby.

"Sir, out of respect to you I am going to tell you everything, but please understand that the only reason I have withheld this information is to protect my men and also to not put you in a compromising position. I take full responsibility for what I'm going to tell you, the whole thing is my idea."

Frank explained how they had identified the whereabouts of Johnny and how the only realistic way to get into the area was by parachute. Time was of the essence. It was now or never and the only unit currently in Afghanistan with the capability to conduct this type of mission was the BRF.

"How the bloody hell did you think you were going to pull this off? I mean, even if you did somehow get up in the air, how will you get over your target? And then, how would you know when to jump? You could land anywhere! Seriously Frank, what the hell are you bloody thinking?

"They're going to kill him Sir. They will torture him, cut his head off, and dump him in the gutter. I can stop it. I can save him… We can save him. Will you help us Sir, please?"

The Squadron Leader replied "Even if I said yes, there's no flight path over the mountains you're talking about. What were you going to do, hijack the plane and force us to divert?"

Frank twitched uncomfortably, unable to look him in the eye.

"Jesus Christ! That's your plan! That is insane!" The pilot said angrily.

"If we can get out at twenty-five-thousand feet, we could fly under a canopy to the mountain from fifty kilometres away." Frank replied

"Yes in theory you could, but the winds would have to be perfect. It is bloody windy at altitude here you know, we're talking 150 knots at twenty-five-thousand feet. Get it wrong and you could end up in bloody Pakistan. Not to mention the temperature up there, that could be minus thirty degrees. Have you really thought this through Frank?"

"I have sir, and that's why I want you to help us. With your help we can make it work. All I need is someone to get me close enough, the rest is up to me and my blokes. I know we can do our part if we can just get up in the air. I'll tell them I put a gun to your head! What do you think sir, will you do it?"

"You bloody Paras, you really are a bunch of lunatics. Give me some time to think Frank, I will meet you back here in an hour. This is between us, right?" The Squadron Leader stood with his hands on his hips, looking down at the ground, head shaking slightly. His shoulders were rounded forward as if a heavy weight had been put on them and that was how he felt.

"Of course, sir." Frank assured him. "I will wait for your decision, nobody else will know about this conversation."

The next hour passed slowly for Frank as he waited. His fate and the fate of the mission lay squarely in the hands of the Squadron Leader. Hopefully, he would not return with a posse of Military Police and march him straight off to jail. He did not. Instead he returned with the news that he would fly the mission and that he'd already amended the flight route to get closer to the target.

"I was going to retire after this tour anyway." Said the Sqn Leader. "Might as well go out with a bang!"

Frank shook his hand once more. "I owe you sir." He said sincerely.

CHAPTER FOURTEEN

The Rescue Mission

The lights on board the R.A.F C130 Hercules aircraft changed to a dim red in order to allow the soldiers' night vision to adjust. Reece spoke out loud to himself nervously under his oxygen mask, his muffled ramblings unheard by anyone else as he tried in vain to convince himself that everything would be ok. He looked across to the men sat opposite him wondering if they were nervous too, but with their helmets and masks covering most of their faces it was impossible to tell, all that was visible of each soldier was his eyes, wide open and alert the men were focused on the task ahead, experience had taught them all their own way of dealing with the nerves and apprehension, to shut them away. Instead they concentrated on the mission, rehearsing the details in their minds. The plane continued its rapid ascent, the four powerful engines droning loudly. It was a bumpy journey and the plane banked sharply, climbing in a tight spiral above the airfield so as not to alert the enemy of their intended destination. Reece looked at the altimeter on his wrist to see how high they were, but it appeared to be stuck at 8000 feet. After tapping it several times and shaking it to no avail he began to worry, he was sure they were still climbing. In his best effort to appear calm he gained Frank's attention by tapping his arm. Frank looked him in the eye and raised his eyebrows. Reece pointed at the dial, tapped it and raised his shoulders with his palms toward the ceiling to signal his confusion. Despite the circumstances Reece found this method of communication very amusing, using eye movement and hand gestures to convey messages, but it was surprisingly effective. Guessing the anxious passengers concern correctly Frank reassuringly patted him on the shoulder, showed him his own illuminous altimeter which also read 8000 feet, gave him a thumbs up and patted him on the shoulder again before turning away again as he started to don his leather flying gloves which he always wore for freefalling. The assurance this gave Reece was instant, he knew everything was going to plan. Frank's confidence was inspiring, he thought. As a military tandem master Frank had taken dozens of non–parachutists on jumps and knew from bitter experience how dangerous a nervous passenger could be, they needed to be alert and responsive when they left the aircraft or the descent could become a real struggle. A passenger not adopting the correct body posture during freefall could make them unstable, they could spin and tumble and that could affect the safe deployment of the parachute canopy.

Only once had he been put in danger by a passenger, but it was an experience he had no wish to repeat. Earlier that year during training in America he was ordered to take a senior US Navy officer for a jump. It was the RAF's way of saying "Thank you" to the Commander for the use of his facilities on base and a regular event on overseas detachments. Frank understood the politics and agreed but started to regret it as soon as he laid eyes on the cargo. The station commander was a huge man, 6'1" and obese at 19 stones weight. Obviously worried, he sweated profusely and talked nervously, feigning a laugh at every opportunity. Frank briefed him in detail stressing how safe the descent would be and gave him simple instructions to follow, but despite Franks best efforts the moment they exited the plane the commanders fear overcame him. Arms and legs flailing they started to tumble out of control toward the earth at 120mph. Frank tried to carry out his drills but could not get them stable enough to deploy his drogue parachute. Realising the situation was getting dangerous he took the old school approach to regain control of the terrified passenger. One punch to the side of the head later he got his attention and the commander suddenly remembered what he was supposed to be doing. Frank got them stable and deployed his drogue followed by his main canopy, that was enough freefall for one day. Once on the ground he apologized to the American, but the exhilarated officer had no recollection of the tumble and thanked him for the experience.

"My pleasure sir" Frank grinned as he looked at the small lump in the corner of his eye. It wasn't every day he got to punch an officer in the head and get away with it.

Reece's altimeter was working perfectly ok, because although they were now at 22000ft the aircraft was pressurized at 8000ft. A few more minutes and they would be at jump height, 25000ft.

The Parachute Jump Instructor waved his hands to gain the soldiers attention and held up a small black board that had "P-8" written on it in white chalk. All the men responded with a thumbs up to acknowledge they were parachuting in eight minutes. The PJI then went along the two rows of seats, disconnecting the men from the large oxygen tank tethered to the floor in front of them, and connecting them to the small oxygen bottle that was strapped to the side of their parachutes. Once he was content that everybody was receiving oxygen from their bottles, he held up another sign that read P-4. Frank stood up and held out his hand to assist Reece getting to his feet. He pointed to a large metal box near the back of the plane and Reece gingerly walked to it and straddled it, just like they had done in rehearsals. Frank moved up close behind him and attached the buckles to the back of Reece's harness, ensuring they were tight. The PJI helped Reece secure the small rucksack packed with water, ammunition and a few rations to the front of his harness. Now he was really uncomfortable, with weight pulling down on him in all directions and Franks rifle digging into his ribcage. His ears were also feeling pressure as the plane was depressurised and when he looked again at his altimeter, he saw the needle moving quickly through the numbers from 8 to 12 and then all the way round again, finally stopping on number 1, which actually meant 25000ft.

While this was going on the rest of the men had also stood up and connected their rucksacks to the front of their parachute harnesses. Because of the oxygen containers and seats, it was difficult to form a neat line but the men were roughly in order as the Loadmaster gave the hand signal before opening the ramp at the rear of the plane. The ramp opened with a loud screeching noise, splitting in half, with the bottom half lowering slowly to horizontal and the top half tucking neatly into the roof with a clunk. The PJI held up another board, P-2. Frank tapped Reece's shoulder and gestured upwards with his thumbs. Reece awkwardly shuffled backwards in time with Frank until they were both on their feet. Frank turned them towards the ramp.

The dispatcher put his left hand on Franks shoulder and ushered him forward with his right, walking slowly backwards towards the dark void at the back of the plane. Strapped so tightly to the front of Frank, Reece found it impossible to walk, so he waddled in a low squat trying to step in time with him. Now there was no denying it, he was as frightened as he'd ever been. During his career he'd done some daring and risky things but had always felt in control. This time he was completely at the mercy of Frank, and gravity, they would decide his fate and it was reasonably predictable. Although doing a parachute jump had always been one of his ambitions, this was more than he'd bargained for.

"You're o.k mate, just a parachute jump, perfectly safe, nothing to worry about." His talking became a shout as he moved closer to edge of the ramp. Reece was experiencing what the paras called "disco leg," part due to the stress of the half squat position he was adopting and exacerbated by his worsening fear. Despite his best efforts to control it, his legs shook violently beneath him

and although terrified the proud young reporter felt hugely embarrassed, certain that everyone must be able to see his involun-
tary spasms. No one had noticed, the other paras were all busy
getting themselves ready and soon were all lined up behind the
tandem pair, carrying out their equipment checks one last time
before the order to jump. Frank patted him on the shoulder and
extended both thumbs in front of his face for one last bit of re-
assurance and he responded with his own thumbs up just as the
red "prepare to jump" lights came on ahead of them on the side
of the airframe. The dispatcher beckoned them forward again to
bring them right to the very edge of the tailgate and they edged
forward, shuffling their feet.

"Oh fuck, this is it, fucking idiot, idiot, idiot." Reece was convinced they would fall out at the next step before he was ready,
the mask and equipment strapped to the front of his body made
it impossible to see the aircraft floor.

Frank also couldn't see the floor but knew to follow the directions of the dispatcher. He would bring him forward until
Frank's toes were virtually hanging over the edge of the tailgate
to ensure he could get a clean dive away from the aircraft. Behind
them the remainder of the patrol were now bunched up tight
together, hands on the parachute pack of the man in front to enable them to exit as close together as possible. When the green
light came on the whole patrol needed to get out as fast and close
together as possible to avoid separation in freefall. A mere few
seconds would mean hundreds of feet spread between the first
and last man out. Once out they would follow Frank and Reece
in freefall until they reached 20,000ft then split up and deploy
their parachutes at 19000ft. Frank would fall to 18,000ft before
opening to ensure he was the lowest man, and the patrol would
then follow him to the landing zone.

Frank reached around, grabbed Reece's wrists and crossed them
over his chest. Reece grabbed the webbing straps where he had
been told and felt his head getting pulled back just as they had
rehearsed. It was time.

"Here we fucking go!" As he snarled through gritted teeth the red light changed to green, the dispatcher gave a thumbs up and he felt himself tipping out of the plane as Frank propelled them forward into the dark abyss high above the desert. Including their equipment, they had a combined weight of 450lbs, so they dropped like an anvil away from the plane going upside down momentarily. The spectacle of the others jumping out behind them en masse was amazing, Reece even spotted the dispatcher waving goodbye as the plane quickly disappeared into the moonless sky and headed for Kandahar. There was no going back now.

There was no sound but the wind blasting him in the face as they fell. Reece maintained the arched position that he'd been briefed, and they were nice and stable when Frank deployed the main parachute canopy. The freefall had been short but exhilarating and once the parachute silk had paid out with a thump, there was a good canopy above their heads. The sound of the other canopies deploying could be heard close by and Frank did a 180 degree turn to close the gap between him and the remainder. Using his night vision goggles he scanned the sky and identified the others, confirming their status on his radio which was fitted to his helmet. Once he was happy, he started to navigate to the Drop Zone using the GPS on his wrist, the other 17 canopies stacked neatly behind him, silently gliding toward the enemy. At such height the temperature was bitterly cold, but warmed up gradually as they descended. Even with the night vision goggles it was difficult to identify features on the ground below, which appeared as shades of green and black, with no sense of depth. In practice the soldiers would always have something on the ground to orientate by such as a big fluorescent arrow laid out, pointing into the wind, or some lights set out in a recognisable configuration so they knew where to land and which way to approach the landing site from, but not this time, it was pitch black and they would have to get it right. This pressure fell on Frank, but he would rather be leading from the front and was confident he could reach the drop zone. By 7000ft they were over the mountain and Frank initiated a slow turn over the top, scanning below for anything that resembled the aerial photography they'd studied. Gradually shapes emerged and he could make out the compound walls by the time he'd descended to 6000ft and began to set up the landing pattern for the others to follow when he reached 4000ft. The drop zone was at 3000ft and it was still a bit breezy, so he did a short downwind leg before turning back into wind for the landing. Reece did his part, releasing the container from the clips on his chest when instructed, and felt a heavy tug on his harness as it dropped to the end of its rope to hang below them.

"Feet up, feet up." Frank spoke into Reece's ear. The idea was for Frank to take the landing, not Reece, and he duly responded, lifting his feet as high as he could just before the equipment hit the floor. The landing was perfect as Frank pulled down on his steering toggles as hard as he could, gently landing on his feet. He immediately collapsed his parachute by pulling one of the steering toggles all the way in to ensure a gust of wind could not re-inflate it and then after a quick scan of the area unbuckled himself from all of the equipment attached to his body, including Reece.

"Here, take this and get in to cover over there." Frank whispered. Reece nodded and took his small, but heavy rucksack from Frank, quickly moving into the cover of the stream which Frank motioned towards. As he crouched, he could hear his breathing, it seemed so loud. But in his efforts to control it by shallow breathing, he made it worse and started to gasp for air. His heart pounded beneath his body armour, it was racing, fuelled by adrenaline. Suddenly he felt sick and began to sweat. He withdrew his inhaler from his pocket and took a shot to prevent an asthma attack.

Through his NVG's Frank saw Reece fidgeting and pulling his collar away from his neck. He moved across to the ditch and knelt next to him.

"You ok Airborne?" He asked.

"I'm no Airborne, I think I'm going to be sick." Reece replied quietly.

"No, you are fucking not! Listen to me mate, we're all nervous but we're going to be ok, so long as we keep it together. That includes you Reece. We need you as much as you need us. You've already proved you've got the bottle to do this by jumping out of that plane strapped to a nutter like me. Now fucking snap out of it, cos we're gonna go kill some Taliban scum and get Johnny out of this fucking shit hole. This time tomorrow your story will be in the news all over the world."

Frank scanned the area through his NVG's looking for the remainder of the patrol and any sign of the enemy. He counted thirteen and watched as they hastily prepared their kit. Within a couple of minutes, they had all rendezvoused at the stream and cached their parachutes in the stream ditch, hastily covered with some foliage and dirt. Hopefully, nobody would stumble across them and compromise the mission.

The remaining four men were the two sniper teams. They had landed a few hundred metres to the north and were making their way up a steep ridge that overlooked the small village. Once in position they would provide overwatch and fire support from the north and east. They ascended slowly and deliberately, not wanting to dislodge any loose rocks that could tumble noisily to the ground, alerting the enemy below. They carried their rifles in the alert position, butt firmly in the shoulder, thumb on the safety catch, finger hovering over the trigger, ready to react, but occasionally had to sling them behind their backs so they could use both hands to scramble up the slope. The going was hard but they were able to move relatively fast and silently, utilising goat tracks most of the way. The first team reached their position within thirty minutes and begun setting up their fire positions and scanning the target area through the oversized thermal, telescopic sights attached to their weapons. The second team followed close behind and continued past, towards their chosen position about three hundred metres further along the curved ridgeline, reaching their location about ten minutes later and setting themselves up quickly to cover the assault.

While the snipers were carefully climbing the hill, Tonto had been leading the assault group up the stream until they came level with the compound where they intended to gain entry. Silently they crawled for about 40 minutes, stopping every few seconds to listen and look for the enemy. Moving so slowly was laborious and required a lot of discipline as the adrenaline in their bodies energised them massively, urging each one of them to get on with the job and release their pent-up aggression. Surprise was important though, if the enemy saw them coming, they could be pinned down in the ditch right from the get-go and that would drastically tip the odds against them succeeding. Patiently they paused again to observe and listen, slowly raising thermal imagers to their eyes to scan for enemy movement and breathing as quietly as possible. A small flash was seen in one of the corners of the target compound roof as a cigarette was lit by a Taliban guard standing sentry, the small flame flickering for a couple of seconds to reveal a bearded face, which drew the attention of the soldiers lying prone in the ditch. Their excitement heightened further still, the enemy now a tangible object. Through their NVG's the stealthy soldiers could see the Talibs face in more detail as they neared, illuminated by the glowing tip every time he took a draw on his hand rolled cigarette. As they got closer, he began speaking loudly as he was joined by another man who borrowed his cigarette to light one of his own, before returning it. The first guard carried an AK47 slung across his back, the second man had a Rocket Propelled Grenade launcher slung behind him, a rocket already inserted into the muzzle. The way they were acting it was obvious they were not expecting company. So far, so good. The assault team stopped when they drew level with the compound and adopted herringbone formation, each man taking alternate arcs to ensure they had all round defence. The rear man faced back the way they had come and Tonto faced forward. It had been hard graft crawling through the dirt, rocks and trickle of water and everyone was sweating with several cuts and grazes to their elbows and knees. Frank raised the snipers on the radio.

"Sniper Teams 1 and 2, this is Frank, send sitrep, over." He held his microphone close to his mouth and spoke as quietly as he could. There was a brief pause before the situation report came back as requested.

"Sniper Team One is good to go. I have visual of your call sign plus two enemy sentries on the north west corner of the compound, one with AK47, one with RPG, both facing into compound, no further enemy seen, over." Ginge's gruff voice was unmistakable over the radio, a gnarly Lance Corporal from 2 Para, at 32 years old he was the longest serving member in the BRF and hugely respected by all ranks for his soldiering skills. Although Ginge had never attended a sniper course his marksmanship was legendary. Born and raised in the Scottish Highlands, he had been shooting rifles since a young boy when he would go hunting with his father, a gamekeeper for a huge country estate owned by the royal family. He could judge distance and wind without the help of modern technology but seemingly just as accurate and never missed. During operations in Iraq the sniper in his patrol had been wounded during a firefight and he had taken over his weapon. The resulting decimation of the Iraqi ambush by the undiscovered sharpshooter saved the lives of many BRF soldiers and established his place in BRF folklore. Even though the rifle he took over was zeroed to another man, he was able to work out his adjustments within a couple of shots and then quickly located and killed seven concealed Iraqi gunmen firing on the BRF patrol, causing the remainder to abandon their positions and withdraw over the hill from where they were hiding. Another two fell from his fire as they retreated. When it was over, he had killed more of the unwitting enemy than the rest of the patrol put together.

Ginge's partner was a new member of the BRF called Mac. At twenty years old he was paired up with Ginge to learn the ropes after passing his sniper course just before deploying on tour. He had qualified as top sniper but was learning more from Ginge than he would ever learn on any course.

"Sniper Team Two in position." Whispered Danny as the crosshairs of his Long-Range Rifle rose and fell slightly on the head of his intended target in time with his breathing. Danny and his sniper partner Taff had worked together extensively over the last two years and were a formidable force, meticulously planning every detail of their missions and cross checking each other's calculations. Both men were expert snipers and took turns as the primary shooter on missions, racking up eleven confirmed kills between them in three months. Taff measured the distance to the target with a laser range finder before handing it over to Danny. Both agreed on the range and wind calculations to ensure an accurate shot before Taff took up position to cover the rear while Danny concentrated on the task.

Danny continued on the radio. "I cannot see you guys, but I do have eyes on the two sentries in the north west and an additional sentry in the south east corner. South east target appears to be a lone man sat down behind the wall, possibly asleep, AK47 on the ground by his feet. I'm good to go, over."

"Roger, wait, out." Said Frank, taking a few seconds to think.

Ginge was disappointed that he had not seen the third sentry and adjusted the focus on his sight to inspect the south east corner in more detail, noticing what looked like a small heat source emanating from just above the wall. As he studied it, it moved slightly, and he felt confident it was the top of the sentry's head. He spoke into his radio.

"Frank, this is Sniper One, I have eyes on the sentry in the south east corner now too. Partial clear shot. Awaiting orders. Out."

"Partial clear shot my arse! Cheeky fucker is trying to nick my target!" Danny turned and said to Taff, who was hearing everything through his own headset.

Taff, a man of few words agreed. "A bit cheeky that is boyo!"

Danny pressed the presell on his radio firmly to talk. "Frank, this is Sniper Two, I have a *clear* shot on all three targets. Awaiting orders. Out."

Both teams were now in position, ready to initiate the assault and both wanted to claim as many lives from the enemy as possible. Frank knew what was going on.

"Roger. Sniper Two, can you hit one of the targets in the north west? Over." Asked Frank.

"Sniper Two, roger clear shot on either cigarette smoker, over." Replied Danny.

Ginge interjected. "Sniper One, roger, you take RPG man, I'll take AK47 man, then I can switch to Sleeping Beauty and take him too. Over"

"Sniper Two, roger, but I can take Sleeping Beauty." Danny replied instantly. "Clear shot on both." He reiterated.

The snipers understood Frank's intention; if they could simultaneously hit the two men stood together on the roof it would reduce the chance of the remaining terrorists being alerted and maintain the element of surprise.

"O.K, engage on my order, then both switch fire to Sleeping Beauty." Frank confirmed what they had anticipated and both men settled into position for the shot. "Report when clear and be prepared to cover us as we assault."

"Sniper Two, roger, ten quid says I'm there first." Danny took out his chewing gum and placed it on top of his telescopic sight before taking off his safety catch, awaiting the order to fire.

"Twenty quid says you're not." Came the reply from Ginge, the challenge was set.

Frank gave them a few seconds to settle down and turned round to look down the line of men behind him to check they were following proceedings over the radio. A few thumbs up gestures from the soldiers satisfied him that everyone was in the loop, before counting down.

"Sniper One and Two this is Frank. Engage on three...... One...........Two.......Three"

Simultaneously the snipers squeezed their triggers sending two copper plated bullets from their barrels with only a whisper of sound as their silencers suppressed the weapons noise. In less than a second the bullets had travelled the quarter of a mile to the two unsuspecting terrorists stood on the roof and the snipers felt a brief sense of satisfaction as they saw their perfectly aimed shots strike the targets, one in the side of the head and one in the middle of the forehead. A mist of blood and brain sprayed into the air as the bodies collapsed onto the roof, both dropping to their knees and falling forward in perfect synchronicity, colliding and holding one another up in a freaky kneeling position. Danny and Ginge quickly shifted their rifles and attention to the lone sentry on the opposite corner of the compound. Oblivious to his comrades' fate, he was still sat against the wall fast asleep, head leaning back and to the side, mouth wide open with dribble running from the corner onto his shoulder. Within three seconds another two shots had sealed his fate, entering the back and side of his head and exiting at the opposite point, removing half of his head and his entire face with the massive force they produced, propelling his body sidewards to a crumpled heap on the floor in a bloody mess.

Ginge reported to Frank first. "Sniper One, all sentries neutralized, no further enemy seen on north or west walls, over."

"Sniper Two, all's quiet on the south and east sides too." Danny said. "Three enemy confirmed dead, over."

"Roger, good shooting gents. Moving now. Out." Frank acknowledged. He turned to the others.

"Right lads, prepare to move." Frank stood up, he would be leading from the front as always, the others were ready to go right behind him, adrenaline surging through their veins in a mixture of excitement and anticipation. He looked at Reece. "Stay close mate. Ready?"

Reece looked him in the eye. In the darkness it was hard to tell but for the first time he was sure Frank was smiling, his white teeth shining in contrast to his camouflaged face. "Ready." He replied.

"Move!" Frank said vaulting from the cover of the ditch, landing in a crouch position and started his sprint across the open field between them and the target compound closely followed by Reece and the remainder of the men. It was only a short sprint, no more than one hundred metres, but the out of shape reporter found himself unable to match Franks speed and was soon being overtaken by a few of the others. Reaching the wall gasping for air he was ushered back to his place by Leon.

The entire group had made it across the field safely without alerting the Taliban, but not without disturbing a dog inside an adjacent compound which began to bark loudly the second Frank reached the 8-foot-high mud wall. Now there was a sense of urgency, it was a matter of time before someone would investigate what was upsetting the dog and potentially compromise the men before they breached the wall. Leon put his back to the wall and cupped his hands together between his legs and Frank used them as a stirrup to get up high on the wall to peer over, his rifle slung behind his back. The remainder got ready in pairs to do the same. On seeing Frank go over they would follow, stopping on top of the wall for a second to pull their partner up behind them. He put his hands on top of the gritty wall and slowly inched his head up to look inside the compound and to his horror came face to face with one of the Taliban who was also peering over the wall to see what the dog was barking about. The Talib gasped when he saw a camouflaged face inches from him, but before he could raise the alarm, Frank reached over and grabbed him around the back of the head with both hands and pulled down with all his power. The snipers could not see into the compound from their positions so were unable to see the bearded Talib as he'd climbed onto a table by the wall. First thing the others knew about it was when Frank came crashing down with the shocked man in tow, hitting the ground with a thud as both men landed on their side on the floor. Frank instinctively straddled the shocked man and snaked his forearm around his head and under his chin before he had the chance to raise the alarm. He grabbed his wrist with his other hand and pulled tightly, squeezing on the man's throat, choking him. The Talib was making a gargling noise as his arms flailed in desperation. Two of the others quickly pinned his arms to the ground as he put up a good fight. Frank adjusted his grip and twisted as he arched his back to apply maximum torque to the neck. The man's body went limp with a sickening crack as his neck finally broke under the tremendous strain being applied. The fight had lasted seconds and been relatively quiet, the soldiers sat in silence for a few seconds, listening for any sign that the enemy were alerted to their presence but all was quiet they still had the element of surprise on their side. It was a minor hiccup. Time to carry on task. Nobody spared a thought for the young man now lying dead on the floor beside them, he was merely an obstacle in the way of their mission, none of the BRF even looked at him.

Reece had seen many dead bodies during his time as a reporter and dealt with many unpleasant stories including massacres, but nothing had prepared him for what he had just seen. He looked down at the lifeless figure next to him and felt sad. Was he somebody's son, father, brother? The insignificance of that man's death to the soldiers was a symbol of their focus on the mission.

The soldiers were all over the wall within seconds, working in groups, one helped up the first who then helped pull up the second, both then sat on the wall and pulled the next up between them by grasping an arm each and hauling upwards as the soldier scrambled up the wall with his feet. When it came to Reece's turn, he had a man on each foot providing a stirrup, and a man on each arm pulling. The combined effort almost catapulted him over the wall and he quickly grabbed hold of the top to avoid crashing down the other side. Once over the obstacle the men moved quickly forward, weapons in the aim, silently scanning the compound for signs of the enemy. The courtyard was bare, apart from a few clothes hanging on a washing line and an old-fashioned bicycle leant against the wall, a mixture of a 1970's racing bike and a girl's shopper, obviously put together with salvaged parts. The layout was exactly as Reece had briefed, there were four doorways, two on the north and two on the west, so they had no problem identifying which one to head for. They lined up on both sides of the entrance, which was covered by a hanging blanket, some standing, some kneeling, all intently watching their arcs, covering each other's backs. Frank whispered in Reece's ear "You sure it's this one?" He pointed at the entrance.

"This is it, I'm sure." Reece replied confidently, giving the thumbs up.

The other three doorways led to a toilet a storeroom and a room that the ladies would use when they visited. The men carefully checked all three before reporting them clear to Frank.

Frank positioned himself at the doorway and paused to listen. Opposite him, on the other side of the opening stood Leon who acknowledged him with a nod. Through the straps and equipment on his face, Frank could see that he was smiling broadly, revelling in the excitement of doing what he loved, he was in his element. Frank grinned. Suddenly Leon raised his left hand to give the "halt" signal. Frank looked at him and Leon cupped his ear and pointed to the doorway, he had heard something. Now they could both hear it...footsteps! They froze, someone was on the other side of the blanket moving around. Being compromised at this stage could put the whole operation in jeopardy and give the enemy time to escape or execute Johnny. Frank raised his weapon so that the barrel was about chest height, inches from the material of the door. Leon quietly slung his weapon by his side and withdrew the knife he carried on his left breast, gently pulling downwards to prise the six-inch blade from its leather sheath. The blanket moved, slowly being pushed from the inside. Suddenly a shadowy figure burst out from the darkness, launching at Leon and knocking him to the floor. He felt a searing pain in his shoulder and a heavy weight on his chest as he was attacked, momentarily confused before realising it was a dog, a massive Afghan Wolfhound. Grasping the knife tightly, he drove it into the snarling beast, repeatedly stabbing it in the body. After a few strikes the dog was subdued enough for him to take an aimed shot and he thrust the blade into its neck, right up to the handle before sawing through its throat, half decapitating it. The enormous dog went limp, slumping on top of him as its final gargling breath could be heard exhaling through its open neck. The weight on Leon's chest pinned him to the ground before two of the others pulled on its rear legs as he pushed it off. All the others could do was watch, not wanting to shoot in case they'd hit Leon. He stood up, his face covered in blood from the dogs spurting arteries which he wiped with his sleeve. He replaced the knife into its sheath after wiping the blood on his trousers and bent down to pat the dead dog. "Good dog, sorry mate." He said softly. A wave of sadness washed over him briefly as he looked at the slain beast, he loved dogs, and this one was only doing his duty. He looked up at Frank.

"Fucking good bloke!" Frank said sarcastically. "He only wanted to play fetch!"

Leon looked across to H who was shaking his head disapprovingly. He grinned and stuck his fingers up; the others would never miss an opportunity to wind him up.

"You ok?" Frank asked.

"Yeah mate, his bark was probably worse than his bite." said Leon.

"We'll never know, will we?" "You fucking killed it before it even got the chance to bark, you cruel twat!" Tonto taunted as he maintained his fire position in the doorway where Leon had been standing.

Another soldier reached up and removed a shirt from the washing line and placed it over the dogs' head as the pool of blood expanded across the dusty floor, the last of its blood now trickling from the wound.

Standing close to Frank, Reece was perplexed by the whole situation. Minutes earlier a young man had been brutally killed and nobody had raised an eyebrow, yet this dog had stirred emotions in the soldiers. To them, the dog's life was more important, it didn't deserve to die. But the Taliban who had captured their commander, they were worthless scum, who deserved everything they were about to get. There would be no remorse when they were killed, none at all. Everybody re-took their positions, the killing of the dog had fortunately been quiet and there was no sign of enemy movement.

Frank spoke into the radio "All callsigns, courtyard secure, we're going in now over"

The sniper teams replied in turn.

"Sniper One, roger, nothing to report, over."

Sniper Two, roger, all clear, over."

"Roger, out." Frank finished.

Two men remained in the courtyard to cover the withdrawal and watch for enemy as the remainder disappeared into the building in single file behind Frank.

They moved quickly down the dark corridor, weapons at the ready. Reece was still not used to the night vision goggles and bumped in to Frank at the first junction. He pointed to the left. Two men quickly went right and discovered a metal gate secured by a padlock and chain. One remained at the junction as the others continued. Leon leading, Frank tightly behind him and Reece following closely to give directions. Leon stopped, there was a doorway ahead and another to his right. He watched forward.

Reece pointed straight ahead to signal the way to go but Frank needed to clear the room on the right first. Using hand signals, he instructed the two men behind Reece to clear the room. They filed past and moved stealthily into the room. It was some kind of communal area with a television in one corner, some cupboards and several mattresses on the floor. One of the men noticed something move on the ground and carefully walked towards it to find two men asleep together, spooning. Despite the Taliban's condemnation of homosexuality, it was common knowledge that many of them practised it. These two would have to be neutralised to ensure they didn't wake up and use the AK47's which lay beside them. The men stood over the targets, suppressed weapons pointed to their heads and fired 2 rounds each, almost simultaneously into their skulls, killing them instantly while they slept. In a court of law this would be called murder, but there were no courts here, the law here was kill or be killed, big boys' rules. Content that the room was now secure they returned to the corridor, pausing briefly to inform Frank of the two enemy dead. He acknowledged them and signalled to Leon to advance. The doorway in front of them was the top of a steep stairway that led down to the caves. It was so dark, even the night vision goggles were not working effectively, so the men used the built in infra-red torches on them. These were invisible to the naked eye but lit up the building like it was daylight through the goggles. Leon began to descend the narrow stairs, the safety catch on his rifle was off and his finger rested lightly on the trigger. At the bottom there were more stairs. On his left and straight ahead they went up, to his right further down. Reece's memory had served him well so far and Leon correctly anticipated the right turn. One man stayed at the stair intersection as the remainder continued underground, the air becoming noticeably colder the deeper they went. Halfway down the flight of stairs Leon's goggle picture started to become bright. He halted and switched off the infra red torch, there was light ahead.

Crouching into a half squat he slowly moved, one step at a time. The light was getting brighter, so he tilted his goggles upwards to see with his own eyes what was there. There was an orange glow at the bottom of the stairs which flickered slightly, probably a fire or lamp of some sort. As he watched, a shadow was cast across the floor, quickly moving from right to left then across the wall. A voice shouted from below in Arabic, making him jump.

"Simba!.......Simba!"

It was the owner of the dog, calling his name. The shadow appeared again, almost blacking out the corridor.

"Simbah!.....Simbah!

The shadow was moving and becoming smaller, he was heading straight for them.

Leon's heart was beating so hard he could feel it against his body armour as he brought his rifle into the aim.

Frank was just above and behind him on the stairs doing exactly the same. It was about to go noisy.

The dog owners sandaled feet came into view, then the bottom of his dish dash and the barrel of his rifle which he was carrying idly by his side.

"Simb.........."

The first round struck him in the centre of his chest as he called his pet for the last time, immediately followed by nine more as Leon and Frank fired while moving down the last steps. Leon got to the blood-soaked man first and quickly put one more shot into his head before continuing forward.

"Leon, go firm!" Frank said sharply

In the corridor was a table with an oil lamp and two chairs. On the table dominoes were placed neatly in several connecting rows and nobody played dominoes by themselves he thought.

"There's another one." Frank warned.

Just then a rifle appeared at the end of the corridor, discharging a burst of un-aimed gunfire as the Talib fired around the corner ricocheting rounds off the walls and ceiling but miraculously hitting none of the men. Leon and Frank returned fire and moved forward at a fast pace to the table but the enemy had escaped.

"Everyone ok?" Asked Frank

"All ok Frank." Replied H. "Leon, you never told us you'd been teaching the Taliban how to shoot!"

"Dick!" Leon retorted.

"Right lads, they know we're here now so we need to move fast." "We need to get to the boss before they get the chance, so it's MFV from here, maximum fucking violence, no prisoners!"

They set off apace, weapons pointing in every direction, scanning, looking for the enemy, the rear man facing backwards.

Shouting was heard ahead, echoing in the tunnel.

"Allahu Akbar, Allahu Akbar."

The terrorists were praising their god, they cared not if they lived or died, to them death in battle carried a promise of eternity in paradise.

Another tunnel appeared on the right.

"Straight on." Panted Reece.

"Keep going forward Leon." Relayed Frank. "Tunnel right." He warned the remainder.

As they sped past the tunnel the soldiers pointed their weapons down it in turn, but there was no time to investigate it. The last man instinctively took up position next to the entrance to secure it as the others rushed ahead. He turned to watch them depart, feeling somewhat isolated as they went and wishing them luck. As he turned back, a man ran from the tunnel, crashing into him at full speed before he had time to react, knocking him off his feet and onto his back with a thud. His head snapped back, the Kevlar helmet protecting his skull as it bounced on the hard ground. His rifle, on its sling was pinned underneath him as the Talib sat on his chest and gripped him by the throat with both hands, a crazed expression on his face as he squeezed with all his strength, the white of his eyes exaggerated by the black eye liner that surrounded them, his oversized teeth snarling as he growled and spat. The soldier gripped his wrists tightly, trying to remove his hands from around his neck, his eyes bulging as his brain was starved of oxygen. As he began to lose consciousness his vision narrowed like he was entering a tunnel, his brain was shutting down. Suddenly the pressure on his windpipe subsided and he felt the sensation of warm fluid spraying on his face like a hot shower. As he came around, he immediately sat up and instinctively scurried backwards, away from the liquid that was spurting into his eyes and mouth. Blinking rapidly to clear his eyes, he began spitting as he recognised the salty taste. It wasn't water, it was blood! Warm, salty blood. His vision cleared as he processed what had happened. One of the BRF, the rear man, had heard something and gone back to investigate when he'd been attacked. On discovering his comrade being choked he'd grabbed the Talibs head from behind, yanking backwards on a fistful of oily black hair, and ferociously thrust his knife into the side of his neck, all the way to the black resin handle. That strike alone caused a fatal wound but, just as he had always practiced, he'd forced the blade forward with a fast sawing motion to completely cut through the windpipe, half severing the head. The Talibs blood spurted and poured all over the young soldier before his flaccid corpse slumped on top of him, eyes still wide open, staring toward him as he wiped the blood from his face. "What the fuck happened there man?"

"You're alright mate, the fucker got the jump on you, but you're alright, shake it off and get back in position." H replied casually.

"Thanks H, I owe you one." The soldier replied, immediately before throwing up on the floor, adding to the putrid mess already there.

H waited while the soldier straightened himself out and made sure he was ok before turning to depart after the others. "Oh, by the way, give that twat a lozenge will you. Apparently, he's got a sore throat." And with that he disappeared back down the corridor, weapon in the shoulder.

Sporadic gunfire and shouting continued as H hastily moved along the passageway, passing another BRF member at a stairway. He nodded as he moved past, and the soldier returned the gesture and patted him on the back as he went by. He could tell who was firing, because the Taliban were firing bursts of automatic and the BRF were using aimed, single shots, which were still very fast, but much more accurate. Within twenty seconds H had caught up with Frank and the remainder of the assaulting BRF troops. They had stopped at a corridor T-junction and were taking fire from both sides. Frank acknowledged H's return with a thumbs up and a nod and H did the same.

Not wishing to lose momentum Frank quickly issued orders to the men. Him, Leon, Reece and two others would go left toward the cell area. H plus the remaining two would provide cover and secure the right. H gathered two White Phosphorous grenades and one High Explosive grenade and got into position. Under covering fire, he threw the White Phosphorous first, down the right corridor, three seconds later, with a dull thud, the low explosive detonated, sending hundreds of pieces of white hot Phosphorous into the confined space that concealed the enemy. Screaming from at least two men could be heard as the bright, burning pieces seared through their clothing, skin and flesh as they frantically tried in vain to extinguish the flames. Seconds later the second Phosphorous grenade landed in the same spot, sealing the fate of the wounded and injuring or deterring others from moving. One of the injured men ran towards the BRF, his hair and clothing alight as he emerged from the smoke screaming in agonising pain. He was not attacking them, but rather trying to escape the immense pain, arms flailing, patting himself down desperately, pieces of skin and flesh were hanging from his arms and body as he neared the T-junction. Several bullets hit him at the same time as the BRF ended his misery, his contorted body on the floor smoking and hissing as the phosphorous burned out. H now threw the High Explosive grenade down the left corridor. Frank and his team were ready, and as soon as he heard the explosion he was off, quickly moving down the corridor to engage the enemy while they were still shocked from the massive blast and shrapnel as they turned the corner. Leading from the front, through the dust and smoke, Frank saw two Talibs, wounded from the fragmentation grenade, crawling towards a door, one of them coughing violently, spitting blood, the other sobbing and mumbling incoherently in Arabic. A third lay motionless, face down in the dirt, his entire jaw and teeth exposed where the skin and flesh had been completely removed from the left side of his face, his eye hanging from its socket. Frank closed in on the wounded pair, silencing the first with a single round into the back of the head, quickly switching to the second, administering another two shots before returning to the first to fire one more round. Leon did the same to the third man, two shots to the head was a robust method of ensuring the enemy was neutralised. Reece moved close to Frank, placing his left hand on his shoulder.

"The cells are through that door." He whispered. Pointing to a doorway beyond the one obstructed by a dead Talib, his hand was visibly shaking, overloaded with adrenaline and anxiety. His words came out quieter than intended because of the dryness in his mouth and throat, so he forced a cough, licked his lips and repeated the information. "The cells are through that door Frank."

Franks unblinking eyes remained focussed ahead, but he acknowledged Reece with a deliberate nod. "Roger that mate."

The door that Reece pointed to accessed one last corridor which had a further two doors within it, one on the right, and further down, one on the left. Both were typical prison cell metal doors, with large hinges and small hatches at head height, and both were closed. Frank and Leon pushed forward through the doorway, their boots crunching on the human remains beneath their feet. Reece followed closely, placing each footstep more carefully. Frank took up position by the first cell door and glanced inside through the hatch. Inside he saw two men. The first was sat on a small, metal chair in the middle of the room, wrists and ankles secured to the frame by pieces of electrical cabling, the white wire painted red with blood, caused by the tight application and obvious struggle, and pools of blood beneath each restraint where it had dripped onto the dirty floor from the open wounds. The captive wore an orange boiler suit that hung open at the front where buttons had been ripped off, his feet were bare, covered in lacerations on the soles and instep. He sat motionless, head slumped forward, the slight rise and fall of his chest the only indicator that he was still alive. Frank was almost certain it was Johnny, but it was hard to be sure because of the blood, swelling and slumped position of the body.

Outside, the first burst of gunfire had woken enough of the Taliban to raise the alarm and they ran throughout their compounds shouting out loud to awaken the others from their sleep. Screaming could be heard from all the other compounds and lights were turned on and torches shone in all directions as armed Taliban fighters scurried around to identify where the shots had come from, ready to defend their base. Once the grenades detonated, they were left in no doubt where the fight was taking place and the blasts acted like a beacon to the Talibs who immediately turned their focus onto the target compound. On the hillside the snipers adjusted their fire positions, aiming their weapons at the other three compounds. To exit, the enemy fighters would most likely use one of the doors or gates, an obvious choke point where they could be ambushed by the sharpshooters. Three of the four snipers were now facing towards the targets, with only Taff securing their rear to ensure they weren't attacked from behind. Ginge and Mac covered one of the western compounds each and Danny the one to the south.

Mac was the first to fire at the reinforcements. The gate he was observing opened slowly, the creaking metal hinges just about audible across the open ground, and he saw a man peering from the inside nervously. Deciding it was safe the man stood up tall in the gateway, looking back into the compound he ushered those behind to follow him, waving frantically. Mac resisted the urge to fire immediately and lay patiently, the crosshairs were perfectly placed in the centre of the targets head. Another head came into view as the two men conversed, deciding on their next move. Mac knew he couldn't kill them both with one bullet, but this was the next best thing he could do. He breathed in through his nose, took up the first pressure on the trigger, then breathed out through his mouth, steadily squeezing the trigger all the way as his lungs expelled air and his rifle expelled the bullet. The second Talib reeled backwards as pieces of his friends shattered head sprayed across his face, the metal gate ringing like a tolling bell as the bullet passed through its target and struck the steel behind. The remaining men were shocked and decided to stay where they were for the time being, contemplating their options. Mac fired another shot into the chest of the limp corpse to assure them it was the right decision.

The compound to the south had burst into life with fighters deploying to the roof to defend it from what they presumed to be an imminent attack. Four men climbed up from the same place, a ladder against the northern wall, before Danny managed to get a shot off, felling the fifth with a shot to the stomach just as he reached the last rung. Falling to the ground below screaming in agonising pain as his intestines spilled though the open exit-wound, he dissuaded any others from further attempts to climb the ladder and also took them out of the battle as they tended to his injuries. The four men already up the ladder had no idea where the shot had come from and took cover behind the low parapet wall that ran the circumference of the roof. From his vantage point two of them were afforded no protection at all and were in complete view as they peeked over the wall, desperately looking for sign of their attackers. Danny aimed at the one presenting the biggest target mass and fired again, this time striking the back of the upper torso and killing the target instantly as his heart and lungs were obliterated. The next fighter was already fleeing when Danny fired his next round, just missing and blasting a hole in the wall next to him.

"You jammy little bastard!" Whispered Danny as he quickly but smoothly re-cocked the weapon, ejecting the spent cartridge and replacing it with a new one.

The terrified Taliban propelled himself headfirst over the parapet as he sprinted for his life along the roof, preferring the odds of falling to being shot. Landing awkwardly on the hard ground below, the fall had fractured his femur and dislocated his shoulder, but he at least felt like he'd evaded execution. Witnessing the fate of their comrades the two remaining fighters had also decided to vacate the roof, both scrambling to the opening in the centre and executing a hanging jump to safely land in the courtyard below. Danny had not even noticed the two men escape as he'd kept his attention on the man who had jumped outside and who was still unaware of where the shots had come from. The injured Talib had three options; Stay where he was, crawl left, or crawl right. All Danny could see was part of the foot on his broken leg which glowed white through the thermal sight but didn't justify firing another round. If the man stayed still or moved to his left he would disappear behind the protection of the wall. If he moved to his right, he would expose himself to Danny once more. A few seconds later Danny fired again. He had chosen wrong! The round struck his already dislocated shoulder, half severing his arm, leaving it hanging uselessly by his side. Danny fired again.

"Just die you stubborn twat!" He said. Frustrated that it had taken so many shots to finish him off.

The fighters in Ginge's compound took a different tactic. Inside were three men and they had obviously decided that the best form of defence was offence. Sprinting at full speed out of the gate they evaded Ginge's first shot easily and it ricocheted off the door frame and into the compound harmlessly. Splitting up immediately they ran in an extended line parallel to each other towards the target compound. Ginge was impressed by their speed but also aware of his own capabilities.

"Can I borrow you for a minute mate?" He asked Mac.

"Me?" Mac questioned.

"Obviously! Yes you!" Said Ginge sarcastically. "I've got three of the fuckers legging it towards the compound."

"Say no more." Mac interrupted.

Three seconds later both men fired a shot at the middle target who spun as he fell face down in the dirt.

"Did you shoot the middle one?" Asked Mac.

"Yes mate." Ginge replied.

"Ah shit, so did I!" You take the left I'll take the right." Mac directed.

The remaining two runners had maintained their momentum, making a beeline for the compound.

"Roger that mate." Ginge acknowledged, quickly firing another shot.

Mac also fired again, this time the bullet cracking over the head of the target and causing him to dive into the cover of some large rocks.

"Did you hit him?" Ginge asked.

"I Don't know mate. I couldn't tell if he dived or if he fell." Mac replied disappointedly.

"Mine definitely dived." Said Ginge. "He's hiding in them rocks like a little rat!"

Suddenly a burst of gunfire thudded into the ground above their position, not that accurate but close enough to make them duck their heads to the floor instinctively.

"That's the end of that game of hide and seek then!" Said Ginge. Acknowledging that their position had been identified. The muzzle flash from the fighter Mac had engaged confirmed he was indeed still alive and had given away his position and both snipers scanned the rocks looking for him. Mac saw a flash in the periphery of his sight picture immediately followed by the crack and thump of a bullet passing close by and impacting in the soil. "Well that one was closer!" He said, almost giggling.

"I think he might actually be shooting with his eyes open now!" Joked Ginge.

Ginge had noticed that the other fighter was withdrawing towards the compound he had came from, this time employing some tactics and sprinting from one piece of cover to the next, only exposing himself for a short period each time, but the priority was the man shooting at them.

"We need to kill this annoying prick!" Ginge said seriously.

"I concur." Mac replied in a mock posh accent.

As the Taliban fighter crawled along the ground on his belly, moving to a new position to fire at the snipers from, they watched intently through their sights. The rocky outcrop he was using was only small and there were only a finite number of places for him to utilise. If he wanted merely to survive, he could stay still and hide, but his goal was not survival, he wanted to kill the intruders as much as they wanted to kill him.

"Got ya!" Mac whispered. A slight change in colour was visible in his sight picture right beside one of the rocks, caused by the exhaled air the fighter was breathing. The tiny swirling colour contrast would be missed by most, but Mac was very good. He was right, the Talib was hiding behind the rock, breathing heavily as he prepared to expose himself one more time to fire towards Mac and Ginge. Mac set his sights just above the rock so that when the enemy popped up, he would be ready. The fighter psyched himself up before moving, jumping out to the side quickly and adopting a squatting position while firing another burst of bullets to where he thought the snipers were hiding. Mac was caught by surprise and shifted slightly right before returning fire quickly with a single shot. This time the rounds from the AK47 were very close, striking the ground right in front of the paratroopers and spraying them with bits of dirt and stone. Mac's shot proved more effective. The round had actually struck part of the fighters AK47 and deflected upwards, tumbling and entering his head through the lower jaw, exiting through the top of the skull, the blood momentarily ejecting upwards like a macabre fountain.

"Nice shot mate!" Said Ginge who pivoted just in time to see his fleeting target sprint back through the gate into the compound. "You little shit!" He snapped.

While preoccupied supporting Ginge, one of the fighters from Mac's compound had managed to stealthily escape over the wall and make his way to the same stream the soldiers had used undetected. Without realising it, he was incorporating the same tactics against them as they had used against him and he crawled up the wet ditch like they had, but with a greater sense of urgency, covering the distance much quicker. He had heard and seen the shots being fired and the screams of the wounded and knew that his team wasn't faring well but wasn't about to give up. Halting in the same area that Frank had done earlier he scanned the open ground between himself and the compound wall. Content that it was free of obstacles or soldiers he next observed the compound walls to see if any sentries were posted. It seemed that there was nobody there. The fighter did a final check of his equipment before committing to the run, removing the ammunition magazine from his rifle to check it was full, making sure his waistcoat buttons were fastened so the spare ammo wouldn't fall out and offering a quick prayer towards the sky. Squatting like a sprinter in the blocks he pumped his arms and moved his legs as fast as he could toward the compound.

During his brief pause at the top of the stream, little did the Talib know that Ginge had seen him through his weapon sight. "Mac." He said.

"Yes mate." Replied his partner.

"We didn't leave any blokes outside the compound, did we?" He asked. It was odd that someone was in the same place the assault group had been in earlier.

Mac considered the possibility. "No mate. They are all inside. Why?"

"There's someone sat in the stream where the blokes were earlier, but I can't make out who. Check in with Frank to make sure mate. I'll keep eyes on."

The sights were very good, but the man in the ditch did not look like the other fighters they had engaged, he seemed to be wearing a uniform and he had a waistcoat similar to what some of the BRF wore to carry their equipment. From Ginge's vantage point he could not see the AK47 that was resting on the ground and the crouched position the man was in produced a difficult sight picture. He was in fact wearing an Afghan army uniform that he had once worn as a member of the A.N.A before deserting and joining the Taliban.

Mac raised Frank on the radio and asked the question while Ginge kept watch.

"No mate, we are all inside the compound except you four snipers out there. Anyone else is fair game." Frank replied clearly.

"Roger, out." Said Mac. He looked at Ginge who had heard the conversation through his own earpiece.

Ginge acknowledge with a nod and took up the first pressure on the trigger.

At that point, by pure luck, the Talib shot out of the ditch and began his sprint. Ginge sighed and began tracking him with his rifle, stopping a short distance in front of him and firing. The round missed by a whisker but served as a motivator for the afghani who accelerated further still.

"Fucks sake!" Snarled Ginge.

"Need a hand there mate?" Asked Mac, still scanning the two compounds to the west.

"No. I've got it. One more round." Replied Ginge deliberately calmly.

Nearing the compound wall, the Talib did not appear to be slowing down at all. Ginge tracked him again thinking that it would be an easier shot once he hit the wall and would have to turn straight towards him. He assumed that he would be heading for the gate as the wall was too high to negotiate on his own. However, he underestimated the athleticism of the fighter who propelled himself into the wall, hitting it hard with one outstretched foot and using that to gain height. He grabbed the top of the wall with both hands and pulled himself upwards, using both feet to scramble up the rough surface. It was an impressive feat, but as he reached the top and flopped forward to lie on the wall, he was static long enough for Ginge to take his shot. His body hardly moved as the bullet penetrated his ribcage and he remained draped over the wall, legs hanging on one side, arms and body the other. Ginge fired again to ensure he wasn't playing possum.

Back inside the compound, stood behind the prisoner, with the barrel of an AK47 pressed into the back of their head was another Taliban fighter, a young man wearing all black, except for a green canvas waistcoat that carried four additional ammunition magazines and a large knife. He shouted out to Frank "You mother fucker bastards, fucking let me go or I can promise, to fucking shoot this fucking British pig dog!"

Leon looked at Frank "That's a lot of fucks!"

Frank replied. "My men will not harm you, if you put your weapons down and let the prisoner go."

"How I can trust you? You must promising!" Came the nervous reply.

Reece dashed to Franks side. "I know that voice! That's Zar, the guy I gave my boots to." He whispered.

"You sure?" Quizzed Frank.

Reece slowly peered into the hatch with one eye. Before turning back to Frank. "It's him. He's still wearing my boots." He declared proudly. "He's a good lad, let me talk to him, if we let him go, we can get Johnny back, and get the hell out of here."

"Okay, do it." Frank conceded.

"Zahir...Zahir...It's me, Reece, from England.....I gave you those boots you're wearing." Reece shouted, slowly revealing his face through the hatch.

"Fucking hells Reece, you are my friend, you help me my brother?"

Reece could see the fear in Zar's eyes and hear it in his voice. He'd always hoped they would meet again but never dreamed it would be under these conditions. He looked at Frank. "Can we let him go. Give him a chance?"

"Frank shouted through the hatch. "Drop your weapons, and when I open the door, kick them over to Reece. None of my men will harm you, you have my word."

Zar looked at Reece anxiously.

"You can trust him Zar" said Reece triumphantly. "He's a good man. Just do what he asks, and he will let you go."

"Okay my brother, I will doing it."

Zar placed his rifle on the ground and pulled his waistcoat over his head, hanging it by his side.

Frank motioned to Leon who gripped the door handle and pulled it open on its creaking hinges, the weight exaggerated because of the unlevel walls and floors.

Zar swung his waistcoat backwards to create momentum and slung it through the open doorway, his rifle skidded across the floor as he kicked it over.

Leon scanned for further weapons. "He's clear Frank."

Frank pivoted through 180 degrees on his left foot, landing squarely in the centre of the cell door, staring into the eyes of the Talib.

Zar feigned a smile. "Thank you Sir. Now I go home, yes?"

"Wrong answer!" Answered Frank, and he fired a round into the unarmed enemy's chest, propelling him backward, arms flailing, into the wall. Sliding down into a seated position he left a trail of smeared blood on the wall where the bullet had exited his back. Gasping for air, he tried to speak but Frank put another round into his chest before the words came out. "Not fucking interested!" Muttered Frank as he squeezed the trigger.

Reece fell to his knees, head in his hands. "Bastard! You said you wouldn't hurt him! You gave him your word! How could you do that?"

Frank replied in a matter-of-fact tone. "No Reece, I told him my men wouldn't hurt him. And they didn't, I did. So technically, I didn't actually lie!"

Leon was already attending to Johnny who was barely recognisable through his battered face. Both eyes were swollen almost shut, and his deformed nose and jaw were obviously broken. Blood ran from his nostrils and mouth as he tried to speak, but he was so weak and injured, barely a sound came out. He was severely dehydrated, so Leon took out a water bottle and poured it into his mouth, supporting the back of his head with his free hand.

"We've got you Boss, you're going to be alright mate, don't worry." Leon gently patted Johnny's shoulder, conscious of his injuries. "You'll be home soon, hang in there buddy."

Johnny sobbed, tears running down his cheeks, dripping from his disfigured jaw, mixing in with fresh and clotted blood on his already soaked clothing.

"You showed them fucking pussies Boss!" Said Frank. "Nobody is gonna hurt you now, the blokes have smashed these fuckers up."

Frank handed Reece a knife. "Help Leon get him out of those restraints while I finish clearing this place." He spoke into his radio. "All callsigns this is Frank, we've got the Boss, he's wounded but he'll be alright. One room remaining to clear, then we're out of here. Prepare to move in two minutes. Sniper One call for extraction"

"Sniper One roger out."

Reece tried to cut the wire with Franks knife, but the pulling and sawing motion caused Johnny to cry out in pain.

"Sorry Johnny, so sorry mate, I'll untie you, it will be easier. Hang in there buddy, we'll have you out of here in no time mate." Reece placed the knife on the ground and hurriedly set about untying the mass of knots that secured the wire in place. "Jesus Christ, you can tell these lot didn't go to Boy Scouts!" He joked to Johnny as his hands slipped on the bloody wire which was wound around several times with multiple, hastily applied knots. "A couple of half-hitches would have done the job, but they've gone with the old "Bunch of Bastards" here Johnny." Reece's jokes were not only to distract Johnny, but also himself. A few feet away Zahir's lifeless body sat slumped against the wall, eyes open, staring towards the open door, a haunting look of sadness etched on his face.

Johnny raised his head slowly and looked Reece in the eye, his pain evident in his voice as he responded in a gruff voice. "If you can't tie knots…. tie lots!" His eyes fixed on Reece as the corners of his mouth turned upwards slightly, the whites of his teeth briefly visible as he grinned gruesomely.

"Ha Ha, very good. Still got your sense of humour Johnny." Acknowledged Reece.

Lowering his head slowly, Johnny noticed the knife on the floor as Reece finally released his hand and quickly moved onto the wire around his ankle. Leon was already untying the wire on the other side.

"Tilt him backwards and we'll slide him straight off the chair legs." Leon said.

"Good idea" replied Reece as they both steadied the chair, leaning it backwards a few inches. They pulled gently on Johnny's ankles, teasing the wire over the ends of the chair legs. Johnny let out a loud groan as his legs were freed. His joints had been locked in position for several hours and straightening his legs brought a combination of huge relief and excruciating pain.

"Take your time Boss." Said Frank calmly. "We need to check you over before we can move you."

Suddenly Johnny launched himself out of the chair in a low crouch, snatching Franks knife from the ground as he propelled himself towards Zahirs lifeless body, stabbing the blade deep into his rib cage. In a frenzied rage, sobbing uncontrollably he thrust the weapon repeatedly into the body, every strike making a deep thud, like the sound of hitting a punch bag, before switching target to the neck and face. The sound of the knife striking the bones of the face and skull was like two rocks hitting each other, until the final blow. Johnny summoned all the strength he had left, raising his hand high in the air before bringing it downwards like a hammer, driving the knife straight into the top of Zahirs head, fracturing the skull and embedding itself deep inside his brain. If he wasn't dead before, he was now! Johnny slumped to the floor beside him in the foetal position, exhausted. The attack was left by the others to run its course. Even if they'd had time to stop it, they wouldn't have done, Johnny needed some closure, some revenge. The men had no idea what had happened between the two men, only Johnny knew, and they would never ask, that was his business. Not knowing made it easier to deal with.

Frank looked down at the corpse, the knife sticking out from the skull had cost him over $100 from a hunting shop in America and he had grown quite attached to it. He reached down to extract it but as he pulled, he brought the whole body with it like some kind of sick puppet show. Realising it was drawing attention he placed his foot on the head and pulled hard to retrieve it out quickly, then replaced it into its sheath on his chest harness.

Reece looked at him in astonishment. This was not normal behaviour! But a discrete look at the others let him know that they were not disturbed. They would have all done the same thing.

Frank noticed Reece's discomfort. "Your knife is your life Reece. Your knife is your life!" He said unfazed.

The medic entered the room and immediately knelt beside Johnny.

"Has he had any morphine yet?" He asked.

"No. Just some water." said Leon.

The medic retrieved a morphine auto injector from his pack and administered it to Johnnys thigh, he did not need to ask if he was in pain, it was pretty obvious. He passed a 1 litre intravenous fluid pack to Leon.

"Square that away while I check him over please mate."

"Roger." Leon replied.

All members of the BRF were trained to a high level in First Aid and regularly took part in Detachments with the London Ambulance Service to gain hands-on experience. Some practised putting intravenous fluids into each other after a heavy night of drinking to rehydrate and cure a hangover. After a quick primary survey, the medic assessed that although Johnny was badly beaten up, he was safe to be moved, with no immediate, life threatening injuries. Using a thick green rubber band, he applied a tourniquet tightly to Johnny's arm to engorge the veins, and cannulated him in the forearm, just below the elbow with the biggest needle he had. Leon passed the tube from the fluid pack which he'd suspended on a nail in the wall to keep it elevated. Once the saline solution was flowing into the bloodstream the medic took hold of the pack and started to squeeze it, forcing the fluid in quicker. He had another fluid pack ready to go as soon as the first was empty, this time using plasma solution to aid with the clotting of blood throughout Johnny's wounds.

While this was going on Frank talked to H and the other soldiers within the compound to get a situation report. The sniper teams above ground also gave him an update while he simultaneously directed his men to clear the final room.

H and his team had successfully cleared the right-hand corridor, where they had earlier thrown the phosphorous grenade, killing another two Taliban in the process, and had discovered a significant cache of stolen U.S military C4 explosives. The C4 was stacked to the ceiling, intact in its original packaging, emblazoned with U.S Marine Corps insignia and serial numbers. On discovering the explosives H had been shocked, not because they were there, but because he realised, he had been throwing grenades two minutes before, about fifty feet away from a pile of explosives that could have killed them all. Luckily, the tunnel walls were very thick and had shielded the stockpile. No doubt, those explosives were destined for the numerous IED factories around the province. Once there the bomb makers would create hundreds of mostly crude devices to be used against the coalition. Pressure plates, trip wires, command wires and vehicle borne IED's were causing casualties to soldiers and civilians on a daily basis and this find would save countless lives. H had already taken the initiative and wired the explosives with detonation cord and safety cord, so they could be destroyed in situ when they departed.

The Sniper Teams had also been busy, between them killing another seven Taliban who had attempted to reinforce the bunker compound. The remaining Talibs were pinned down in one of the small compounds to the west, drawing fire every time they exposed themselves for a second. The shots that the terrorists returned were ineffective. Pointing their weapons around corners or over walls to fire un-aimed bursts at the hidden sharp shooters the green tracer rounds could be seen harmlessly zipping across the night sky like angry green hornets. The snipers couldn't be sure how many there were but guessed at three or four. Danny had raised the alarm to the Brigade HQ when he requested helicopter support for their withdrawal. The secrecy of the mission had led to a lot of confusion and a heated, lengthy authentication process to establish who they were, but assets had eventually been launched, including attack helicopters. Aboard one of the support helicopters was an angry and confused Chief of Staff, who'd been sent by the Brigade Commander to oversee the mission. The BRF were his elite. He wanted answers.

Danny called through to the recovery force on his radio.

"Hello Ugly Zero Two, this is Mayhem Three Two Delta, ECAS request over."

ECAS was Emergency Close Air Support. The Apache helicopters escorting the recovery force were each armed with a 30-millimetre chain gun and sixteen "Hellfire" guided missiles that could destroy a tank from up to ten kilometres away and had an excellent track record in Afghanistan. As a close support weapons platform, the Apache had been used to devastating effect during the campaign. The psychological impact on the enemy of their apparent enthusiasm to engage, and ruthless ability to destroy was huge, often causing the Taliban to flee at the first sight or sound of their arrival on scene. In contrast, the positive psychological effect on the coalition, when they were in support was immeasurable. Morale and confidence would go through the roof upon their presence. The capabilities of the Apache were revered by the soldiers on the ground, and because they were piloted by Army pilots, not Air Force, the soldiers regarded them as one of their own, a feeling shared by the two man crew.

"Ugly Zero Two, you are loud and clear, we are inbound your location. We are four Uglies and two Pegasus, ETA two zero minutes, send target information, over." The British pilot replied, letting Danny know that there were four Apache's and two CH47 "Chinook" helicopters en-route. The signal wasn't great but good enough to work with, probably because they were flying low across the terrain. The Chinook helicopters were also armed. Although their primary use was transporting troops and equipment, each had a mini gun mounted on the right side and a machine gun at the rear which meant that all together a phenomenal arsenal of firepower was about to reinforce the BRF.

Danny couldn't help but break into a broad grin on hearing this amazing news, before sending clear details of the target to the Apache as requested. This short brief ensured that the crew knew exactly where the enemy position was and how to attack it without causing friendly casualties. The pilot read the information back to Danny to double check he'd recorded it correctly.

Danny listened intently, tilting his head to the right to wedge his radio handset tightly against his right ear with his shoulder and pushing the index finger of his left hand into his left ear hole. His right index finger traced a line underneath the coordinates written in his notebook as they were recited back to him correctly.

"Mayhem Three Two Delta, readback correct, call sixty seconds, over." He said. A rush of excited anticipation making his hairs stand on end.

"Ugly Zero Two, roger out." Came the reply. The pilot would give Danny a call when he was one minute away from the target.

Without missing a beat Danny hooked his handset back onto the webbing of his shoulder strap, where he'd fashioned a holder from a small piece of green bungee, while simultaneously unclipping the fist-mike, 2 way speaker from the opposite side with his left hand and spoke into that.

"All callsigns this is Sniper One, be aware the recovery assets are inbound. ETA about eighteen minutes. Four Apaches and two Chinooks. We will take out the last few Ragheads out here with their Hellfire and get them in the overhead before you withdraw. Frank acknowledge over."

Frank answered quickly. "Roger that Danny, let them know that we'll need to be getting off the ground quick, because we've found a big cache of explosives and we'll light the fuse on our way out, over."

H spoke quickly into his radio "Frank, this is H, I've got five minutes of safety cord. I'll light it on your call, over."

Frank replied. "Five minutes of cord, roger out."

To close the conversation Danny also replied. "Sniper One, roger out."

As seamlessly as before Danny switched radios, not even pausing for thought. "Hello Ugly Zero Two, this is Mayhem Three Two Delta, message over."

The pilot answered promptly. "Send, over."

"Be aware that we have a large amount of UXO that we will be detonating on withdrawal, so you will need to be clear of the pick-up-point ASAP, once pick-up complete, over." Danny warned of the unexploded ordnance.

"Roger, confirm you have remote detonation device, over." The pilot wanted to know how the explosion would be detonated.

Danny explained. "Negative. We are using safety cord. Five minutes delay, over."

"Roger, five minutes delay." The pilot read back. "Pegasus will be turning and burning for quick extraction, over."

"Roger, out" Finished Danny.

Before extracting Johnny, they needed to make sure there were no undiscovered enemy left behind that could follow them up so Frank ordered two of his men to clear the final room, which

Reece had confirmed as another cell. Danny and Leon quickly entered the cell that remained unchecked, quickly discovering it was empty of enemy but did have one occupant.

"Jesus Christ!" Gasped Leon.

"Poor fucker!" Said Tonto, shocked to see a man hanging lifelessly from the ceiling by a length of rope tied to his wrists. Stripped naked and covered in blood which had dripped to form a pool on the floor beneath him, the man had been hoisted off the ground by his wrists, which had been bound together behind his back. Both of his shoulders had dislocated under the strain, tearing his tendons and ligaments, and leaving him hanging in a deformed position that was so unnatural it was hard to process. In the corner of the cell a camera was mounted on a tripod, facing the man. Leon walked behind it and noticed the red recording light was flashing.

"Get him down quick!" He said, grabbing the man's legs and lifting him up. "Cut the rope! Medic!... Medic!" The camera still rolling might have been an indication that he had been alive moments before. The medic ran into the room, as Tonto frantically cut the rope with his knife and the limp body flopped over his shoulders like a fireman's carry. Leon placed him down on the ground quickly but carefully for the medic to carry out his assessment. Kneeling beside him the medic pressed his knuckle hard onto the bridge of the casualty's nose and rubbed it across while shouting. "Wake up, wake up mate!" If he were alive, that pain would surely be enough to wake him up. There was no response. He placed his ear to his patient's mouth and placed his hand on his chest, listening and watching for any signs of breathing. Still nothing, they were too late, he was dead. Without saying a word to the others, the medic straightened up to a kneeling position and delivered a hard, hammer fist punch to the chest of the casualty sending a shudder through his entire body that made his limp arms move slightly. The others looked on with surprise. "What the fu.." Leon was about to query the tactic when the casualty suddenly opened his eyes.

"Cardiac thump." Said the medic, smiling proudly. "Mad Ronnie taught me that years ago on a medical cadre in 3 Para. You've got to try these things."

"Every day is a school day. I Never knew that." Said Leon, very impressed with the outcome.

"Me neither. Happy with that!" Agreed Tonto.

The cardiac thump was an old school method no longer taught in the military and widely disputed by medical professionals as to its effectiveness. Anecdotes of a quick strike to the heart reviving a casualty were well known in the world of front-line first responders, and still practised by some, but only when the patient was in cardiac arrest, and as a last measure before initiating CPR.

The casualty began to cough, so the men tilted him onto his side, supporting his head so he could spit out blood from his mouth. Obviously confused, he attempted to talk, but the words were slurred and garbled.

The medic consoled him, gently patting his shoulder. "Try and relax mate, we'll look after you." He said.

Tonto exited the room and crossed the corridor to inform Frank about the discovery of another captive in the final cell.

"Who is he? Is he one of ours? Is he ok?" Frank asked.

Johnny spoke. "Marine. He's a Marine. I Thought he was dead."

"I thought he was dead too!" Tonto said. "In fact, I think he actually was dead."

Frank followed Tonto back into the cell to see for himself, arriving as another intravenous drip was being administered.

"Where are his clothes?" Frank asked.

"Not seen." Replied the medic.

"Dog tags?" Frank said, hoping the man would still be wearing his identity discs if he were a soldier.

The medic double checked. "No, nothing."

The patient was still mumbling incoherently in his delirious state, the effect of morphine making him even drowsier.

"Tattoos! Check for tats. The Royals love their tats." Frank instructed. If Johnny was right, and he was a Royal Marine, there was a good chance he would have a tattoo. Like the Paratroopers, the Royal Marines were fiercely proud of their unit and lots of them had commando tattoos, usually on their shoulder or chest.

The medic wiped away the blood on the man's shoulder to reveal a tattoo.

"USMC." He read out loud. "He's a Yank!"

"United States Marine Corps." Frank acknowledged. "Christ knows how long he's been here." Frank held the man's hand gently and spoke to him calmly. "You're going to be alright mate. We are British Army. Helicopters are inbound to take you home."

The man squeezed Franks hand, moaning out loud with the pain it caused to his arms and shoulders, nodding his head slightly in recognition.

Reece had also followed into the cell and was rapidly scrolling through the photographs on his camera screen, stopping on one and zooming in closer to the face. "Fuck my old boots, it's O'Malley!" He blurted excitedly. "It's Sergeant O'Malley!" He dropped down beside the casualty opposite Frank, grasping his other hand. "Are you Sergeant O'Malley from the U.S Marines?" He asked softly.

The battered man nodded, and tears trickled down his cheeks.

Reece showed Frank the picture from the ODA compound wall and despite the significant injuries he could tell it was the same man.

"Find him some clothes." Frank ordered.

Leon looked at him puzzled. "What? Where?" He said.

"Ask one of the blokes out in the corridor if you can borrow theirs. I'm sure they won't mind." Frank said sharply, pointing outside the room towards the dead Talib.

"Ah right, got ya." He replied before moving to the nearest corpse and de-robing him of his trousers. After a quick check he decided not to take any of the available shirts as they were all soaked in blood and riddled with holes. He placed the trousers onto the American carefully, assisted by the medic.

Frank updated his men on the discovery of the US Marine and ordered them to prepare to move.

Outside, Danny relayed the message about the POW to the recovery flight, which was then again relayed back to HQ.

"This is going to hurt mate." The medic briefed the American. "So, I'm giving you another shot of morphine to take the edge off it."

The Marine responded with another quick nod as his body shook and he groaned in pain. Carrying him out through the confined spaces and stairs was going to be difficult and aggravate his injuries so he was given another injection of morphine. Johnny received the same, welcoming the second shot to lessen the immense pain he still felt despite the first dose.

The two casualties were picked up by the soldiers. Those doing the carrying handed their own backpacks to one of the others to carry so the casualty could be slung over their backs. Although they could not effectively use it, they still carried their rifles in one hand. Dust and smoke were everywhere, still settling from the shockwaves of the explosions, but the tunnels were still navigable. The smell of cordite, phosphorus and burnt flesh was strong as there was no through-wind to disperse it deep underground as they moved quickly back along the corridor. As they linked up with the other soldiers who were securing the route there would be a quick exchange of glances and pat on the back as they went past.

Bodies were strewn at every turn and doorway and discarded weapons littered the floor as they navigated their way back. It had seemed much quicker on the way in. H plus one other stayed behind with the explosives. They would light the safety fuse at the last safe moment to afford them maximum time to withdraw. Leon led the way, checking a couple of times with Reece for directions but mostly navigating by memory or by following blood trails and spent ammunition cases, reaching the courtyard in a couple of minutes and linking up with the soldiers who had stayed there. Outside it was still dark but the stars in the clear sky and the small crescent moon provided some ambient light. The fresh air felt cool and clean as it filled their lungs and Leon drew in a full lung of air before spitting out as he exhaled to clear the smoke he'd inhaled. Shots were still being fired and a body lay on top of the wall where a Taliban had almost made it over before being taken out by the snipers. Pock marks had been made high in the walls where the Taliban had been shooting harmlessly into the compound, not only missing the BRF but also giving away their position to the snipers.

Frank called Danny on the radio. "How long until the air support?"

"Three minutes." Replied Danny

A burst of incoming gunfire rattled overhead, one of the shots striking the wall and creating a new hole above where they stood.

"How many enemy are left?" Asked Frank. They would not be able to extract until the enemy were taken out.

Danny replied promptly. "At least three enemy in the compound to the south. One confirmed RPG still in action."

Ginge cut in quickly with his update. "There's still three or four in the compounds to your west, but we think they are moving between the two. We think there must be a tunnel system connecting them, because they keep popping up all over the place."

"Roger, out." Said Frank, turning to face Reece. "Reece, are these compounds connected by more tunnels?"

Reece had completely forgotten about the tunnel system that interlinked the compounds until now. "Um, yes, I think there are a few." He replied nervously, well aware that this information would have been helpful a lot earlier. The tunnel system was in fact quite complex, a maze of hand-dug passageways that connected the compounds and led to several exit points on the mountain that could be used for escape. During his previous stay Reece had not been given access to the tunnels and had no idea of their scale.

"What about this one? Is this compound connected by a tunnel?" Frank asked, pointing down to the ground.

"I don't know about this one, but I'd guess so." Reece closed his eyes to concentrate, recalling the layout of the other dwellings. "I remember that the one over there, and the one over there, both came out in the Women's Rooms." Reece pointed towards the two compounds where they were taking fire from as he spoke.

"And which one is the Women's' Room here." Frank asked, speaking very clearly.

Reece gestured towards one of the doorways and walked towards it. "This one." He said, stepping inside a large room, knowing that the soldiers had already checked it earlier. Frank followed him inside, switching on the torch attached to his rifle as he stepped through the doorway to illuminate the dark space. The room was large but quite bare. There were two beds, two wardrobes and an old chest of drawers that had partially collapsed. Frank shone his torch left and right, up, and down. Clearly nobody had occupied it for a while, the wardrobes were empty, and the beds piled high with junk. Frank turned back to face Reece, his rifle held in his right hand with the muzzle and torch pointing to the ground. "What do the tunnel entrances look like?"

Reece's eyes were suddenly drawn to one of the wardrobes which stood in the corner of the room against the wall behind

Frank. Something had moved. His head turned slowly to catch up with his eyes, looking over Frank's shoulder. The back panel of the wardrobe slid quietly and deliberately sideways to reveal a secret doorway. A shadowy figure silently emerged from the opening malevolently. The man, wielding a large knife had not noticed Reece, Franks broad frame shielding him from view in the dim light, and he thought he could attack Frank from behind. Franks knife was right in front of Reece's face, strapped to his chest and Reece grabbed it, yanking downwards to release it from its sheath. Reece threw the knife with all his might as the Talib lunged towards Frank, only noticing the journalist as he launched the blade at him.

Frank spun around quickly to face the silent attacker, startled by Reece's actions. The knife missed the target, bouncing off the wardrobe and sticking into the ground and the unscathed attacker continued his charge. Frank brought his right knee up and drove his foot into the middle of the Talibs chest, stopping him in his tracks, almost taking him off the floor. He brought his rifle up into his shoulder and fired rapid shots into the man's body before he had a chance to regain his balance. A look of shock was etched on the Afghanis face as his arms fell to his sides, still clutching his knife. Frank continued to fire rounds into his body as he reeled backwards with the force of the bullets and fired a few more after he had fallen to the ground dead, knife still in hand.

Leon entered the room, weapon in the shoulder, followed closely by some others. "You alright Frank?" He said.

"All good mate. Found the tunnel." Frank replied, pointing to the wardrobe.

"You alright Reece?" Leon asked.

Reece was stood motionless, in a daze, staring at the dead body. He knew that was a close call. His ears were ringing from the shots that had been fired right next to his ear and his hands were shaking.

"Old Phil Taylor here is alright aren't you mate!" Frank said, slapping him on the back.

"What?" Answered Reece.

"Phil, The Power, Taylor!" Frank joked. "I tell you what, that wardrobe won't mess with you again!"

"Oh, right. Phil Taylor. Darts champion. Funny." Reece mumbled.

"Keep an eye on that tunnel entrance until we bug out lads." Frank instructed the soldiers. If anyone else came through they'd be ready this time. Come on, let's get you out of here." Frank said, picking his knife up from the ground before putting his arm around Reece's shoulders and ushering him back outside.

The snipers were confident they had pinpointed the location of the two remaining fighters in one of the compounds and were firing shots intermittently from both sniper positions to keep them pinned down. Danny's radio kicked into life.

"Mayhem Three-Two-Delta this is Ugly Zero Two, sixty seconds over." The Apache pilot informed Danny he would be on target in sixty seconds time.

Danny replied promptly. "Roger, confirm attack-heading two seven zero degrees? Over" He asked, confirming that the helicopter would be approaching from over his left shoulder, flying from east to west.

"Roger, heading two seven zero. Do you have any target update for me? Over." The Apache pilot knew what his target was and that the soldiers were close by, but any additional information would ensure Danny got the service he required.

"Roger, we are taking small arms fire from the northwest corner of the target compound and we believe there is a tunnel linking the target to the adjacent compound to the west, over." Danny explained.

"Copy that, we will take a look at the compound to the west

as well. Confirm all friendly forces are north of the target." Acknowledged the pilot.

"Roger, we have friendlies in the compound to the north of the target, danger close but in hard cover, and one sniper team 300 metres further north plus one sniper team 300 metres north east." Danny clarified.

"Roger, copy that. I am visual target and visual team to the north. Confirm you have two men on the hillside to the north at approximately eleven hundred metres elevation?" The pilot said, watching Ginge and Mac sitting patiently amongst some rocks.

"Roger. Sniper team is north on facing slope, over."

The Apache was hovering, peeking over the mountain using the imaging technology on board to build up situational awareness which they shared electronically with the other aircraft in the sortie so that everyone could gain a clear understanding of the battle picture. The pilot asked one more question to confirm he had selected the correct target before committing to the attack. The cluster of compounds were close together and a mistake could be catastrophic.

"Can you confirm that the friendly force compound has what appears to be a horse lying down in the courtyard next to the men in there?" He asked, studying the thermal image on his display screen.

Danny could not see into the courtyard, so sought clarification from the men on the inside.

"Wait, out." He said to the pilot, switching to his other radio to call Frank. "Frank this is Sniper One, be aware the Apaches are in position now, but want to confirm that you have a horse in your compound. They can see it through the thermal. Is there a horse there?" He asked, well aware how much of a random question that was.

For a second Frank was confused but then he looked at the huge dog laying on the ground with a sheet over its head and realised the easy confusion.

"It's a very big dog!" He replied. He then started to perform star jumps. "Tell the pilot I'm now jumping up and down waving my arms, right next to the dead dog, over."

"As you do." Said Danny. Danny relayed the information to the pilot who was already watching the scene.

"Wow that really is a big dog!" The pilot said. "Tally target, tally friendlies. Take cover, weapons firing on your call."

"Roger, wait out." Danny replied.

The helicopters were lined up tactically, out of earshot and sight but ready to fire. Two of the Apaches' had programmed their Hellfire missiles to strike the compound where the majority of the fire had come from and where the Taliban shooters were hiding, the other two gunships had selected targets identified earlier in the mission where shots had been fired from. The two Chinook helicopters that would carry out the extraction were holding off further to the east awaiting the call to execute their pickup.

Frank had been doing star jumps for quite a while, slowly spinning around in circles as he did so because he didn't know where the helicopters were watching him from. He stopped when Danny called him once more on the radio.

"Frank, this is Sniper Team One, Hellfire mission on your call. Compounds to your south and south-west targeted, over."

"Roger, fire now." Said Frank, breathing heavily from his exercise. "Sniper Team Two acknowledge." He said, ensuring that all groups knew to take cover.

Ginge had been following the conversation intently and answered immediately. "Sniper Two, roger over." He replied. Mac and Ginge looked at each other excitedly, both grinning widely.

"This is going to be fucking mega!" Mac said.

"Fucking SMASH!" Said Ginge expectantly.

"Roger, firing now." Replied Danny. "All callsigns, take cover! Out."

Danny switched to his other radio. "Hello Ugly Zero Two, this is Mayhem Three Two Delta, fire now over."

The Apache pilot passed the order to his fellow pilots and weapons operators instantly, then responded to Danny.

"Ugly Two Zero, in hot!" He said. Signalling he was about to fire.

"Continue hot!" Replied Danny, which was the final command to fire.

The helicopters rose vertically in formation, cresting the ridgeline, but remaining invisible to the targets, the sound of their engines just about audible between the sporadic shots being fired by the snipers and Taliban.

The BRF in the compound had all moved back inside to take cover from the potential secondary missiles and blast, but Frank stayed outside with Leon to maintain eyes on the targets and watch for enemy movement. Frank had also allowed Reece to remain outside so he could capture the moment on camera. The three men lay on the roof behind a low parapet wall, keeping as low as possible while peering over the top, Reece with his camera at the ready.

A sudden huge bang exploded, followed by a ripple of more bangs and whooshes as sixteen supersonic Hellfire missiles struck their targets. Night became day as the explosions lit up the mountain top with bright flashes, sending shockwaves and debris through the air. Flames engulfed the compounds with plumes of smoke rising like small mushroom clouds high in the sky. The men on the roof ducked behind the parapet as projectiles made of metal, wood and stone, caused by the blasts whirred horizontally out from the impact points. Other pieces of debris rained down from the sky like meteorites, thudding and clanging loudly on impact with the ground. Reece held on tight to his camera and continued snapping away blindly, his face pressed into the dirt of the roof as he held the camera up above his head with one hand, the other hand protecting the back of his skull and neck.

The bombardment was over in a few seconds, with the secondary explosions from fuel and ammunition stores continuing for a few seconds more, before the scene started to settle, revealing the damage.

Frank knelt on one knee to observe the damage. Surprisingly, the compounds had withstood the onslaught quite well, although they were damaged, they were still standing, albeit with some holes and scarring, and fires still burning inside. The firing had stopped.

The Apaches flew closer to the target, scanning for any movement, the sound of the four machines getting louder as they neared.

Danny called them on his radio.

"Hello Ugly Zero Two, this is Mayhem Three Two Delta, BDA targets destroyed." He said, letting the pilots know what the battle damage assessment was.

"Roger, no further activity seen. We will secure the area for Pegasus to land." The pilot replied, ascending to a higher altitude so that they could support the Chinooks during the extraction."

Danny updated Frank and the others on the goings on over the patrol radio before calling the Chinook pilot to update him on the landing site.

Frank ordered the sniper teams to collapse their positions and make their way down to the football pitch for pickup.

The distinct sound of the Chinooks approaching energised the men, the mission was almost complete.

Unbeknown to the BRF and the aircrew, just before the missile assault, a counter-attack was about to be launched by the Taliban. Ten fighters who had rallied together in the tunnel system had been about to attack the main compound from three separate locations simultaneously, three of them wearing suicide vests laden with C4 explosives and filled with nails, nuts and bolts. The fighters were experienced, battle hardened men, fresh from the front line where they had been conducting attacks against the allies and Afghan Army for months. They had been sent to the mountain for some rest and recuperation before rejoining their comrades in the north. The fighters had been surprised by the assault from the air but still determined to avenge their losses. The famous "Wocka wocka" sound made by the Chinooks was just as distinctive to the Taliban as it was to the soldiers, giving them early warning of their impending arrival. The fighters had a good understanding of western tactics and correctly guessed the Chinooks would be coming to collect the soldiers on the ground. They also knew the aircraft would be at their most vulnerable once on the ground, so decided to remain concealed in their underground positions until the helicopters landed.

Danny and Taff were first to arrive at the nominated landing site, the football pitch, and took up fire positions amongst some rocks to observe the area and secure it for the others, informing Frank over the radio of their progress. Ginge and Mac were also descending from their sniping position, traversing the loose rocky slope carefully to avoid falling or creating too much noise. They stopped regularly to scan the ground in front of them and the enemy compounds, checking for any movement through night sights and thermal cameras. Complacency at this point could be their worst enemy, the mission was not over until they landed back in camp.

H had been waiting patiently with the underground explosives cache with his three team members, keeping up to date via the radio. The Hellfire attack had caused a lot of anxiety to them down there, the tunnels shaking during the assault, dust falling from the ceiling and the shelving rattling. They would be glad to be out of there. The plan was for them to light the safety fuse at the last safe moment. They needed to make sure they had time to get out of the tunnels, onto the landing site and into the aircraft, while at the same time ensuring the Chinook would not have to wait for them on the ground any longer than necessary. Frank decided that he would give H the order to extract the second the Chinooks' wheels touched the ground.

H had collected the safety fuse from the other soldiers that carried it and altogether that made ten feet, which burned at about 1cm a second, equating to five minutes burn time. The safety fuse would be lit by a match then burn slowly, giving them time to withdraw. The safety fuse was connected to a short length of detonating cord which had a knot tied into its end before that was inserted into a piece of PE4 plastic explosive which would create the initial explosion. This had been tactically placed against the C4 cache which would detonate thereafter.

Frank organised the casualty evacuation group and left the compound with the two casualties who had been loaded onto lightweight stretchers that the soldiers had assembled as soon as they exited the confined space of the tunnel. The Apache crew watched them from above as they left the walled compound through the gate and headed through the open spaces to the football pitch. Soldiers stopped at every turn or every 25 metres and took up a fire position, not only to secure the route but also to maintain a link back to the compound to ensure verbal communications was achievable back to H and his team at all times. When H withdrew, the line would collapse behind him, bringing everyone back together at the landing site.

The two casualties were placed on the ground at the southern end of the pitch and Frank, the medic plus two others stayed with them. The remaining men spread out north and west to secure the landing site for landing. Both sniper teams were now together on the eastern edge of the pitch, ready to go.

Within seconds the first Chinook was overhead, the percussion and downdraft of the rotors pulsating in the bodies of those below and blowing those kneeling off balance.

It landed square in the middle of the pitch, descending rapidly, forcing the hydraulic suspension to work hard to absorb the impact. A section of eight soldiers sprinted out from the lowered tailgate to reinforce the security perimeter, diving to the ground and setting up their weapons in the prone position.

Frank gave the order to H to light the safety fuse which he did immediately, staying only long enough to confirm it was alight by watching it track up the black cord as it audibly fizzed, before running away with his team. The four men sprinted through the tunnels, up the stairs, into the courtyard and out through the gate, picking up the waiting soldiers as they raced to the landing site.

The stretcher bearers picked up the casualties and moved quickly to the back of the helicopter where they were met by the loadmaster and medics who ushered them to where they wanted them put down. The BRF medic immediately began to brief the on-board paramedics and doctor on the casualties and Frank instructed the other two BRF soldiers to remain on-board. As he turned around, he came face to face with the Chief of Staff, who poked Frank in the chest and began shouting angrily.

"Who the hell authorised this!? You are finished Cutler! Do you hear me!?"

Even without the deafening noise of the idling engines above them Frank could hear nothing, if his hearing was bad before, after all the shooting and explosions it was even worse now. He watched the agitated Majors' lips move for a second, recognising by the body language and intensity that he was receiving a bollocking. Frank looked downwards slowly, his head tilting forwards to look at the finger prodding his body armour, pausing for a second and taking a deep inward breath, his eyes closed momentarily before he lifted his head and gaze back up, until his eyes refocused on the enraged officer. Frank leaned forward, his nose almost touching the nose of the officer, his frown half closing his eyes and his jaw pulsing as it clenched biting down hard on his teeth.

"Fuck off!" He snarled loudly through gritted teeth, spit ejecting from his mouth into the COS's face. Thrusting both hands hard into the chest of the officer, his shove took him off the floor and sent him crashing into the side of the helicopter, falling onto his backside. Filled with adrenaline and aggression it was fortunate for the Major that Frank had more pressing matters to deal with and he walked back down the ramp to organise the BRF extraction.

"RPG!!" Shouted one of the soldiers on the western flank. Gunfire erupted once again as the BRF soldier sighted a Taliban fighter appear from the cover of a stream holding a rocket propelled grenade launcher in the aim, facing toward the Chinook.

The soldiers' reaction was very fast, and the red glow of his tracer rounds had guided the others onto the target quickly, but not before he had fired the RPG. The Talib dropped under a hail of bullets from four different soldiers and fell back into the stream that he had been hiding in, dead.

The rocket missed, but not by much, and fragments of the warhead scattered close to the target, one piece cracking the windscreen of the aircraft in front of the pilot.

Suddenly the other Taliban simultaneously launched their attack, engaging the soldiers and aircraft from the west and south. The soldiers returned fire ferociously, deterring some of the attackers who dived back into cover, but not all. From the south one of the suicide bombers emerged, running at full speed towards the aircraft and screaming loudly, not fully appreciating the advantage of night vision aids. The loadmaster ran to his machine gun on the tailgate and quickly sat behind it, releasing the safety catch as he adjusted the weapon. The Talib was still at least 100 metres away when the gunner opened fire, not even using the sight to aim. Instead he watched through his PNG's and guided the tracer rounds onto target as he fired. The vest detonated as he fell, either intentionally as a last-ditch effort or because a tracer round had hit the right place. Still about fifty metres away most of the projectiles fell harmlessly away from the helicopter, but a few did cause some damage. A couple of fragments had struck the fuselage of the chinook, one tearing a hole in the external bodywork and another disabling one of the hydraulic extension arms that raised and lowered the tailgate. A third fragment, a copper screw had embedded itself in Reece's camera, violently knocking it out of his hands when it struck as he took a picture. Frank saw him scurrying around on the ground and ran over, thinking he may have been hit.

He skidded to a halt next to him and grabbed his arm. "Are you hit?" He said.

"No, it's worse than that!" Reece replied, looking directly into the lens of Franks PNG's. "My camera has been hit and I can't bloody find it!"

Despite the chaos of bullets and explosions around him Reece was distraught at the thought of losing his camera. Frank leant down.

"Do you mean this camera?" he said. Holding Reece's damaged possession in front of him. "The one that's attached to your body?"

Reece grabbed it with both hands desperately. The sling he kept it on was still intact and had arrested it.

"Thank you. Thank you." He said, inspecting the damage.

"Now get on that fucking helicopter before the next one takes your head off!" Frank replied, pointing to the Chinook.

The original plan was for the first Chinook to take the casualties plus the snipers and the second to pick up the remainder, but that needed to change.

The proximity of the enemy made it impossible for the Apaches and second Chinook to engage with their weapons.

Frank spoke on his radio. "All callsigns this is Frank. Everyone on the Chinook now. I say again, everyone get on the Chinook now. H acknowledge."

"Roger that mate." shouted H answering without needing the radio as he came running towards Frank with the other soldiers in tow. They ran past and onto the helicopter, pushing as far inside as they could without interfering with the medics.

Frank spoke into that mic again. "Danny, tell the aircrew we're all getting on this lift. Anyone left behind will be fair game. Anyone with the QRF tell them to withdraw. Out."

Frank wanted the men off the ground so that the Apaches could utilise their weapons. He watched as the men got to their feet and sprinted to the Chinook and ran there himself to speak to the loadmaster, who gave him the thumbs up, seemingly enjoying himself. Frank grabbed the first soldier from the aircraft that he saw and told him to account for his 8 men, before beginning to count his own troops, including Johnny, the American and Reece. The QRF soldier reported in to Frank.

"All my lads are on board." He shouted. Holding up 8 fingers then giving a double thumbs up."

"Roger." Replied Frank. "Buckle up."

The remaining BRF were firing and manoeuvring their way back to the aircraft, laying down a deceptively large amount of fire to keep the enemy's heads down as they withdrew. They all knew that once they stopped firing the Taliban would regain their momentum and come back at them hard.

Danny and Ginge were the last two to board. They had been using their sniper rifles to cover the others until the last safe moment. Frank grabbed their equipment straps to assist them up the ramp. Everyone was accounted for. He shouted into the earpiece of the loadmaster.

"That's it. That's everyone. Let's go, go, go!"

The loadmaster immediately spoke into his microphone, informing the pilot and the other helicopters that all friendly forces were off the ground and the helicopter began to rock as power was generated for take-off. As expected, the Taliban rediscovered their appetite for battle and concentrated all their fire on the one target left on the ground, the helicopter. Rounds were hitting the Chinook down its port side, ripping through the thin metal and ricocheting around the inside of the cabin as it lifted rapidly, turning through 180 degrees as it ascended to bring its weapons to bare. The gunner who had been assisting the medics up until that point because the mini-gun had been redundant on the starboard side took up position behind his weapon as the loadmaster began engaging from the rear with his machine gun. The mini-gun operator started firing as soon as he had line of sight, the stream of tracer rounds directed to the muzzle flash he saw from an AK47 firing at him. Frank was also firing his rifle out the back, stood next to the loadmaster, balancing himself against the side wall. The Apaches were now in no fear of hitting friendly forces and unleashed their arsenal of Hellfire missiles into the compounds, the underslung chain guns also being used on targets in the open.

The second Chinook was also engaging with its minigun adding to the immense amount of firepower being delivered. The few remaining Taliban had retreated back into the tunnels, to stay above ground was suicidal, although for some that was a conscious choice they made, a glorious death in battle meant a guaranteed place in eternal paradise.

The sight was something none of the soldiers or crew had ever seen before as they laid waste to every heat source, light, and moving object they saw. The millennium celebration fireworks were pathetic compared to this!

The firing ceased as they extracted from the mountain and the soldiers looked out the back at the flames as they moved away.

Frank felt a tap on the shoulder and turned to see one of the soldiers pointing to H. H tapped the watch on his wrist and shouted out to him. "Ten seconds."

Frank acknowledged him with a nod and looked back to the compounds. A few seconds later another explosion went off with a dull thud. The C4 cache was destroyed, collapsing the tunnels and torture chambers and burying the dead.

Frank looked across to H with a rare smile and gave him the thumbs up.

A few seconds later another series of unexpected explosions detonated, much bigger than the others with an almighty blast and a shockwave that could be felt inside the aircraft.

Frank looked to the loadmaster who did not appear surprised.

"What the fuck?" He mouthed.

The loadmaster stood up and shouted into Frank's ear.

"U.S Air Force." He said. "The Yanks don't mess about when their blokes get tortured!"

The U.S had ordered the air strike as soon as they had heard about the discovery of their Marine. The likelihood of anyone surviving the helicopter attack was slim, but the ordnance they had just dropped had probably flattened the mountain. There would be nothing left.

During the extraction, more injuries had been sustained than the rest of the mission and the medics were hard at work treating those who had been hit inside the helicopter. The US Marine and Johnny had been stabilised and the new priorities were gunshot wounds. One of the BRF soldiers had been shot in the lower leg with a large part of his calf muscle hanging by his foot, and one of the reinforcement troops suffered a shot to the shoulder that also required urgent surgery. The medics treated them as best they could with morphine and dressings in the cramped space of the Chinook and the other soldiers supported them until they were handed over to the medics at Kandahar who were waiting to receive them with a fleet of ambulances. Reece squeezed himself into the smallest space he could find, keeping himself out of everybody's way. The scene was like a subdued Hell as the medics worked overtime to treat the casualties, the urgency of the situation written on their faces as the soldiers reassured their friends they'd be ok. A few sat in stunned silence, unblinking eyes staring at a fixed point with a haunted expression. However, the worst news was not discovered until they landed back at Kandahar and started to de-bus. Taff, who had seemingly been sleeping throughout the flight had been hit in the back of the head by a bullet and killed instantly just after take-off. Thinking he was sleeping the others had left him alone to rest. The bullet had not left an exit wound as it had been slowed down by the aircrafts materials before it penetrated the base of his skull. He looked peaceful, there had been no suffering, but that did little to ease the pain the others felt. Frank encouraged the men to go and get some rest and stayed on board with his fallen warrior until the medics came to take him away, helping them carry the body from the helicopter, onto a stretcher and then into the waiting ambulance before returning to his seat on-board. As the ambulance pulled away and disappeared into the darkness, Frank suppressed his emotions to stop himself bursting into tears. A dry gulp, a few sniffs and some rapid blinking, followed by some fidgeting with his watch strap almost masked his sadness, but a few tears managed to escape and dripped from his nose to the metal floor between his feet.

A large American contingent was also waiting for them at Kandahar. An ambulance and military police vehicles with flashing lights came to ensure the quick extraction of the U.S Marine who was whisked off to the American Medical Centre. Several Humvee vehicles also arrived as the Chinook came to a halt. After the casualties were quickly taken away and the soldiers departed Frank sat quietly by himself. The Chief of Staff had left the helicopter but waited outside for the casualties to be removed before he spoke to Frank, still intent on disciplining him for his reckless actions. He made his move as Frank sat slumped in his seat, head in his hands. Stepping onto the ramp, he approached, and as he did Frank looked up, sensing his presence. There were tears in his eyes and a tiny puddle on the ground from where he had been crying. Frank wiped his eyes and looked at the angry officer, anticipating his reprimand, but before he got the opportunity to speak a loud, deep, American voice shouted out.

"Sergeant Cutler?"

Behind the Chief of Staff at the base of the ramp stood a huge man, dressed in U.S pattern camouflage, with a chest full of medals and a peaked cap with four gold stars across the front. The Chief of Staff recognised him immediately and quickly came to attention, respectfully saluting. "Good morning General." He said nervously.

"Good morning Major." Replied General McGraw of the U.S Marine Corps, the senior officer in Kandahar.

Frank also recognised the General as he had seen him on the T.V many times and was well known to all the soldiers for his gung-ho approach to operations, earning him several nicknames including "Mad Dog McGraw", "Quick Draw McGraw" and "Marine Corps McGraw."

Frank also stood to attention. "Hello Sir." He said. "I'm Sergeant Cutler, how can I help you?"

The General saluted Frank with vigour, looking him straight in the eye intently before breaking into a broad smile. He walked past the COS who stepped aside to let him through and stood in front of Frank, towering over him at 6ft 5 inches tall. He extended his hand to shake Franks and when Frank mirrored his action, he grabbed it and pulled him towards him, shaking it while he patted him on the back hard, but affectionately.

"Let me tell you something son." He said. "You already have helped me. Me and the entire Marine Corps. What you just did is bad ass! The question is, how can I help you?"

"Thanks sir." Frank replied solemnly. "But I'm all good thanks. I just need to make sure my blokes get fixed up and get some rest."

"Damn right." Said the General. "Anything you need, you got it Sergeant. Anything! Now go get some sleep and I will talk to you later. I want to personally thank your men too. We'll have a beer and some meat tonight. Okay? Do you guys like beer and meat?"

"We love it Sir, and we also love pizza, long as you are buying." Said Frank.

"You got it Sergeant, make sure you're hungry!" The General chuckled as he turned to leave.

The COS stood to attention and saluted again as the General left, the wind taken from his sails. The telling off would have to wait.

The General paused before getting into his Humvee, shouting back towards Frank. "Hey Sergeant, do you need a ride somewhere?"

Frank quickly grabbed his rifle and equipment, slung it over his shoulder and jogged down the tailgate.

"That would be mega Sir, yes please." He replied.

General McGraw opened the rear door of his vehicle for Frank and he got in, loading his kit in first and taking a seat, ignoring the COS as he brushed past him.

The major watched as the Americans departed in their Humvees leaving him behind, Frank giving a cold stare as the vehicle pulled away. Standing alone, the major cast a lonely figure in the aircraft as the loadmaster turned out the lights.

The barbeque laid on by the Americans that night was impressive, not only was there a full hog roast over an open fire and a hot-dog stand, but there was also a jacuzzi and a bar with a selection of ice cold beers on tap. British and American flags were proudly displayed side by side and music played from an old-fashioned juke box covered in neon lights. Next to the bar was a large picture of Taff mounted on a wooden frame, below it 4 wreaths, one from each of the U.S Armed services including the USMC. Frank recognised the picture from the 2003 Iraq tour they had deployed together on. It showed Taff wearing his Parachute Regiment beret and desert fatigues and had been taken after a patrol to the Iranian border. In the picture he was looking away from the camera as if he was unaware it was being taken. Staring into the distance he looked serious, deep in thought. In reality, that was a brief moment of sensibility during a period of mucking about and play fighting. When the BRF arrived, General McGraw excused himself from the group he was talking to and intercepted them as they approached the bar.

"Welcome to my little piece of America!" He bellowed. "Get these warriors a beer and keep em coming!" He ordered the barman, who promptly began filling plastic pint glasses with Budweiser beer, two at a time. The General made a point of shaking hands with each soldier and thanking them before putting his arm around Franks shoulder and ushering him away to a small table.

"Frank, what you and your men have done is truly amazing, and I want you to know that it will be acknowledged by the United States. Taffs death is our loss as it is yours, and it has already been agreed that he will be awarded the Purple Heart in recognition of his sacrifice. Along with all the men in your team, he will also receive the Silver Star medal in recognition of the gallantry you guys showed. I know you are going to take some heat for this mission Frank, but let me tell you something, I will do everything in my power to protect you and those brave men over there." The general pointed and moved his arm in an arc across the gathering to include the aircrew and everyone else involved in the mission, who had also been invited.

Later in the evening he would reiterate his gratitude and promise of support to the entire group during a heart-felt awe inspiring speech to his guests. He was a master orator and his words resonated with everybody there, leaving them feeling humbled and proud.

The remainder of the night was filled with drinking, eating and storytelling between the British and American soldiers, Marines and airmen. Even Reece was treated as an equal, now fully adopted by the BRF as an honorary member and assumed to be an actual member by some of the Americans. By midnight most had retired to their beds with only a handful remaining. Now sat at the bar, Frank and the General were both well-greased. A half empty bottle of Kentucky Bourbon whiskey rested in a bucket of ice between them along with their respective beers on the table-top. The alcohol had reduced their inhibitions and dissolved the normal awkwardness and etiquette issues between a senior officer and soldier, they were just two soldiers having a drink together. During the night they had discovered that they were very similar characters with a shared passion for soldiering, combat sports, music and political view. They also shared a harsh, dry sense of humour, swapping anecdotes and laughing loudly. At 0300hrs the General ushered his duty driver to take Frank back to his tent and made his way to his accommodation after shaking hands and saying goodbye.

CHAPTER FIFTEEN

What Next

While Johnny recovered in hospital after being flown back to the UK, the next couple of days were frenetic for the BRF, and even more so for Reece. The mission had been a huge success, the Americans had been celebrating the recovery of their soldier who had been missing in action for almost a month, with public acknowledgement from General McGraw on television interviews. Even the U.S President had mentioned the British Airborne during a speech from the gardens of the White House.

In the U.K, the media coverage had placed a great deal of pressure on the MoD who remained intent on investigating the mission and all those involved despite the overall success and amount of positive publicity, not to mention a huge morale boost to the coalition forces. Meting out punishment for the mission now, while the troops were being lauded would not go down well with Joe Public. Instead the MoD conducted their investigation more covertly and awarded their punishment discretely after the dust had settled.

Johnny's injuries were substantial, and it would take many surgeries and physical therapy sessions before he would get back to any sort of normality. Although still officially an officer, he would spend the next two years on sick-leave as he cycled through surgery and recovery. The psychological damage was not so obvious but it was there in equal abundance, enough in its own right to ensure he would never soldier again. After two years of treatment Johnny would be formally medically discharged from the army, before pursuing a career in banking in the city.

Squadron Leader Hudson, the pilot that had flown the paratroopers into the mission, was encouraged to take retirement. After thirty years' service, his pension was a healthy amount and he was still young enough to start a new career flying for a civilian company. Although he was effectively being sacked, his testimonial from the RAF was outstanding and he was able to retire honourably and seemingly of his own choice and transition easily into civil aviation.

Sergeant O'Malley, the US Marine that was rescued was stabilised in Kandahar before being flown to a U.S garrison in Germany, where his wounds were treated, and he began his long road to recovery. It would be a month before he returned to the U.S and over a year before he would walk again, but despite his physical and psychological injuries he would make a good recovery and eventually leave the Marines and write a book about his experience. The title was "When all hope is lost" and it was so successful it was turned into a movie.

Reece's story made the front page of the Daily Telegraph and was then serialised every day for the next week, with his photographs earning worldwide acclaim and commanding vast sums of money from foreign publications. The photograph used for the front page showed Taff carrying Sergeant O'Malley on his shoulders as he ran towards the Chinook, behind him another BRF soldier is firing his rifle from a kneeling position towards a building that is ablaze with bright orange flames. That picture became iconic and synonymous with the campaign. Unfortunately, his story also received interest from a terror group of Islamist fundamentalists who issued a fatwa on him, forcing him to change his lifestyle in London, adopting a more vigilant and security savvy personality. He stayed in touch with several members of the BRF, especially Johnny and Frank and met with some of the soldiers when they came to London to party.

Frank was told in no uncertain terms that his soldiering career was over by an angry Brigade Commander, accompanied by his Chief of Staff. They had been forced into some quick thinking and retrospective planning by the mission and, only because of its high-profile success, came out of it relatively unscathed. However, the unauthorised execution of a multi-asset, highly dangerous rescue mission could not go unpunished and Frank was sent back to the UK under the guise of compassionate leave for the birth of his baby. Fortuitously his wife gave birth to their first child six days after his return, which was two weeks premature. In memory of his friend and comrade the baby boy was named Bryan. Frank would not return to Afghanistan, instead while on paternity leave, he received a posting order to go and work as a Training Analyst within Army Headquarters. In his absence, H was selected to take over as Platoon Sergeant and promoted in the field, finishing the tour after several other successes and no further casualties. Frank followed their progress closely via email and the occasional phone call but did not interfere, H was more than capable and he did not want to undermine his position. On their return they would all meet up to celebrate, mourn and say their farewells.

CHAPTER SIXTEEN

Career Change

O n arrival to the large open-plan office in Army HQ where he was allocated a desk, Frank was introduced to his new boss, a morbidly obese civil servant who held the rank of Major in the Army Cadet Force and encouraged people to address him as "Sir."

"Good morning Sergeant Cutler, I am SO2 J357." He said loudly.

Frank extended a hand to greet him, well aware that he was carrying items in both hands. "Morning Jim." He said, noting the name on the identity card he wore on a rainbow coloured lanyard around his neck.

His new boss held a bacon roll in one hand and an oversized "Army – Be the Best" plastic coffee cup in the other and fumbled to put one down before shaking hands.

"I hear you're in the Cadets?" Said Frank. "I ran some training for the Cadets last year. We might have met before." Frank started as he intended to go on, establishing the civilian versus military hierarchy. He had been warned about Jim.

"Yes maybe." Replied Jim. "Well get yourself settled in and we'll have your welcome interview before lunch."

Frank spent the rest of the morning being shown around by a

Sergeant called "Nik-Nak" from the Royal Artillery who introduced him to the people spread about in the half empty office and familiarised him with key locations such as the Admin Office the NAAFI shop and the vending machines. Strangely, all the officers introduced themselves by job title, not rank and name and while doing the rounds he met "SO3 J35," "SO3 J7," and "SO2 J8" before asking the Artillery Sergeant to explain the coded language. Nik-Nak explained how it represented their rank and appointment before Frank interrupted to summarise. "Basically, they're "Sir" or "Ma'am." He said.

"That'll do, yes." Confirmed the Sergeant.

"And why do they call you Nik-Nak?"

The chubby sergeant pointed to his head with both hands as he answered. "Because I've got a head shaped like a Nik-Nak!"

"Where's the gym?" Frank asked.

Nik -Nak paused. "Hmmm, good question. I think it's over that way, by the back gate." He said, rising on to his tip toes and pointing over a large building. "I've only been here a few weeks myself, so I'm not sure."

"Where do we parade for P.T then?" Frank quizzed, already concluding that they were not going to get on.

"What P.T?" Said the Sergeant, looking confused.

"Morning P.T!" Frank said. "Morning P.T!.. 0800hrs!.. Where do we RV?"

"We don't do P.T." Replied the Sergeant. "Some people train at lunchtime but there's no unit P.T. We start work at our desks at 8 o'clock and finish at 5 o'clock., there's no time for that. The Major says it's not a priority"

"You're joking right?" Frank said seriously. He had done P.T at 0800hrs every day since he had been in the Parachute Regiment. "If you train at lunchtime, when do you eat lunch?" He asked, genuinely baffled. "Lunchtime is for eating scoff!"

"Most people just have a Pot-Noodle or some crisps at their desk for lunch." Said the Sergeant. "But we do have a sports afternoon on Wednesdays, the Major likes his sports afternoons."

Frank was puzzled further. "How come you don't know where the gym is if you do sport every week?" He queried.

Nik-Nak explained. "Well, I say sports afternoon, but what happens is, the Major brings in cakes and we all have a beer and a game of FIFA on the PlayStation. We hook it up to the projector, we've got our own league."

Frank looked around the office space glumly. Everything and everyone he looked at agitated him. The people all looked out of shape, their bellies hanging over the belts of their un-ironed trousers, their boots unpolished. Ringing telephones were ignored, the bins overflowed with junk food wrappers and empty cans of fizzy drinks, and signs were plastered everywhere, warning people to follow one pathetic rule or another or face disciplinary action by another nameless person. One person was blatantly playing Solitaire on their computer with piles of untended paperwork stacked in their in-tray. At that moment he knew it was over. There was no way he could continue serving like this, it would break him.

"Fuck this!" He said and without explanation left the building by the nearest fire exit. Heading directly to the married quarter he had just moved his young family into, he sat down with his wife to discuss their options. Normally Frank didn't show his emotions, not even to his wife, but the sadness in his voice demonstrated how much it hurt him to admit defeat. Being a Paratrooper was a huge part of Frank's life but knowing that he would never work in a battalion or the BRF again and would be desk bound until his retirement date was something his pride would not allow. The Brigadiers' decision to relegate him outside of the Brigade would never be reversed, because no officer would dare to undermine him, it would be career suicide. The Brigadier would one day be a General for sure. Franks wife knew it was the right decision, she knew him well enough to know that he needed to be around like-minded people. Frank would get depressed during leave periods if he weren't able to see his mates or do regular fitness, like many other soldiers he was institutionalised or more accurately in the case of paratroopers indoctrinated. His wife made them a sandwich and a brew of tea which he ate in silence before returning to the office for his interview. Arriving five minutes early, he waited to be called in, and sat down on the plastic chair already facing Jim's desk.

Jim began his well rehearsed brief. "Welcome to the team, I hope you 've had a chance to take a look around what I call the "Puzzle Palace" and meet some of the crew."

Frank got straight to the point. "I'm going to be totally honest with you Jim." he said. "I can't do this, I can't work here, this isn't for me. I am a paratrooper, not a clerk or an analyst and if I can't soldier, I can't stay. Nothing against you, or your team, but I can't!"

Jim was taken aback. He looked either angry or concerned, Frank couldn't tell which. He cleared his throat before speaking.

"Okay Sgt Cutler, I will also be straight with you. First of all, you need to understand that I am an SO2, which means I hold the equivalent rank of Major and therefore, as a senior NCO you shall address me as Sir!"

Frank took a deep breath as his hand began rubbing the side of his head and he started blinking rapidly, the first signs of his irritation.

Jim continued. "Secondly what we do here is soldiering too! It may not be as glamorous or exciting as swanning around the desert in Afghanistan, and we might not get the medals, but we are working just as hard as the guys and girls out there! Thirdly..."

"Get out!" Frank said quietly. He was rubbing his head with both hands now, his eyes fixed to a spot on the ground.

"I beg your pardon!?" Exclaimed Jim.

Franks head lifted but he avoided eye contact, his eyes were darting from side to side rapidly as violent thoughts raced through his head. He knew that if he looked at Jim and saw any sign of anger or aggression, he might lose control. "Get out!" Frank snarled menacingly.

"How dare you tell me to get out of my own office! Who do you think you are talking to?" Jim said, shocked by Franks' behaviour.

"I'm talking to a fucking slob, that never had the guts to join the Army and pretends to be a Major! I'll make you a fucking Major if you don't get out in the next five seconds!" Frank paused and looked up, staring him in the eye. "A Major fucking casualty!" Frank stood up, and leant forwards, his hands on the desk. "Now fuck off!" He shouted.

With that Jim stood up and ran from his office, holding on to the waistband of his trousers as he went because he had unbuttoned them where they were too tight.

Frank sat back down, head in his hands. After gathering his thoughts for a couple of minutes he reached into his breast pocket and pulled out his wallet. Wedged tightly behind his Army I.D card and Driving Licence was General McGraw's business card. Frank extricated it and read the details on the front before flipping it over to read the short, handwritten message on the back "I.O.U!" and a personal cell phone number. He checked his watch, 1133hrs. It would be early morning in America. He slowly reached forward and picked up the telephone on Jim's desk, holding it to his ear while contemplating his next move. The dialling tone changed after a long pause to an annoying beep and Frank lowered the handset onto his thigh, deep in thought, oblivious to any sights or sounds other than the telephone, almost in a trance. Suddenly he sat upright, momentarily replaced the handset onto its base to reset it, then dialled the number on the back of the card.

A familiar voice answered. "Hello."

Frank spoke. "Hello General, it's Sergeant Cutler from the British BRF here, sorry to bother you, is it okay to talk?"

"Fallshirmjaeger Frank! Is that you?" Shouted the General excitedly.

"Affirm Sir, it's me." Frank replied with a grin. He did not expect the General to remember so easily.

The General was genuinely pleased to hear from Frank as they had got along so well in Afghanistan. "How the hell are you buddy? How can I help you? You want to cash in that I.O.U?"

"Funny you should say that Sir." said Frank. "You said there was a job for me at your Recon School in Camp Pendleton. What's the weather like in California?.........

The End

ORIGIN OF THE STORY

In 2006 I was sat in a small camp in Helmand Province, Afghanistan with some of my fellow soldiers. We were feeling frustrated because after a fair bit of planning and preparation, the patrol we were all geared up for was cancelled. That was the second or third time it had happened, and I wondered how many more times it might happen before we got out on the ground to do our job. The reason was probably down to a lack of support such as a Quick Reaction Force (QRF) and / or medical cover. As the Advance Force Reconnaissance, we were ahead of the Main Battle Group and relatively isolated in the location, compared to the bigger, established bases. The main occupants of the camp were small contingents of U.S and U.K Special Forces units who were in the process of handing over their areas of responsibility to conventional forces. Although there was plenty of work to do, there are only so many times you can study a map or clean machine guns, so to keep my over-active brain occupied I started to write a little story in my notebook, in pencil. Not really knowing how to begin, I simply started to describe the scene in front of me to see where it went. After a couple of days, one of the blokes called Adie, who was an attached Vehicle Mechanic (VM) from the REME offered to lend me his laptop and I used that, ending up with a few thousand words. Adie read the start of the story and gave me really good feedback, which encouraged me to carry on. Between patrols and tasks, I'd try to carry on, adding to the story slowly but never getting the opportunity to focus on writing.

During that tour I was extracted back to the UK because my wife had given birth to our first child. I got to see him within 24hrs of him being born, thanks to a good friend who somehow got me on a flight back to the U.K. The day after I returned to Afghanistan, I was waiting in Camp Bastion for my unit to collect me when an old friend from 3 Para visited the tent I was in. I will never forget that day. He told me that someone from 3 Para, my old battalion, was MIA (missing in action.) A while later another old friend came by and informed me that the MIA soldier was Bryan Budd, a very close friend of mine who I had served with in 3 Para and the Pathfinders.

"You know that bloke that's MIA?" He said..... "It's Bry Budd!"

My heart sank, but I knew that Bry was an extremely capable soldier and had a good chance of getting himself out of the shit. Over the next half an hour or so a few more old friends from the battalion popped in to tell me the worrying news. Everyone was anxious, but hopeful that his Company would find him safe and well as they fought their way back into the area that he was last seen in. Sometime later another friend came to visit me. He knew me and Bry were mates. I was sitting on a camp cot in the shade of a green canvas tent. It was 12ft x 18ft and the doors at either end were rolled all the way up to the roof to let some air flow through. There were a few other camp beds in there, but I was the only occupant at the time.

"Steve." He said. "I'm sorry mate, they've found Bry, he's dead. Sorry mate."

"Ahh fuck!" I sighed. My head dropped, nodding slightly as I rested my forehead in my hands. "Thanks for telling me mate." I said. Conscious that was probably as hard for him to say as it was for me to hear. Like before, I received the news from a few of the blokes from 3 Para, each one telling me with a shared sense of loss and sadness, I suppressed my emotions that day, if no-one was around I would have probably cried like a baby, and I probably should have. In the years since I have cried many times thinking about my old friend, an awesome bloke and even better soldier. That was probably the worst day of my life. Before my son was born my one wish was that I would live to see him, and I was grateful that I did. Bry never got that luxury, he was killed while his wife was pregnant with their second child, a terrible injustice.

Later that day I was picked up by my own unit, who diverted a patrol to collect me as they returned from a tasking. The soldier driving my vehicle looked tired and during the drive back to our base camp confided in me that he had awoken every day for the last few weeks convinced that it would be his last, that he would die that day. I looked him in the eye and could see that he meant it, it was sad to see. He'd spent weeks thinking he was going to die. I don't know if he'd told anyone else.

"Mate, it's a good time for you to go home." I said.

That patrol was the last one he was scheduled to make and it was just as well. He was mentally exhausted. We got back to base safely and he returned to the UK shortly afterwards. Last I heard he was a policeman.

I never thought I would still be writing this story 14 years later. Between 2006 – 2020 my career took me in several directions, both geographically and professionally, and occasionally I would be incentivised to write some more. In March 2020 I had just finished a career of almost 27 years in the Army and started a new one in the Health and Fitness industry when the Coronavirus, COVID 19 pandemic struck. I had written about 30,000 words at that point. Being on "Lockdown" was the perfect opportunity to finally finish the story. This story is fiction, but all the characters and events are influenced by people I've met or heard about and events or situations that I've experienced, heard stories about or envisaged.

At 46 years old I am still physically fit as I've always maintained an active and healthy lifestyle, however, like most old paratroopers my body has been battered, which means I have to tailor my training around a lot of old injuries. A physiotherapist once told me I had a classic case of "Old-soldier-itis." She had asked me to draw circles on a sketch of a human body wherever I had regular pain but there were so many circles she ended up starting again, this time marking the places that didn't hurt instead. I also have tinnitus quite badly in both ears which means they are constantly ringing with a high-pitched buzz. The quieter my surroundings get, the louder they seem to ring, again quite common among soldiers. Hearing loss, also attributed to my service, means that I have hearing aids which I wear when in meetings or presentations. Also, despite my initial dismissiveness I was diagnosed with PTSD in 2014 and underwent treatment with the Department of Clinical Mental Health (DCMH) up until 2019. I know there are a lot of soldiers out there suffering with mental health issues, many of them having endured experiences far worse than anything I have ever seen or done. Some have told me themselves, others I have witnessed decline. Most don't seek help because of pride or the worry that they will be medically downgraded if they do, which could have drastic consequences on their career. Usually people tell me they will address at the end of their military service so that they can soldier on and not worry about losing their income and pension. Everyone knows somebody with mental health issues and I personally think that the stigma attached to it only exists among a minority of ignorant, self-appointed "tough guys" these days. A cynical friend asked me about PTSD once. He knew I was undergoing treatment and taking medication and I tried to explain to him how I didn't think I was in any way exceptional and that in my opinion there were lots of us who were on the verge of crazy, probably including him. We were sat in a car in Exeter City during heavy traffic and a man was walking in our direction on the pavement. I asked him. "See that bloke walking towards us?"

"Yes." He replied.

"Are you thinking about what you're going to do if he tries to get in the car and attack us?"

My mate Marty said. "Yes. Why?"

"So am I." I replied. "Have you thought about what you'll do if he pulls a knife or gun?"

"Well, yes, of course." Marty said. "But that's normal!"

"So have I." I said. I pointed to the car in front of us, also stationary, with a man sat in the driver's seat. "See that civvy in front?" I said. "Do you reckon *he's* thinking about how *he's* going to kill this fucker if he tries to get in *his* car? "Or do you think he's just sat there chilling out, listening to the radio and wondering what he's going to have for dinner?

Mine and Marty's minds had probably raced through a dozen scenarios within seconds of seeing this man, just as they had all day prior to that, whenever someone got close, made a sudden movement or looked suspicious.

"Problem is mate." I said. "It's actually not normal. Normal people don't think like we do."

I knew he would have been thinking the same as me, I bet 95% of my peers would have too, because in a military environment, when you are with people who have gone through the same or similar experiences and training, that is normal, because everyone is thinking the same.

Hypervigilance is common amongst soldiers that have been in hostile environments and it causes or exacerbates anxiety. I can tell you that living in a state of perpetual high-alert and the physiological and psychological effects it causes is exhausting. Before medication and psychotherapy my mind would be racing all day, every day as I envisaged violent outcomes with every passing person or group of people that I assessed as a credible threat. In my mind every scenario ended the same, me killing them, or dying trying. Within a few seconds of seeing someone I would assess their threat, think through my reactions if they said or did something aggressive to me or my family, think through how far I was prepared to go, bearing in mind that they might be equally prepared, then think about the consequences of killing them. Going to prison for murder and the effect that would have on my wife and kids, or being killed, and my kids being left without a dad were the two common outcomes. Living like that is not only exhausting, it is depressing, you never stop to enjoy anything, you just move from threat to threat and never even get the release of the fight, because generally people don't actually want to randomly attack you when they are shopping at Tesco or out walking their dog.

Watch out for friends and family that might be suffering with mental health and support them where you can. Equally, seek support if you need it.

Printed in Great Britain
by Amazon

82953527R00142